OF LIFE AND DEATH
Tales of Aenar

Thrice Nine Legends

Joshua Robertson
J.C. Boyd

CRIMSON
EDGE
PRESS

Dedication

To those who can tell the difference between fiction and
reality, but pretend it is all real anyway.

There once was a time when the gods were gods without question. When men were men without example. When heroes were only the frivolous dreams of lurid mortality. It was a time when truths and untruths were indistinguishable, hatred and love were equally excusable, and life and death regaled all of humanity in the same breath. Myths of old were realized and legends were born from the very dust man was formed of, to be told and retold until the grace of time altered them beyond knowing or forgot them completely. Still, some tales were preserved deep within the hearts of mankind, for reasons that could not be fathomed. Perhaps bearing the fruit of some profound truth or kept alive merely by the strength of the men who lived them. Some tales would never be forgotten.

Thrice Nine Legends Saga

The Blood of Dragons by Joshua Robertson & J.C. Boyd
ANAERFELL*
HESHAYOL*

The Kaelandur Series by Joshua Robertson
MELKORKA*
DYNDAER*
MAHARIA*

Other Thrice Nine Legends Saga by Joshua Robertson & J.C. Boyd
WARDEN OF THE ASH TREE*
UNDERSUNG*
A SONG AND SILVER*
STRONG ARMED*
WHEN BLOOD FALLS*
THE NAME OF DEATH*
THE SKINCUTTER'S DAUGHTER*
THE HIGHBORN LONGWALKER*
OF LIFE AND DEATH*
DEATH AT DUSK**

Additional Works

Legacy Series by Joshua Robertson & J.C. Boyd
BLOOD AND BILE*

THE HAWKHURST SAGA*
GRIMSDALR*
THE PRINCE'S PARISH*
JACK SPRATT*

Published by Crimson Edge
**Forthcoming by Crimson Edge*

Table of Contents

WARDEN OF THE ASH TREE

Thrice Nine Legends

Month of Harvest

Fourth of Warmth

46 CE

Chapter I

Maksim Artur cowered a hundred paces from Jana Pearka's window in the recently plowed field, reluctant to miss the regular, nightly exhibition. He presumed she was innocent when leaving the drapes drawn back like they were; though, he fancied the thought that she enjoyed being viewed when undressing in her bed chamber. The fictional musing not only made him gutsier when watching, squatting out here in the open, but it kept him coming back to her window almost every night since summer began.

Only an hour had passed since the sun dipped below the Valarun mountains, blanketing the world in shadow, but the darkness made no difference to him. Whether noble or commoner, every Vucari had darksight, including Jana. So, even tonight, with the sky absent of Myestera's moonbeams, he was no more hidden in the field than she was in her bedroom. She could look over her shoulder at any moment to see him gawking, while fighting to keep his hands from his trousers.

He scarcely heard the scamper of light footsteps before his friend, Levin Kovach, skidded to a stop next to him. The lithe man bobbled his head in his perpetual excitement, arching his neck to peek at the window. He asked and answered his own question in a heated whisper. "What did I miss? Oh! She started already."

"Shush." Maksim warned, darting his eyes to the back of Jana's head. She did not give any sign of hearing Levin. He examined her carefully from a distance, stroking his chin with admiration. She kept her back to him, staring at the unadorned wall of her bed chamber like she did most evenings. His lip found its way between his teeth, while she slowly pulled her stitched tunic from her shoulders, exposing her olive skin, and then released it from the tips of her fingers to the floor. Her thick, black hair hung loose between her shoulder blades, reaching down to the small of her back. He sucked in a mouthful of air. Her freckled flesh was dry and coarse from working the fields with the other landless. He had never seen a noble girl with her complexion.

"What do you mean *shush?* We are not exactly taking precautions out here," Levin said with a snort, peering up at him with a boyish grin.

Maksim ignored his friend. He did not want to answer questions. He wanted to admire Jana's speckled skin. He followed the bow of her body, curved to perfection from breast to buttocks, counting the familiar, tanned dots along her back. His breath poured from his lips, instinctively moving his hand from his chin to his chest as though grasping at his shirt might slow his heartbeat.

Levin nudged him. "Hey! When exactly did we start standing in the open while peeping? You know anyone passing on the road can see us, right? The other landless can surely see us through their own windows. We should be switching into birds, or mice, or *something*."

Maksim winced at the suggestion. The magic-wielding southerners called his people *skin-switchers*, because of their sacred power to physically alter their bodies into the likeness of animals. Each Vucari could transmute into different creatures, determined by their bloodline. The noble classes had the purest bloodlines, with some—like Maksim's lineage—having the power to transform into a *bies*. The horned brutes were said to be the very spawn of Wolos, the God of the Dead. The landless, on the other hand, had diluted blood. They barely had the strength to hold the shape of a wolf or bear.

"Not very talkative tonight, are you?" Levin wiggled his eyebrows at Maksim. "Oh! I forgot you fell *in love* and lost your mind. Nine Lands! I bet you want Jana to catch you!"

"I am not in love." Maksim snapped, feeling the heat tickle the tips of his ears. He cautiously held his gaze on Jana; she delicately brushed at her shoulder. A bit of dust.

"I do not want to be any part of a fantasy where we get caught. No, sir. I like when we had a dozen women we rotated through," Levin said. "Malia, Niviada, Breena…"

"Stop it," Maksim muttered. He and Levin had spied on women together since puberty struck, almost half a decade ago, when their ability to change into fauna sparked. The magic was meant to help them guard the Ash Tree; though, to Maksim's knowledge, very few, if any, Vucari had seen the fabled Tree of Life. Regardless, instead of changing into an owl or shrew, Maksim remained out here in plain sight. He reiterated his position. "I do not want to get caught."

"Sure," Levin sarcastically muttered. "I suspect you are only days from finding the courage to call out to her." He chortled. "*Oh, Jana*...I bet you would like a handful of *felpoppies* right now."

Maksim unhappily pulled his attention from Jana and slugged Levin in the arm, pushing away any thoughts of what his true feelings might have been for the landless girl. Of course, Levin would suggest they weaken the girl with *felpoppies*. The plants were usually used as a sedative when the injured needed limbs hacked off. "Stay quiet. We are not boys any longer. The Khagan will not be slapping our hands. We will be hanged."

"Hanged?" Levin scoffed with disbelief, his dark eyes wide. "The old codger will more than likely ask us for details. He is not going to hang us. We are his best students."

"He has hung apprentices before," Maksim said.

"Yeah. Forty years ago, and none even remember the crime or the name. If anything, I bet it is a story they tell all future Wardens to scare them," Levin retorted with a shake of his shaggy head. "I will bet you a silver Jana will be yelling at us before the week is out."

"I am not betting with you," Maksim said. "You always win."

"So, you agree then?" Levin asked.

Maksim rubbed his nose. "No, I don't agree...fine. I bet you she won't be yelling at us about anything."

Levin slapped Maksim on the back. "But it won't happen tonight. She is gone."

Maksim's frowned, following Levin's eyes back to the window. He was right. Jana had already retired from her chamber and escaped to some other room in her home. He stared hopelessly for a moment on chance she might return.

When she did not, he stood and grabbed Levin's arm to pull him away from the house. "Come on. Let's go."

Instead of jerking free, Levin leaned into Maksim and swooned. "Oh! Are you taking me back to your place or should we go to mine? All this time, I thought you invited me out here to watch the girls. I would have never thought…"

He pushed his arm away. "Do you speak to your ma with that mouth?"

Levin grinned, his feet crunching against the thick grasses as they snaked toward the well-worn path leading to the main settlement, Ayral. "What has gotten into you? Did you have a rough day listening to the Khagan rattle on in the temple?"

Maksim looked back at the many homes of the landless scattered on the outskirts of Ayral. Not a single home had a flame burning in the window. And they would not. The Vucari had little need for fire. Besides their gift of darksight, their bodies were unaffected by heat or cold. Fire was a weapon for war; not a necessity for life. Sometimes they may use it for cooking, but even then, Vucari could eat their food raw without any concern.

"When is the temple not a place of turmoil? Especially after the rumors circulating from last winter?" Maksim muttered, pushing the red-brown bangs from his eyes, and focusing on the road ahead. He could see the outline of wooden homes in the distance. "Five months have passed and still no message from those at Anaerfell."

"The Wardens will give word when they are ready," Levin said.

Maksim hummed at the boring response, realizing this was the first he had seen Levin since morning. "Where were you today anyway?"

"It was my day to preach to the landless. Though, I cannot say how much I accomplished. Scythia says the Reds killed Wolos," Levin smirked, "and all the Wardens who had gone to meet him at the solstice."

"Scythia Gergo? The rat bastard!" Maksim kicked at the dirt with his boot. "He is looking for any reason to convince the people to worship Myestera instead of Wolos."

Levin scrunched his nose. "We know the Reds made it over the ice last winter. They buried Charreni under a mountain. Surely, you do not think they crushed the village and then went back home?"

"They were probably looking for revenge after our assault on Lairhein," Maksim said.

"Come on. Our forces did not even breach the city walls, and they defeated Torn'ash in open battle," Levin argued. "I hardly see anything for them to avenge."

Maksim frowned, recalling the recount of the story he had heard from the few warriors who returned. He would have never thought the Reds could defend against a dragon, let alone rout it back to the Shade Fells. Torn'ash was said to be the *Viy*, the Father of Serpents. Not a single dragon was more feared than him. "I don't know." Maksim swung at the air with a fist. "But, Nine Lands, they did not traipse into the mountains and kill the God of the Dead."

"Scythia—" Levin started again.

"—is a plague to our people," Maksim finished. "I do not understand why anyone would listen to him when the Khagan has said otherwise. We would be better off seeing him hanged."

Levin paused to take a breath, the air whistling between his lips. His eyes hung on Maksim for several footsteps, his aggravation hidden behind a thin smile. "You did not have to interrupt me, you know? You should know I support the Khagan more than anyone."

Maksim shrugged and grunted.

"Great apology. You should work on saying sorry before courting Jana. Women do not care too much for men who cannot form words. Your ma did not teach you anything, did she?" Levin said smugly.

"She taught me how to crush the skulls of loudmouths." Maksim said, lifting his fist to hit him in the shoulder again.

Levin lifted his arm to stop him, pointing to the village ahead. "Who is that? Balogh? What is he doing out here?"

Maksim followed the finger to see the familiar, middle-aged watchman standing in the makeshift road, nearly three-hundred paces beyond the palisades surrounding Ayral. He squinted at them across the distance.

"Yeah. That is Balogh," Maksim finally replied. "I would recognize his old, bald head anywhere. He should be helping the Khagan close the temple."

"Do you think he spotted us in the fields?" Levin asked worriedly.

Maksim was already shaking his head back and forth before answering. "We were too far out…I think."

Balogh lifted his hand to salute them, and then started walking in their direction. He held his back straighter than the stone-tipped spear he held at his right side. He had a definite sense of duty about him, bounding awkwardly down the road at a half-run.

Levin loudly cleared his throat as Balogh closed the distance. "What are you doing out here so late?"

"Fetching you," Balogh said, rubbing his forehead with the back of his hand. He slowed to a stop, towering a head taller than either of them. The black beard hanging from the tip of his chin bounced with each word. "What are you doing out here wandering among the landless? I must have searched the entire town twice this past hour."

Maksim gulped, looking over his shoulder as though he were searching for an answer. The fields were quiet.

Levin was quick to answer. "Spending a full day studying to be a Warden is exhausting, you know? We sit for hours listening to the histories, and reciting the histories, and discussing the histories. Oh! I tell you, knowing who beget who, and then who they beget…so much begetting. We try to get outside the walls to clear our heads. I am *really* surprised you haven't seen us come and go before today."

"I did not ask for a speech, Levin. I know well enough what it takes to be a Warden. Nine Lands. You run your mouth like your ole da. Not a pleasant quality," Balogh said, as Maksim twisted back to face him. Despite the bald nobleman's frustration, Maksim noticed he had an eerie, impassive gaze smeared across his face. Something unnerved him. As if adding weight to the suspicion, Balogh stood silently for a bit longer, nervously gripping the spear in his hand.

"Is everyone in a mood tonight?" Levin asked, lifting an eyebrow at Maksim.

"Shut up," Maksim said. His tone was less playful than he intended. Levin whistled and took a step back. Maksim did not bother correcting himself, turning his attention to the watchman. "Were you going to tell us what you wanted?"

Balogh raised his finger at Maksim, darting his eyes. "Let me catch my breath, boy. Okay? Bad enough that I am running errands for the Khagan. I do not need to hear your lip, too."

"My lip?" Maksim mouthed the words in confusion. "I am just—"

"Khagan Rhirgwe sent you?" Levin interrupted, seeming to notice Balogh was troubled. Maksim could only shake his head while Levin barked questions. "For us? Why?"

Balogh grimaced. "Gonna try to twist it out of me, are you? Well, I am not going to speak the Khagan's mind. He would have my hide if I said a word, especially out here."

Maksim gazed through the charcoal air to Ayral behind Balogh, comforted that the summons had nothing to do with him and Levin peeking on Jana. "I suppose we better go see what this is all about."

The three returned to Ayral in silence, traipsing past the palisades and through the colossal, stone pillars into the settlement. Maksim glanced to the many skulls, positioned within the niches of stone. After any battle, the surviving warriors would customarily collect the heads of the Vucari's enemies. Some were humanoid, belonging to the Reds from Lairhein. Others were animalistic in nature, or even monstrous, reflective of the bipedal wolf-like Vulkodlak haunting the mountains of Valarun. The edifices were monuments to Wolos, symbolic of the Vucari's devotion to remain Wardens of the Ash Tree.

A handful of sentries lounged inside the wooden gate leading into Ayral, wearing boned breastplates and carrying long spears on their backs. They had little to guard against. The Vulkodlak stayed in the mountains, and the Reds had never traveled to Ayral, but they vigilance was better than death.

Maksim followed Balogh down the hardened road. The rectangular, single-room houses—the homes of the nobles—lined either side of the street. Levin's and Maksim's own homes were not far away. He imagined his little brother was already down for the night. His ma was likely drinking her evening tea.

As if he were poking around in Maksim's head, Levin bumped him with an elbow. "How is your ma holding up after your da fell last winter?"

"Her and Jersi are doing well," Maksim said, meeting Levin's wide eyes, knowing his friend had lost both his parents nearly three years ago in another war. He did not remember a year without a war between the Vucari and the Reds. Levin now lived alone in his parent's home. "Ma is not a stranger to war and death."

"That is the truth. Your ma and I fought in wars before you were born," Balogh said, leading them past the Shrine. The sacred place kept a fire burning all-year-round, used to send the dead to meet Wolos at the Kalinov Bridge, where the God of the Dead would lead them to either the Netherworld or Thrice Ten Kingdom. Every winter, the Khagan would sacrifice a landless to please the God of the Dead. Maksim knew the sacrifice was considered a great honor, knowing you had been born to appease the gods. Yet he was glad to be noble-blooded. Balogh continued, "I can tell you she gave the Reds something to fear more than once. You have fighting blood running through your veins. You both do."

Maksim held his tongue, having no need to be patted on the back by Balogh. He knew his family held the sacred blood of the *bies*. If the watchman had fought alongside his mother, he likely knew the same.

"You fought alongside my parents?" Levin asked.

"I was with them when they fell near Lairhein," Balogh answered with a grim smile. "The magic of the Reds is a hard thing to contend against."

"Now, you are smiling?" Levin scowled at Maksim, hitting him in the ribs with his bony elbow. "We are talking about my death of my parents here."

"Pssh. Your days of mourning have passed." Maksim grabbed his side and swatted his friend away; he had barely realized he had a smile on his face. He listened for a moment to the river running to the south of Ayral. "I was thinking how the Reds are blind to the dark," Maksim said. "Can you imagine how well-off we would be in our forays if we kept our attacks to nights such as these?"

Levin scrunched his nose. "The Reds have their magic, Maksim. They would simply create a ball of light and the advantage would be lost."

"We often attack at nighttime," Balogh said, rolling his eyes. "Rarely does it give us the upper hand. Someday, you boys will be in battle. Try not to pretend like you know everything."

Maksim did not waver. "Ah, but what if we were to sneak into their city. We would only need a handful, going from bed chamber to bed chamber. They would not know they were being attacked until they were all dead."

"You are a dreamer." Levin muttered. "We lost more last summer than any raid. Did we not just talk about this? The Reds defeated Torn'ash."

"*Dragon-men*," Maksim said with sarcasm at the reiteration of the Red's victory. "More like *dragon-slayers*. They have no respect for what they once were."

Levin said, "No matter what we think of the magic-wielding snobs, you must admit they are a formidable enemy."

"I—" Maksim sneered, "mustn't admit anything. The swine came across the sea and killed our people. Innocent people."

Balogh grumbled. "Bah! The Reds do not remember what they were. They forget our people were once unified and called friends." He stopped in the road. "Enough about the dragon-men. They have no part in tonight's business, and we are here."

The temple, built from the same stone as the pillars, was likely the largest building in Ayral. Maksim squinted at the thatched roof as they climbed the clay-formed stairs.

Levin joked from behind. "We are forever bound to this place. You barely walk out the doors and back you are summoned."

"Silence, boy," Balogh said. "You should know the blessing of being a Warden by now. Unless you would rather be in the fields with the landless..."

The older man intentionally let his voice trail off as though he were expecting Levin to hurriedly deny any such desire. Maksim, instead, anticipated Levin to say something about not being a Warden until their final trials. Yet the younger Vucari only snickered and continued his ascent up the stairs.

Balogh opened the double doors, giving sight immediately to the large wooden table and chairs stretching the length of the room. Maksim had spent hours at this table with his peers, studying, listening to stories, and being quizzed for hours after. Of course, no books, papers, or maps littered the confines of the temple. The Vucari avoided writing anything down. Instead, they told and retold tales from sunrise to sunset.

Maksim pulled his boots from his feet. Balogh and Levin did the same, tossing them to the wall. Maksim was the first to stand fully, eyeing Khagan Rhirgwe Lechim at the head of the table.

Rhirgwe's beady, grey eyes poked out from wrinkly layers of skin around his face, studying them. Maksim stared back at the Prophet's thinning grey beard, which disappeared under the edge of the table. He knew the length of the loose strands fell beyond the old man's waist, even without his slouch. How he had grown a beard to his knees and kept a bald scalp was beyond Maksim. Most Vucari men kept their hair short and their beards long, but Rhirgwe had taken the extreme.

Rhirgwe leaned against the table, folding his hands neatly on the rough wood. The Khagan spoke with an air of authority. "The hour is late, Maksim Artur, son of Macimus, and Levin Kovach, son of Llorachi. We have not the time for banter, so stand straight and be attentive."

He stood shoulder-to-shoulder with Levin, straightening his back, and looking at the Khagan. His friend did the same, ridding his face of any hint of emotion expressed earlier. Even Balogh remained steady as an ice-covered boulder, although he was not directly acknowledged.

Rhirgwe smacked his lips, clearly satisfied, and continued, "What I am about to share with you is only known by myself and Balogh. And it will remain so." Maksim dipped his head, noticing Levin's same gesture from the corner of his eye. The Khagan went on, "Evil is afoot. Blessed Wolos's name, a traitor has revealed himself. He goes to Anaerfell. He means to destroy our civilization."

"How?" Levin asked.

Rhirgwe lifted his hand as though he kept Levin from saying more. "You surely heard the rumors of the Reds traveling to Anaerfell and slaying the god, Wolos?" Rhirgwe probed, lifting the thinning hairs of his eyebrow. "The whispered allegation has swept through Ayral and all the way to Raccassi."

"Lies," Maksim said.

Rhirgwe coughed, roughly shaking his head. His voice dropped, suddenly husky. "No, not lies."

Levin took a step closer to the table, balancing himself with his hands. His hastened words were more breath than words. "Wait—what?"

The room suddenly spun. Maksim's mouth dried. "Are you positive? You mean to say the Reds—

mortals—killed a god? How could they? Why would they?"

"The *how* and *why* is no longer important," Rhirgwe replied, his long beard swaying with each word. "Whether for their own selfish gain or to mar our culture, the truth remains that Wolos has fallen at the hand of the Reds. This truth, however," he cleared his throat, "must never be known by our people."

Levin could not utter his surprise a second time. His jaw simply fell open and stayed.

"You want our people to continue to worship the God of the Dead...even while he, himself, is dead?" Maksim asked.

"I said to listen." Rhirgwe snorted with frustration. "Our way of life is destined by the gods and our ageless tribute to them. Can you imagine a godless society? I would not even ask you to consider it!" The old Khagan grumbled, shaking his head in bewilderment at the thought. His cheeks jiggled like waves over his face. "Your families would lose their lands, and titles, and standing in this city. The landless would overwhelm those of noble blood."

"I...have no family," Levin winced.

"But you will," Balogh rapidly said. "You will someday have a wife. Sons and daughters. Without Wolos, they will have nothing, despite your noble blood."

Rhirgwe waved off Balogh's testament. "Although true, it is more than luxury. In past centuries, the Vucari failed Wolos, and our people were cursed. You know the Vulkodlak roving through Valarun were once our kin! Do you think those monsters were noble-blooded or weak-blooded?" Rhirgwe rhetorically asked through clenched teeth. "Weak! If the landless were to know the truth, they would abandon their charge for their own indulgences!"

"You speak of the charge to protect the Ash Tree," Maksim concluded.

"Yes," Rhirgwe said. "I speak of the Ash Tree. The landless would forget the noble-blooded are the Wardens of the Ash Tree. We are bound by creation to protect the Tree of Life, or the whole world will fall to ruin. They must believe Wolos is living to keep their place and, in turn, the sacred tree safe."

Maksim bit his tongue. To his knowledge, no Vucari, Warden or otherwise, had been to the Ash Tree. They spoke about the tree often enough in the temple, but not even Rhirgwe knew of its location. If anything, the Wardens protected the idea of a Tree of Life.

"Then, we will go on telling the people that Wolos is alive and well. Rumors of his death will fade. No one in Ayral knows the truth, and..." Levin paused, wincing. "Why would you tell us?"

"I told you a traitor has come to be known," Rhirgwe repeated. "Scythia Gergo, son of Alhfrith, has guessed at the truth. He plans to tell the people."

Maksim scowled at mention of the name. Of course, Scythia would be the traitor. No man among the Vucari was less honorable. "He is a landless. What is his word against that of the Khagan?"

"Bah!" Rhirgwe hit the table with an open palm. "He has gone to seek proof at Anaerfell. Already, he has taken the road with a handful of like-minded fools."

"The Vulkodlak will tear them to shreds before they ever reach Anaerfell," Levin muttered.

"We can hope, but we must be certain he does not return," Balogh said, receiving an encouraging nod from Rhirgwe.

Maksim clenched his jaw, mirroring Balogh's own determined face. Despite what he may have said about Scythia an hour earlier, he was not certain how he felt about personally taking the landless's life. He addressed Rhirgwe. "Khagan, are you asking us to track down Scythia and kill him?"

"Him and any in his company," Balogh gruffly said.

"This task will serve as your final trial to becoming Wardens, proving your allegiance to Wolos and the protection of the Ash Tree." Rhirgwe pulled himself to his feet, his feeble hands shaking against the table. "You will leave tonight. Catch him before he reaches Anaerfell and save yourself a grueling journey."

Levin's shaggy hair fell over his eyes as he cocked his head, processing the strange quest. He visibly gulped before speaking to Rhirgwe. "What will Maksim tell his family? What will the others say when we are not at the temple tomorrow for our studies?"

"Balogh will tell them that you seek to unravel the rumors of Wolos's death on behalf of the temple," Rhirgwe said, his fingernails digging into the table. He coughed once more. His arms shook under his own weight, as slight as it may have been. "Regardless, if you catch the traitor in a mile or a hundred miles, you must not return to Ayral until the end of the Season of Warmth. I do not care whether you travel to Anaerfell or not. But, when you return, you will report that all is well within Valarun, at Anaerfell, and imply Wolos's well-being."

"As you wish, Khagan," Levin said. Maksim did not miss the excitement in his friend's tone.

Maksim only dipped his head. He would not argue with the Khagan.

Chapter II

Levin was as calm as a summer breeze, stepping beyond the plowed field of the landless and into the wilderness. He pulled himself along, using his spear as a walking stick, his brown robe fluttering behind him. "Did you say goodbye to your ma and brother?"

"They were sleeping," Maksim answered dryly, feeling no less irritable now than he had earlier. "Now, stop trying to change the subject."

Levin sighed, resuming the conversation Maksim had started when they exited the palisades an hour ago. He kept an awkward smile on his face. "Fine, but I hope you are not this dull the entire trip." He shook his head. "Your position makes no sense! You were just saying Scythia needed to be hanged. Running him through with a spear is not much different."

Maksim wiped his hands against his black trousers, gliding across the grass beside his friend. The swish of the dried blades rubbing against his boots nipped at his ears. "I am not saying Scythia isn't deserving. Wardens are meant to be righteous, right? How do we know this is not a test?"

"Oh! You think the Khagan wanted us to refuse his command and claim the quest wicked?" Levin laughed, throwing his head back. "I have never heard such folly before. The Vucari do not play in devilish schemes to ensnare one another. We are not Reds, Maksim."

"No, we are not," Maksim agreed. "But to be a Warden, we should be trained to think like our enemy, right? We have not gone far. I think we should return to the temple. Ask more questions."

"We would look like fools. Khagan Rhirgwe is not testing us," Levin said, tilting his head like a mother might toward a child. "We were handpicked by the Khagan. Accept the honor."

"You speak as though we are gifted among those who want to be Wardens," Maksim said. The notion of his family having the blood of the *bies* skimmed the threshold of his thoughts. The knowledge was not something frequently shared; in fact, he was certain that Levin did not know what he could become.

"We are the oldest and the most skilled. We should be honored to have this quest given to us." Levin shrugged.

Maksim turned his head to look over his shoulder at Ayral fading in the distance. A disheveled path was left in the grasses behind them as they trekked toward the mountains. His mind riddled with the lessons he had learned at the temple. "We were taught the narrowest gate will lead to Thrice Ten Kingdom. The wide gate, the gate most commonly traveled, leads to destruction."

Levin scrunched his face. "Rhirgwe told us that our final test is to kill Scythia and I aim to do it. My duty is to Wolos and the will of my Khagan. If he did not want it done, he should not have commanded it."

Running a hand through his hair in disbelief, Maksim gawked at his friend. He pulled his fingers free from his long brown locks. "Listen. Not many would question the command of the Khagan. Most would rush to see the will of the sovereign leader fulfilled. Right now, we are traveling through the wide gate."

"No," Levin argued. "Most would not have the heart to slaughter a traitor. I mean, between the two of us, I would say I am not any fonder of Scythia Gergo than you…but I am more willing to protect our people from his crimes. You have to be prepared to do what others will not."

"His only crime is telling the truth," Maksim said.

Levin leered. "Sure. But, some truths are dangerous. Say, hours ago we were watching the prettiest thing in all Ayral take her clothes off." Maksim bit his tongue. Of course, Levin would take a philosophical discussion and make it personal to prove his point. "Not all truths need to be shouted to the world."

"This is not the same," Maksim said.

"We have been charged to kill a man," Levin said. "The way to Thrice Ten Kingdom is to complete the charge given in this life, right?"

"The charge to slay Scythia was not given by the gods."

Levin scoffed. "No, it was given by your Khagan, who is the voice of Wolos. Now, quit being a coward."

"A coward? I am not a coward!" Maksim growled. Levin stepped away from him, smartly, to avoid a fist from striking his shoulder. But Maksim kept his hand stilled. He took a breath and calmed his nerves. "I am asking questions, instead of blindly following."

"You are meant to blindly follow." Levin said from a distance, squinting his eye. "You want to be a Warden of the Ash Tree? The role requires a bit of faith, eh? You heard what the Khagan said. If we do not do this, the world will crumble."

"Maybe," Maksim replied. "I think we should go to Anaerfell and see what really happened to Wolos. We should know if the world really might crumble."

Levin uncaringly shrugged. "As long as we kill Scythia and return at the end of the season, we can do whatever you want."

Maksim mulled over the words, reaching for the hood of his grey cloak to pull over his head. As a Vucari, he may not have been affected by the weather, but the wool cloak did give him a sense of comfort. And, with the threat of the world *crumbling*, he could use the security.

Thinking the world might fall apart at the admittance of a god's death seemed far-fetched, but Maksim could not say he understood the full consequence. He only knew what the Khagan chose to tell him. His hand rested on the blade of the bronze axe securely tucked in his hide belt. The haft of the axe was sharpened from his great grandfather's femur and kept among his family ever since. He had retrieved it from his home with his cloak and a few perishables for the road. His grandfather, like his father, always followed the Khagan without question. Maksim knew he should do the same.

For the next hour, Levin and Maksim trudged through the grass and rock toward the mountains with few words. The moon remained missing from the sky. The Lightbringer would not return the sun to Aenar for several hours yet. This night was ruled by

Czern, the Grey-Clad, and he breathed darkness as dark as he could muster. Though, he held no power over Maksim and Levin. Wolos had gifted them with darksight to see through the murkiest shadow without strain.

Wildflowers and rock blended across the tundra-laden terrain, strewn as though the gods had suddenly spewed the scene like a drunkard might do his insides after a long night at the flagon. The far north did not consist of slithering reptiles or scurrying vermin to rustle amongst the weeds. Insects were plenty during the summer, but most had dispersed by this late in the evening. The temperature dropped too far for their busy buzzing.

Without a doubt, the landmass of Rhian frequently brimmed with weirdness and mystery. But, at night, the land was nearly as peaceful as the grave.

"At last! I found their trail," Levin said, kneeling. "How many men did the Khagan say had come with Scythia?"

"He was not specific," Maksim said, stopping behind Levin, and peering at the several footprints outlined in the dirt. "Nine Lands! One…two…three…four…I see nearly twelve sets of footprints."

"Much more than a handful," Levin muttered, standing upright and dusting his hands against his trousers. He scratched at his shaven face, and then shook his head with a sour look. "We best hope the Vulkodlak kill a few before we catch up with them."

Maksim smelled something strange on the evening breeze and rubbed it from his nostrils. Some animal may have settled for the night in the brush ahead; though it smelled like rotten dog. He added,

"Even with their diluted blood, killing a dozen landless will be difficult."

Levin's nervous laugh was short, cut off by the garroted bark of two wolves, one grey and one black, emerging from the brush ahead. Maksim stopped dead, grabbing at Levin to respond to the beasts. He should have known.

With a couple of bounds, the wolves were on them. The grey leaped at Maksim, jaws wide and hind legs tucked. He barely saw Levin lift his arm to deflect the black wolf before the grey crashed into him. Maksim barely dodged the snapping jaws, twisting his body so the weight of the animal crashed against his back and skidded past. The wolf hurdled to the ground on the opposite side, scrambling on its four legs to regain balance.

Maksim took the chance to jerk his cloak sideways and pull his axe from his belt loop. He grasped the bone handle and snarled. "Traitors."

An arrow zipped by his head from somewhere in the distance, robbing anything he might have added.

"We are being ambushed," Levin shouted, jabbing his spear at the black wolf chomping at the air. "I bet you a silver I kill more than you."

"You're on," Maksim said, staring into the yellow eyes of the grey, circling for another attack. Another arrow zinged overhead. "I will find the archer, and anyone else out there."

Levin responded with a growl, flinging his spear at the black wolf and missing. He pulled his brown robe over his head in a fluid motion. Naked to the world, Levin's body swiftly warped into the form of a great bear. Brown, unkempt fur sprouted from his skin; his face breaking into a black snout, beady eyes, and rows of sharpened teeth. With a roar, Levin's legs thickened as he grew almost twelve-foot tall and bawled at the wolves.

Maksim yelled beneath the din of Levin's reverberation, swinging his axe harmlessly at the grey wolf, causing it to skitter back. From the corner of his eye, Maksim saw the black wolf charge Levin with a rumble. Levin swiped at the black wolf with a clawed paw, knocking it to the dirt. The Vucari yelped and frantically pawed at the earth to attack again, but Levin already was advancing.

Maksim fled to the pasture ahead as another arrow flew by him. A pained whine sounded behind him, suggesting the arrow struck its mark. Hoping the arrow hit Levin in the meat instead of a vital organ, Maksim kept his focus forward. He held his axe horizontally across his chest, scanning the field for movement.

The Vucari woman, halfway ducking behind a shrub, was not difficult to locate. Her dark hair was braided behind her head, brown eyes squinting with worry. She swiveled the bow in his direction and nocked another arrow. Maksim ran at a stoop, keeping his eyes on the archer.

She loosed the arrow. The projectile sailed over his head by several feet. She rushed to fit another arrow onto the string.

He reached her before she drew the string back again. She cried out, reeling back as he came at her with his axe, crouching back in anticipation. Maksim did not recognize her paled skin or angular face as he brought the axe down. She raised her bow defensively, keeping his first swing from being a deathblow. The two weapons clacked, bone against wood, his blade hovering inches above her face. She gritted her teeth, fighting against his superior strength.

As a trained Warden, Maksim already had the advantage in close combat. The landless rarely had the chance to battle, unless they were waging a war against the Reds, and even then, they were often frontline infantry. Pawns to distract from the real threat.

Maksim tensed his muscles, pushing against her quaking arms. Her eyes flashed yellow as she tried to shift into an animal. Yellow hair sprouted from her cheeks and sharpened fangs lengthened from her thin lips. Maksim clenched his jaw, pulling back his axe. He arced the weapon over his head and then swiftly swung it sideways. The woman thrusted the bow upwards with the lost momentum, leaving her arms vulnerable. He continued the motion, cutting through her left wrist with the axe.

She screamed, losing concentration, and halting her charge. Blood sprayed across them; her bow fell with her hand still gripped around the handle, hitting her in the chest and face. Maksim ignored the crimson blanketing his vision and hacked the axe into her horrified expression. She returned fully to her Vucari form with her last breath, blood seeping from the edges of her mouth.

He jerked his axe loose, hurriedly skimming his gaze over the terrain for more landless Vucari. The rolling hills were quiet, save the gnashing and gurgling coming from behind him. Scowling, he gripped his weapon and twisted on his heel. Levin had marred one beast beyond reprieve. The black wolf dragged itself away from the ongoing battle at his rear by the front paws. The grey wolf was already trapped with his throat in-between Levin's powerful jaws.

Maksim approached the black wolf, lifting his axe. The wolf's brown eyes lifted helplessly to Maksim as his body shuddered to retake the Vucari form. The black fur shed from his skin, bones cracking and popping, as the male shape reformed against the dusty ground.

"Why did you attack us?" Maksim asked with a sneer. The Vucari man trembled, his back legs broken and bleeding, and back covered with bite marks from Levin. Maksim could also see the fletching of an arrow sticking out from the Vucari's side. The archer could have done with a bit more practice before taking to battle.

Spit, colored crimson, spilt from the man's bottom lip into his short, black beard. He shuddered with a knowing look, his brown eyes half-hidden between his eyelids. Despite his pain, he partially laughed at Maksim's question. "What are you playing at? You came to kill us, thinking only of protecting your lands and titles." The man coughed, spitting up more blood. "But, don't you see? By coming, you have proven Wolos's death. You would not have come otherwise."

Maksim deepened his scowl, sniffing at the air. He did not smell any animal or man. He winced, peering across the landscape once more. Valarun reached for the heavens in the distance, but if more landless Vucari were shrouded in the hills, they remained hidden.

"If you knew we would come for you, where is Scythia and the rest?" Maksim dared to step closer, feeling the weight of his grandfather's femur in his hands. The landless Vucari must have known Maksim would kill him, but he did not have to be gentle in its delivery.

"Beyond your reach," the man replied, laying his head into the dirt. He no longer had the strength to look up at Maksim. "We could not...have known how many the temple...would send."

"A suicide mission to delay us," Levin said. Maksim lifted his eyes to see his friend reaching for his robe and spear. The grey wolf had returned to its female form. The jugular had been torn from her body and deep cuts shredded her soft stomach, the guts slipping out between the folds of skin.

Maksim turned from the gruesome sight. "Are you injured, Levin?"

Levin shook his head. "Not in the slightest. A couple scratches, maybe."

"A failed tactic then," Maksim said, falling to a knee next to the landless. "We will have the rest of their heads by tomorrow evening."

He plowed the blade into the back of the man's neck, causing him to warble and jolt. It took another swing to break fully through the bone and flesh.

"You have a cold heart, Maksim," Levin said grimly, twisting away. "Remind me never to cross you."

"He needed to die, did he not?" Maksim asked, turning from the unfamiliar Vucari. The head rolled away from the body. "Is that not why we are out here?"

"Sure," Levin replied with a heavy sigh, slipping a silver piece from his pocket into Maksim's hand. "But that was our lovely girl's little brother. On the bright side, you won the bet."

Maksim bit the inside of his cheek, accepting the silver mark. His axe slipped in his fingers. He did not know Jana had a brother.

Chapter III

Maksim slowed their pace to a walk around midday with exhaustion clinging to his limbs.

Levin panted from several feet behind him. "We must've gained on them in the night."

Maksim did not have the energy to respond. He and Levin had lost momentum by carrying, and dragging, the dead landless in the early hours of the morning. Neither of them had wanted to waste time burying the corpses, but they also did not want the bodies to be found. So, they took them a couple miles further from the village, and then tossed the corpses into the weeds in hopes the real wolves would find them.

Afterward, they stayed to the trail. But even now, with Ayral fading behind him, Maksim knew they could not keep going like they were. Yet they must.

"The main mountain pass lies ahead, Maksim," Levin said, rubbing at his forehead. He pushed off with the spear in his hand to keep the pace. "I am surprised Scythia would take it, knowing we are following. One of us should fly ahead and see if we can find him."

"I would not risk having us shot down. We already know he knows we are coming. Besides, the tracks have not changed." Maksim said, gesturing at the scattered footprints in the dirt. "We both know the quickest way to Anaerfell is the mountain pass. Any other way would leave Scythia cornered. None want to be cornered in Valarun with Vulkodlak scurrying about."

Levin harrumphed in amusement. "When you put it that way, I suppose we are the lesser threat."

Maksim rubbed his brow, gazing at the sky. Unlike he and Levin, the clouds casually rolled by in no hurry to be anywhere. Maksim looked on to Valarun, the mountains growing as the day passed. He loosened his cloak slightly, feeling the heat from the sun push through the wool. "I would not go that far. We are simply not the immediate threat."

"I suppose so." Levin tilted his head. The man smirked pulling at the tuft of his hair at the edge of his chin. "And what of Jana's little brother? Have you given any more thought about killing Rorik Pearka?"

Maksim narrowed his eyes at his friend. He suspected Levin enjoyed tormenting him with thoughts he had already buried. "I did not know he was her brother, and even if I did, it would not have made any difference. He was a traitor to our Khagan."

"And?" Levin pressed.

Maksim scoffed. "And I would never have been marrying a landless girl." He pushed Levin away from him. "What are you trying to get me to say? Out with it."

"I want you to admit that you would mount the girl given the chance," Levin said. "I already know you love her. You have not spied on any other since we came across her bed chamber. You have nearly taken all the fun out of it."

"You are going to owe me another silver mark. Jana is nowhere around to be yelling out at us, or did you forget the bet?" Maksim smirked.

"No, I did not forget." Levin rolled his eyes. "Way to admit your love without admitting anything at all."

"I did not admit anything." Maksim rubbed the back of his neck. "When we return from Anaerfell, we will stop peeking at the girls. It is about time we both found a decent noble girl and settled down."

"So, you are saying you are going to stop?" Levin asked.

Maksim nodded.

"Oh! I have heard that one before," he laughed.

"Nine Lands!" Maksim said louder than he intended. "I mean it, Levin. We are going to be Wardens. We should start acting like them. No more of this nonsense. If we were caught by the Khagan, we would have our lands and titles stripped."

Levin scrunched his nose, running a hand through his hair. "You are really shaken up about this. I did not realize you were so sensitive."

"This is not about Rorik," Maksim said. "This is about what is right. I want to get to Anaerfell and learn the truth."

"The Khagan already told you the truth." Levin pointed to the horizon. "Besides, we are trekking into the mountains to kill our own people. There is no *right*. There is what you can get away with and what you cannot. And no one will be stopping us from spying on landless girls."

"I have never known you to be so warped in looking at the world." Maksim squinted at Levin through his brown locks.

"The world is a perverted place," Levin said with a simple shrug. "I am but a reflection of its enduring wisdom."

Maksim kept his eyebrows from raising, but only from effort. Levin was so full of himself, Maksim was certain the man did not believe half of the nonsense that escaped from his lips.

"Help me!" A woman screamed from behind them.

"By the gods," Levin muttered, raising his spear to waist level and spinning around.

Maksim followed his gaze to find the voice somewhere among the rolling hills they had traveled over. His stomach turned.

None other than Jana Pearka ran toward them, clutching her skirts with one hand, and waving them down with the other. He saw no immediate threat to the woman as she closed the distance.

With a chortle, Levin nudged him, and Maksim handed him back his silver piece. "I would like to know how you managed this one."

"I did nothing. Not my fault if the gods look on me favorably," he said. "Though, I would give my left hand for some *felpoppies* out here."

"Stop with the *felpoppies* already," Maksim said. "We are not going to do anything to her."

Levin shrugged.

Maksim kept his eyes on Jana, clumsily cupping his hands on the sides of his waist. Levin rocked on his heels next to him, lifting his spear. He could feel his friend darting his gaze between him and Jana, waiting for a sign to shove his blade through the landless girl's chest upon arrival.

"What are you doing here?" Maksim asked when she ultimately stopped, stooping over in front of them. His mind buzzed, trying to understand how and why this *very* landless girl had slogged into Valarun after them. She should be a hundred miles away, at least, working the fields outside Ayral.

"I—" Her mouth opened enough to see the top row of her teeth, air wheezing in and out of her mouth from running to catch them. She gave Levin little mind, brown eyes locking on Maksim with desperation. Her black hair was knotted and tangled behind her head, clinging to her attire with sweat. "I am looking for my brother. He—he left late last night with some other men. He said something about going to Anaerfell."

Maksim's mouth dried. At least the girl had not found her brother's carcass while trailing them. His mind floundered for the right words.

"I saw what looked like signs from a skirmish half a day back. I thought someone might be hurt, but..." Her voice trailed off, looking to either of them for some explanation.

Maksim rubbed at the hair on his cheek, knowing blood from the Vucari he killed was still sprinkled across his face and clothing.

Levin wisely redirected her with his own question, eyebrows furrowing and cheeks tightening. "If you knew he was leaving for Anaerfell why did you not stop him? Why did you not go to the Khagan?"

She batted her eyes to possibly push away tears. Her chin quivered with her words. "I did not think he was serious. He always listens to Scythia's drivel, but never have they done much more than talk."

"We have not seen any sign of them," Maksim lied, dropping his hand to his waistline. "You should turn back for Ayral and return to your work. If we happen across your brother, we will send him back, too."

"But, the blood I found—" she said.

"Wild wolves," Maksim interrupted. "Levin and I made short work of them." He touched Levin's arm so that he might lower his weapon from the landless girl they knew all too well. Levin acquiesced, firmly setting the base of the spear to the earth. "But we have seen no sign of any Vucari."

Jana swallowed a mouthful of air at Maksim's words, giving no indication if she believed him or otherwise. Her brown eyes widened slightly, looking to Valarun. "Tell me, why are the two of you out here?"

He looked to Levin. Clearly, he could not tell Jana the truth. Not fully.

"We were sent here by the temple," Levin offered, his voice a bit calmer than before.

"Why?" she asked.

"Oh! That is none of your concern," Levin said.

She flared her nostrils. Any exhaustion she may have displayed moments ago abandoned her. "I will decide what is my concern, Levin Kovach. Yes, I know who you are. And, you too, Maksim Artur. I see you two strutting about with the Khagan at the temple while the landless pull crops. Now, tell me, why you are out here?" she asked more firmly.

Maksim nonchalantly shrugged. "You know as well as any other the rumors floating around Rhian," he said, looking at Levin from the corner of his eye. "We were sent to discover if anything actually happened at Anaerfell. The Khagan meant to make the announcement this morning."

"Which you would have heard if you were home where you belonged," Levin said. He pointed back towards the settlement. "Go back home. This is no place for a landless."

Jana crossed her arms under her breasts. "I'm not leaving until I find my brother. I will walk all the way to Anaerfell if I must. I will find him."

"You cannot come with us," Maksim said.

"You cannot stop me from taking the same road," Jana retorted with a heated gaze. "What are you going to do? Kill me?"

The tip of Levin's spear angled as he let the base slip back behind him.

Maksim stepped around Levin, closing the distance between himself and Jana. "Of course not. But we are going to make camp."

"It is barely midday," she said.

"And we have been traveling all night," Maksim replied sourly. "You are welcome to head to Anaerfell on your own."

"No." Her eyes floated to the mountains behind Maksim, concern etching her face before looking at him again. Jana folded her arms. "I can wait."

"Suit yourself," Maksim said.

In short time, Maksim and Levin made a makeshift bed against the nearby rocks. Levin grumbled to him, unintelligibly for the most part, while they attempted to rest. Before long, Levin's complaints turned to mumbles, and then the heavy breath of sleep.

Maksim, however, did not sleep as restfully. For several hours, he tossed and turned, hoping the dreams would take him. But they never did.

Eventually, he gave up while Levin snored away. He discovered Jana had escaped to a nearby ledge, leaving him to his thoughts.

At first, he tried to place what kept him awake. The most logical reason concluded that the landless girl was the cause. She may have been pretty to look at, but Jana was the last person he wanted to see right now. A thought tickled at the back of his mind, considering if his own crimes were catching up to him. He never had stolen or murdered, but he had always gawked at the shape of the female form.

For years, Maksim tried to quit his peeping, but his curiosity always got the better of him. One more night. One more woman. Maksim excused his restless desire on the fact that he had never physically been with a woman. He hoped when he settled down and married, the longing to see the naked flesh would disappear. Admittedly, he was terrified the craving would only, at best, diminish in intensity, and never fully be mended.

His lack of sleep, however, may have had nothing to do with Jana, killing her brother, or his lustful mind. The rumors of Wolos's death were far more threatening than his desires for a woman. If the God of the Dead truly had been killed by mortals, then Aenar was in danger. Wolos was responsible for guiding souls from the land of the living to the land of the dead, whether that be Thrice Ten Kingdom or the Netherworld. Without Wolos, Maksim knew from Rhirgwe's teachings that the deceased could only return to Aenar as demons.

The notion of demons roving over the land, killing women and children, and waging wars was terrifying. His histories had never told a tale where a god had been killed. If Wolos was gone, the balance of the world was lost.

Maksim breathed in the thick air of the evening. Levin continued to snore softly.

He listened for a moment when he heard Jana's boots crunching over the scattered pebbles. He gazed at her with her hands swinging on either side of her swaying hips. By the gods, those curves.

He noticed she had straightened her dark hair, intertwining it into a neat, crisp braid. As she neared, her question came quick, as if she had been preparing it while he slept. "Why has the temple only now decided to go to Anaerfell? We have been hearing the rumors for months. I think you would agree it is peculiar that the nobles would choose to investigate only when hearing the landless planned the same."

He may have spent hours watching Jana in her bed chamber, but he did not know the girl. He was surprised at her firm tone, as demanding as the Khagan himself. Most landless he knew were cowardly and shy, hardly willing to make eye contact with nobles. Jana held no such reservations. She stood, perched over him, arms folded under her breasts, causing them to look larger than he knew they were. He averted his eyes from her, suddenly wishing he was still trying to sleep. His mind was too tired to be interrogated. "You assume much," he said. "What is to say that the temple had not planned to go to Anaerfell all along? Word of Wolos's death was not received until mid-winter. We could not have left until the snows melted and the water descended from the mountain." Maksim folded his knees into a sitting position while she drew closer. He could see her worn, leather shoes and the crooked cut of her skirts in his peripheral.

"So, you are saying the temple always intended to go to Anaerfell?" Jana snorted. "They surely would have said something if that were the case."

"I cannot know the mind of Khagan Rhirgwe," he said, trying to side-step whatever blame she tried to pinpoint. "But a Khagan has much to consider in every decision. The road to Anaerfell is a dangerous one."

"You mean the Vulkodlak?" Jana asked.

"Sure. Or the Reds," Maksim said with a curt nod, lifting his chin to Jana. Her gaze had softened considerably, but her arms remained stiff against her sternum. "If you recall, we heard rumors of their presence on Rhian too. What if Wolos's death was a lie told by our enemy?"

Jana pursed her lips at the prospect. She clearly had not considered such a ploy.

Maksim took the expression as a sign of him gaining leverage in the conversation, and pressed, "Sending our people into Valarun is not like plucking the crop from the field. You must trust the temple will do what is right by all the people. They have to think about everybody."

"You don't think the landless care about everyone?" Her brown eyes, filled with shock, looked back at him incredulously.

"Go home, Jana," Maksim said after a long pause. "If your brother is on the road to Anaerfell, we will send him home."

"Will you?" she asked, her tongue strangely clicking against the roof of her mouth. She may have been mocking him, but he could not be sure.

He tried another approach. "You are not prepared for this journey. You have no rations. Your shoes are falling apart. By the gods, you are in a skirt."

Jana looked down at her ragged clothes, dropping her arms to smooth wrinkles. She visibly gnawed at the inside of her cheek, considering his words. Yet her response was oddly gentle, "I will not be any trouble."

"Jana," Maksim started.

She cut him off, quick as lightning. "I said I will take care of myself!"

Maksim bit his tongue under the fiery temperament of the landless girl. She was not nearly as delicate as he had assumed when crouching outside her bedroom window. Khagan Rhirgwe was right. The world was crumbling, and it was starting here, on the outskirts of Valarun.

Chapter IV

Her voice croaked, "I wonder if you were always so blind. Or is this what happens when you spend your life being taught in the temple? Only the nobles could believe the temple does what is in the best interest of the Vucari." Tears touched the corners of Jana's eyes as she argued with Levin. For three days, the two had been at each other's throats. She clenched her fists. "Do you think the landless are stupid? We do not have the same education as you, but we know simple sense when we see it. We till your fields. We eat your scraps. We fight your wars. We..."

"Oh! You what?" Levin dared to ask when her voice trailed off. Maksim could see his neck redden. Maksim was uncertain his heart could take any more of their bickering. Besides, part of him already knew what she was about to say, and he hated to hear it.

"We sacrifice our family. We do more for the Vucari than the nobles and receive nothing in return." Jana scowled.

Maksim's lessons flooded through his lips, backing up Levin's position. "You know why we have sacrifices. The Eternal Flame must burn."

"Yes," she hissed. "To please the gods—*gods* who may very well be dead already. Do you not think we are wise enough to know what is really happening? Why would the gods wish to have the weak sacrificed when strong blooded Vucari are living in Ayral?"

"Who would govern us if we killed the nobles?" Levin retorted with a sneer.

"The landless," Jana said matter-of-factly, "or is that a treasonous thing to think. Are the landless never allowed to excel beyond their position? Are we all but swine?"

Maksim flared his nostrils, turning his eyes from Jana. He had never heard anyone speak so bluntly about the division of class among the Vucari. Then again, he spent his time at the temple or among the other nobles. If all the landless felt as strongly as Jana, he suspected the nobles held less power than they thought.

He could feel Jana's dark eyes tearing through him, her question left to the wind. He knew he should tell her the landless were not *swine*, but she had painted a picture so clear, he would only ignite her ire further by denying the truth she so strongly believed.

After a moment, when Levin chose to keep his mouth shut too, she began talking again. Her voice was softer, but hardly short of authority. "Three years ago, Mosies Fulhow's wife, Trishia, was taken to the Eternal Flame. I suspect neither of you know who they were." Maksim bit his tongue. He did not know who they were, and honestly, the more Jana rattled on, the less he cared. "Trishia did not have any children; she said she could not. But she raised me and my brother as her own child after my mother died fighting the Reds."

"What about your father?" Maksim asked.

Jana replied, "He died years earlier also fighting the Reds."

"Your mother left for war with you and your brother still too young to care for yourself?" Maksim tensed, looking to the pretty girl. The freckles on her skin faded under the redness of her fury.

"At the behest of the Khagan," she said. "I remember the temple knocking door-to-door, demanding the able-bodied to come and fight. Orders came from the Ghan. What choice did she have?"

"None." Maksim shook his head, knowing none could deny the will of the Ghan in Raccassi. He held more authority than even the Khagan. He faintly recalled the decree she detailed. Levin's parents had been summoned under the same ordinance, dying during the raids on the mainland against the Reds. He held his tongue from saying as much, including that his own father had fallen last winter during battle.

He could not think of a greater honor than being killed during war. Jana should be proud.

Jana smoothed her skirts, continuing her tale, "I was there when Elias Navenka took Trishia from her home and dragged her down the dirt road to the Eternal Flame. When Mosies tried to protect her—"

"He forgot his place," Levin interjected with a shake of his head. Levin clearly knew how the story ended. Maksim could make an educated guess. Mosies was executed and Trishia was sacrificed all the same. "What did he think was going to happen?" Levin added.

Jana's jaw dropped in shock. "She was *his* life."

Levin matched her expression. "They put one another—their so-called love—over the will of the gods. We have laws against such ideology."

"We have the laws of the Khagan," Jana said, curling her lip unattractively. "The temple is only hungry for blood, using fear and power to keep the landless bent to their will. I have never had a god come tell me the temple's way is righteous."

"You are speaking blasphemy," Maksim said.

"Which proves the truth of it." Jana swung her arms in the air with her words. "Society should not silence the tongues of their people when they disagree with their words."

"The gods say—" Maksim tried.

"No! The Khagan says!" she cried.

Maksim growled, wishing the woman would stop her frantic argument. "You are a landless woman, Jana. You would not understand."

She stared at him with cold, brown eyes, shoving a finger at him. "You are the one who does not understand. The nobles stand by and watch the landless get slaughtered for their glory, so they can hold to their lands and titles. Someday, the tables will be turned, and the nobles will know our pain."

"That sounds like a threat," Levin said, glowering at her.

She shrugged, slowing her pace. "Take it for what you will."

Maksim eyed her warily as she sauntered back, unwilling to walk near them. He and Levin kept their pace, more than ready to put some space between them. A half hour or more had passed before anyone spoke again.

Levin poked Maksim with his finger as they meandered through the mountains. The river leading from Ayral had disappeared early yesterday, circling north while they continued east. Levin's voice was barely a whisper. "Are you listening to me? What are we doing? If she refuses to go back to Ayral, this will only end one way."

Maksim bit the inside of his cheek. He gazed at the pass ahead of them in the settling darkness; the path winded for hundreds of miles toward Anaerfell. The escarpments had raised on either side of the path to the point the tops could scarcely be seen. Fragments of larger rocks and rubble lined the base of the mountains. Occasionally, they would pass by a hollow or a fissure, quiet as death.

"If she is with us when we catch up to Scythia, she will know the truth of her brother's death. You know she will attack us, Maksim," Levin said. "Let me kill her and be done with it. We do not need another enemy in the fight to come."

Maksim refrained from turning around where he knew Jana staggered along behind them. He and Levin had pulled ahead by several hundred feet as though they were trying to make a point. Though, he was not sure what that was exactly.

"Maksim," Levin said angrily, hitting the butt of his spear against the ground with more force than necessary. "She is slowing us down."

"I know. I know," Maksim said with exasperation. "We need to convince her to turn back."

"She is not turning back. Listen. I know she is pretty to look at, but we have our duty."

"We cannot lose ourselves out here. Landless or not, she is our people." He gritted his teeth. "She has done nothing wrong. She just wants to find her brother."

"And she is not going to find him," Levin replied with a snort. "Will you stop trying to weigh every deed as either right or wrong? Leave decency to history and think about the inevitable outcome." He dropped his voice even lower, if it were possible. "Whether she travels to Anaerfell with us or alone, she must die once we cross Scythia. She is landless. She holds no loyalty to us nobles. If she wanders alone in Valarun, she will eventually cross the Vulkodlak and die. And if she returns to Ayral, she increases the chances of stumbling over her brother's corpse. Best to kill her than deal with that aftermath."

"It is not right." Maksim fidgeted with his hands, before hooking his thumbs into his belt while they walked. He gazed at the discolored rock surrounding him. He did not want to admit Levin was right, but he could think of no other route. Letting Jana live would undoubtedly leave them hamstrung in the end.

"Save your conscience for old age, Maksim," Levin muttered. "She made her decision to die when she left her home."

Maksim dipped his head in agreement. "Okay. But be quick..."

"I bet you a silver she won't even make a sound before my spear is through her," Levin boasted.

"I am not betting on this," Maksim said.

"Oh! You want to tussle around with her first." Levin pushed his brown bangs from his eyes with a grin. Maksim scowled at him. Levin only laughed louder. "Too soon?"

With the smile, plastered to his face, Levin lifted his spear to his waist and turned on his heel. Maksim lifted his eyes to the twinkle of the stars, barely visible with his darksight.

Jana's sudden shriek halted Levin in his tracks. Maksim reeled around, grabbing Levin's shoulder, to see the cause of Jana's outburst. Levin had barely lifted his spear.

The reverberating roar, echoing on either side of the pathway, gave him the answer.

The Vulkodlak, wolf-men of Valarun, materialized from hidden dugouts in the walls of the mountain, buried by oversized rocks and debris. Some advanced on two legs like a man, while others used all four like a wolf. The monsters were covered in fur ranging from white to reddish brown to smoky grey to black. Their long claws were as menacing as the fangs decorating their wolfish snouts. Each monster on its hind legs stood a head and a half taller than Maksim with muscle comparable to a great bear.

Daunting barks and the sound of snapping jaws joined the din of the raucous roars. From the depths of one of the grottos a Vulkodlak howled, giving signal of fresh meat and more beasts ventured forth.

Maksim's first instinct, as the many Vulkodlak shuffled closer, was to protect Jana. Though, he turned in time to see her body twist and transform into the semblance of a sparrowhawk. Feathers erupted from her neck and back, her face crooking into a beak beneath beady eyes. Her skirt and tunic fell away as she shrunk, flying toward the stars with her skeletal legs tucked beneath her.

He grabbed Levin's shoulder. "We should change to birds and flee."

"And risk them destroying our gear?" Levin winced, watching Jana fly safely above them. He snorted. "We are not landless. And I am not going to arrive at Anaerfell naked and weaponless. Let us show these wicked creatures what the true Vucari have become."

Maksim flexed his arm, reaching for the axe at his belt and pulling it from its loop. A dozen or more of the beasts circled around them. He knew the history of the Vulkodlak as well as Levin. The wolf-men were weak Vucari who had once betrayed the faith of Wolos, and now remained trapped in their bestial form. He urged Levin, "We do not have the numbers."

"I bet you we will change that soon enough!" Levin flung his spear at a dark beast with his own snarl. The weapon zipped harmlessly over the Vulkodlak, striking the mountain surface on the other side. The spear bounced to the rocky terrain with a clatter.

"Not with your aim," Maksim muttered.

As Levin removed his tunic and flung it to the side, Maksim turned around to defend his back. He could not leave Levin down here to fight the wolf-men on his own.

He heard Levin grunt while changing into a great bear, muscles rippling from his back and down his arms with black fur springing from his skin. Maksim gripped his axe, keeping his eyes on the circling Vulkodlak. When the first wolf-man sprang forward, he swiped his axe, missing by inches. The Vulkodlak sprang back as quick as it had come. Maksim dared to swing again, but only to keep the beast back. He would not venture too far from Levin and leave them vulnerable.

Behind him, Levin caught a wolf-man in his clawed hands in mid-transformation, throwing the Vulkodlak to the side with ease. The beast twisted in the air, landing on all fours, before skidding against the loose rock to attack again.

Maksim stepped between the Vulkodlak and Levin, bringing his axe down in a fluid motion. The bronze blade cut cleanly through the meat behind the front leg. The beast roared, turning his attention and snapping at Maksim. With a swift arc, Maksim hit the Vulkodlak again under the chin. Blood gushed from the wound.

Two more beasts rushed at Maksim as the first sauntered back. Levin roared at his rear, barreling at those who circled them. Maksim tried to stay close to the Vucari but kept his attention on the two coming at him. He stepped back to avoid the swiping claws of the first, peeking to his side to see where the remaining Vulkodlak were. There was too much movement.

"Stay close, Levin!" Maksim countered with his axe, grazing a hair too high to connect with the Vulkodlak's face. The second Vulkodlak raised on its hind legs, white fur shimmering. Two clawed attacks raked above Maksim's head as he rolled sideways, and then sprung back to his feet.

The moron had ignored him, ambling closer to the mountain among several Vulkodlak. The beasts barked and growled, biting at Levin's legs and arms, repeatedly tearing away chunks of flesh. His friend rumbled with pain but continued fighting as though he were fresh to battle.

Maksim knew he was not going to get out of this fight without changing too. The other Vulkodlak were already surrounding him, and Jana had proven herself to be useless.

Curling his lip, he pitched his axe at the standing Vulkodlak. He swiftly ripped the tunic from his shoulders, standing naked to the world, and watched his grandfather's femur—the handle of his weapon—flip over and over. Time seemed to stand still as he altered his form.

Wolos's blessed blood coursed through him, switching his skin into a berserker of battle, the sacred *bies*. His feet cracked, widening and curling, until they resembled the hooves of a bull. They tore through his boots, ripping the leather to shreds beneath him. Dark brown, scraggly fur sprang across his body from the waist down, and from the neck up. His legs bent and contorted until they resembled those of a fawn, but three times wider, raising him another foot in height. He roared as his arms and chest, remaining humanoid, grew to keep proportionate to his increased size and girth. He snorted with disdain as his face widened, leaving a large wet nose, angled ears, and fanged teeth. He shook his head in pain, feeling the bony ridges form over his eyes, beneath the large, thick antlers erupting from his skull.

He bawled, sounding more animal than human. He could feel the blood churning in his veins, causing the world to blur with each throbbing pulse. Holding the form of the *bies* was not as difficult as staying lucid while in battle. With every blow Maksim took, he would become further enraged, willing to destroy anything in his path, friend or foe.

The axe blade sank into the Vulkodlak about the time Maksim bounded at the snapping wolf-man to his left, who simultaneously leapt at him with jaws wide. Maksim caught the upper and lower jaw in either hand, feeling the sharp teeth cut through his thick skin. With a mighty jerk, he split the beast's face in two; the yelp was only a fraction quieter than the bones snapping from their socket.

A second Vulkodlak appeared, emerging from those circling. Maksim lifted his arms to react, knowing he could not be swift enough. To his surprise, Jana—remaining in her sparrowhawk form—swooped in front of the wolf-man and clawed at the beast's eyes. The Vulkodlak jerked its head, snapping at her ineffectively, spinning around in a momentary daze. Jana returned to the skies as quickly as she had swooped down. Maksim took the opportunity, pouncing on the wolf-man's back, crushing its face to the earth. He held the monster down with a knee and pummeled the head to the dirt again and again. Bone and skin splintered, and brains spilled.

The roar behind him told of a third attacking Vulkodlak seconds before it reached him. He swung his head in an arc, catching the wolf-man's midsection on his curved antler. Blood splattered across his vision. He rumbled, swaying his head to knock the beast from his horn, only to fall to his knee to hold the weight. The Vulkodlak, powerful and unforgiving, fought through the pain and clawed at Maksim's face. The nails ripped through his skin from the boney ridge above his eye to his cheek.

Roaring, Maksim flung his head sideways, using a clawed hand to help propel the Vulkodlak. His horn ripped through the beast's stomach, breaking ribs, and raining a shower of blood over him. The Vulkodlak crashed against the ground on the opposite side of him, whimpering and clawing at the earth to drag itself away.

Maksim did not let him get far.

Levin bellowed in pain behind him as the wolf-men continued their assault, tearing at his flesh with their teeth and claws. Maksim pushed off his hoof cutting across the ground in a flash. He grabbed the nearest by the scruff of its neck and buried his teeth—as white as winter snow—into the Vulkodlak's neck, ripping the throat out. He pulled back about the time he felt sharpened claws tear across his back.

He tilted his head back and roared, dropping the Vulkodlak from his grip. He had barely turned around when the second attack struck him across the chest. The razor claws of the beast split him open.

His vision blurred.

He swiped his own claws in return, connecting with something he could not see. White fur blurred past him, and he swung again. A howl erupted as he made contact a second time.

Levin gnashed his teeth behind him. He could feel the ground quaking under Levin's weight as he collapsed under the weight of the many Vulkodlak. Maksim reached for another Vulkodlak, despite his fogged-vision. He clasped his hands around the neck of the beast. The small bones crunched under his superior strength.

With a mighty bawl, Maksim grabbed at the beasts swarming over Levin, tearing them off his friend. Levin twitched in an attempt to fight back but held little strength. Maksim's vision faded from a ghostly white to crimson red. The howls of the Vulkodlak rang in his ears as he ripped meat from bone, and crushed skulls. He could taste the blood. He could smell the death.

Suddenly, a forced bay erupted from one of the few remaining Vulkodlak, and the beasts scattered, rushing back into the fissures of the crags. Levin stumbled to his feet to chase after them, possibly thinking he would burrow through the rock after them, and then stopped. He huffed in his bear form, blood oozing into a puddle beneath his large frame.

Levin rumbled softly and fell to the earth.

Levin's body jolted, returning to his human form, the grievous injuries still covering his body. Maksim fell to a knee next to him, knowing he was losing blood too. He could feel the warmth slipping down his chest and back.

His hand fell on Levin's stomach as he retook his regular form. In a short moment, he could speak again. "You are a fool."

"We won, didn't we?" Levin cracked a pained smile. "You owe me a silver."

"I do not think we finalized that bet, my friend," Maksim said.

Levin strained his neck to keep his eyes on him. "You never told me you had the blood of the *bies*. By the gods, you are a god in battle."

Maksim frowned, touching the dark blood oozing from his chest. "Not hardly." Levin's cuts were much deeper than his own. He changed the subject. "Your wounds need fire if you have any desire to see the dawn. Lay still."

An hour later, Maksim knelt behind Levin while Jana redressed behind them. He bit the inside of his cheek, sneaking a peek over his shoulder at her pale skin. He could not keep his eyes from lingering.

Levin elbowed him in the side of the leg with a smirk. "I am bleeding out here, Maksim."

He clutched the bandage around his own chest with a free hand and glared at Levin. He could feel his flesh rubbing against the thin cloth tied around his chest, threatening to slip away and reopen his own wound. Levin, on the other hand, was already looking better with the multiple bandages lining his torso. With a grunt, Maksim pulled his shoulder blades back to hold his bandage in place and wrapped another ripped cloth from his cloak around Levin's midsection.

"You will live," Maksim croaked. "We might still make it to Anaerfell."

"You really are set on going all the way," he whispered back with a snort.

Maksim nodded. "Of course."

Levin winced as Maksim tied a firm knot, pinching the dark skin on the Vucari's back. He may lose some circulation from the waist down, but the bleeding would not restart.

"Better than cauterizing them all," Maksim said, twisting his head to gain a view of Jana again. To his surprise, she stood next to him, her crotch only inches from his face. He coughed and tilted back. Her brown eyes buried into him. He struggled to find words to give reason for why he may have turned in her direction. "Would you put out the fire?" he asked.

She grimaced, walking around him and Levin to where the fire crackled at the end of Levin's feet. Jana had started the blaze with scattered brush immediately following the battle, foregoing her clothes to help them. He had heated the fire enough to redden the bronze blade of his axe. The weapon was not ideal for searing their wounds, but it was better than dying from blood loss. The time spent scorching skin and closing wounds was best forgotten.

Instead, Maksim preferred to watch the swaying of Jana's hips. She meandered around them and kicked dirt over the flames. He swallowed and returned his attention to Levin's bandages.

Levin folded his legs under him. "We will need to keep an eye out for elderberries. Even a handful may help us fight off any infection," he said.

"I do not think the curse of the Vulkodlak is contagious," Jana said.

"Not the Vulkodlak, daft girl," Levin mumbled, shifting his gaze to the spear still lying near the mountain. Maksim nearly forgot what they aimed to do to Jana before the beasts attacked them. He was not certain anything had changed, though, he did recognize Jana stepped into the battle for a second to save him from an additional injury. It was not much, but it was something. Levin attempted to explain his reasoning to the landless girl. "We may have kept ourselves from bleeding out, but we are more likely to become sick after searing our skin."

"The burns weaken us and will lead to fever and fatigue," Maksim clarified. "We will need the elderberries to keep the sickness at bay."

"Well," she huffed. "Aren't you two brilliant with all your learning at the temple?"

"It has its perks," Levin sneered.

Jana kicked the dirt with more force, sending a cloud of dust in the air.

Maksim ignored her, seeing that the dirt floated safely away from them. He adjusted the bandages on Levin's bloodied arm. They were already as stained as the ones across Maksim's chest.

"These are not going to heal anytime soon," Levin said, looking to his left arm. A chunk of flesh remained missing from his shoulder.

He cleared his throat, reminding the man, "You are the one who wanted to fight the Vulkodlak. We could have waited them out. You are lucky we are not dead." He looked around for his cloak, only to realize he had used the last of his cloth on the last bandage. He reached his hand out to Jana. "Give me a strip of your skirt. I need another bandage."

Again, Jana darkly peered at him. The starless sky seemed to only add to her haunting visage and hateful look. Half-heartedly, she reached down and tore the bottom of the skirt to split the threading. Then, ever so carefully, she ripped the fabric in a circle around her body.

Maksim wondered how many strips he could snag before she was completely without her garment. The skirt already dipped just below the knee. A beautiful pale knee.

She waved the cloth in front of his face with an outstretched hand. "Do you want it, or not?"

Maksim took the piece of skirt, muttering his thanks. He wrapped it around Levin's left arm and pulled it tight.

Levin chose his words carefully, holding onto his stomach. "I doubt Scythia, your brother, or any other has made it past the Vulkodlak. Maksim and I must continue to Anaerfell and complete our mission for the temple." Levin scrunched his nose at Jana. "You, however, should return home."

"I told you I am not leaving without finding my brother," she said, narrowing her eyes. "You two, *however*, will hardly make it through another battle. If anyone should turn back home, it should be you."

Levin scoffed, standing to his feet. "You are mistaking us for landless. We don't turn back from our duty."

She curled her lip. "Neither do I."

Chapter V

Traveling through Valarun for the next six days were drearily slow. Maksim found few traces of the roaming Vulkodlak, and even less evidence of Scythia and the group of landless. A couple times a day, he would spot a cluster of faded shoe prints against the rocky road, but the terrain was becoming indistinguishable with rocks piled upon more rocks. He could only assume Scythia stayed ahead of them, but in truth, he could have been hiding in one of the hundreds of caves they had passed.

He looked over his shoulder at Levin, who tarried behind at a snail's pace, wiping the sweat from his forehead whenever it began to trickle into his eyes. He had sprung a fever on the third day and stopped speaking more than a few words at a time when he was demanding water. Despite Maksim's attempts at foraging in the late evening, no elderberries were found in the barren environment. He could do nothing for Levin except hope he would have the strength to fight through the sickness. He did keep Levin hydrated, but with the river long behind them, he relied on natural springs flowing from the mountain.

He still had not found one today to refill their waterskins.

Jana hobbled along even further behind. He knew she had several blisters the size of eyeballs on either foot, and the way her stomach rumbled at night, he was surprised she was even on her feet.

Between the two, they were forced to stop multiple times a day to allow for rest. Maksim tried to sleep when he could, knowing his own wounds needed time to heal too. But his cuts were already scabbed over, and hardly limited his movement.

He put his hands on his sides and stopped, allowing Levin to catch up. Once he was in arm's reach, he handed over the waterskin. "Take what is left, Levin. We might as well rest for a few moments and I can try to find more water."

Levin weakly nodded, taking the dried leather and pulling it to his lips. He gulped hungrily.

Jana dragged her feet behind him. "None for me, eh? I suppose I am meant to die out here."

"You were told to go back home," Maksim said, unsure whether he should feel sorry for the landless girl. He shrugged and wiped his sweaty hands on his trousers. "We did not bring rations for three, and Levin is injured."

"He is more important than me?" she asked, squinting an eye. "That is what you mean to tell me?"

"Well," Maksim said, looking at sun beating down on them, "he does hold his ground in a fight."

"I protected you against the wolf-men," she hurried to say, folding her arms under her breasts. "Or have you forgotten?"

"You flapped your wings at a single Vulkodlak," Maksim smirked. "If you are thirsty, go find your own water."

Jana pushed by him to scope the path ahead. "But he will likely die soon."

Maksim rolled his eyes, turning back to Levin, who found the energy to glare at Jana as she walked away. She soon disappeared around the bend in the mountains. "I am not dying."

"I know," Maksim said, helping him sit down. "I suspect you will break this fever any day now."

"I am already feeling better," Levin said, coughing into his shoulder. "Though, I would feel better if you would kill her already."

"I do not think she is the one slowing us down any longer." Maksim smiled. He took the empty waterskin from Levin, tucking it into his belt. Levin took his turn to roll his eyes. "I know she will be a threat when we catch up to Scythia and the others."

"Yeah, she will," Levin said. "Not to mention she has been picking at our rations for the better part of a week. Take my spear and go do it now." Maksim hesitated, looking to Levin's spear laying in the dirt next to him. "I will owe you a silver coin."

"I thought you already owed me one," Maksim said.

Levin scrunched his nose. "Oh! To be honest, I cannot rightly remember who owes who. But I promise to give you a silver piece if you save my ears from hearing her bicker about those sores on her feet."

Maksim reached for the stone-tipped spear. "Fine. I will kill her, but I don't want your coin."

Levin smiled. "I will give it to you all the same."

He attempted to clear his mind while walking to the bend where Jana had vanished. He had urged her to go home multiple times, and she refused to listen to him. He could not save her from her fate any longer. Levin was right. He had been right a week ago when first suggesting as much. Jana had to die.

The path spiraled through the mountains for several hundred feet, weaving in and out of the rock like a snake. He did not see any immediate sign of Jana, but after a couple hundred feet, he did hear water. His first instinct was to run and fill the waterskin at his belt, but the spear in his hand kept his thoughts bound to his duty.

He inched through the ravine, keeping his shoulder to the cavern wall and his eyes on fixated on the towering mountains.

He balanced the spear at his waist, feeling the stone tip weigh down the front.

The glen was unexpected in the rocks. Green trees and grass scattered around a dark blue pond, no wider than a dozen men, reaching across the gorge. Above him, blue, crisp water flowed through the side of the mountain, dropping almost a hundred feet into the pond. He could see no wildlife among the trees, but he did notice reddish-orange fruits hanging from some of the trees.

He and Levin would eat well tonight.

Jana breached the surface of the pond, loudly gasping for air. Her eyes were closed and her smile wide, waving her hands through the water to stay afloat. With a laugh, she rubbed the water from her face and swam to the edge of the waterfall. In short time, she was positioned underneath, opening her mouth and gulping mouthfuls of the fresh water.

Maksim eased closer, while remaining hidden behind the rocks. Jana was noticeably naked in the water, her clothes crumpled on the edge of the shore with her shoddy boots. The water was not clear enough to distinctly see anything, but he could not miss the shape of her curves.

His mind tickled at the thought of joining her in the water before running her through. Nine Lands, nothing was stopping him. Levin would probably encourage him to have some fun before killing the landless girl.

She splashed ahead of him, swimming to the opposite shore.

He dipped lower to avoid her gaze, if she turned around, but kept his eyes fixated. Even at a distance, his Vucari eyes gave him full view of her pale skin and freckles as she walked from the pond. Her black hair was a dark tangled mess against her back, clumped together like moss.

Maksim bit his lip, wondering why he was stalling. No one was out here, save him, her, and Levin. By the gods, he could only think he was afraid of touching her. If he touched her, he may very well fall in love with her. He was not certain that is how it worked, but he could not risk loving a landless girl.

His hand trembled, knowing he could not do what needed to be done. Levin would have to be the one to kill her.

Jana tiptoed to the nearest tree, her hips rocking with every delicate step. She reached for one of the low-hanging fruits, carefully plucking it from the stem near the triangular leaves. Maksim never had—

The gurgled cry echoing through the canyon stole his thoughts with his breath. He twisted away from

Jana, slamming his back too hard against the uneven rock. He gasped, gripping the spear in his hand at the sound of another warbled scream.

The Vulkodlak had come!

Forgetting Jana, Maksim bolted.

He propelled around the bend of the mountain, expecting to see hordes of wolf-men tearing the flesh away from his friend. Instead, he witnessed something far worse.

A stone-tipped spear, much like the one he was holding, had been shoved down Levin's gullet, and out his backside into the ground. His friend twitched with the wooden shaft forced between his teeth, his insides pouring out from his back. His eyes stretched wide, staring at the heavens. His fingers scraped at the earth uselessly. He would be dead in seconds.

Maksim's jaw quivered with rage, raising his eyes to Scythia Gergo, who nonchalantly let go of the weapon. The landless man tensed his cleft chin, sticking out his bottom lip at Maksim. He knelt to shield his torso behind Levin, rubbing casually at the brown rags he wore. Maksim lifted his spear to his ear, noticing the dried blood splattered across Scythia's wool clothes.

The man flipped his greying, scraggly hair over his thin shoulder. A quarter of his front teeth were missing, causing his words to slur. "So, you planned to kill us, did you?" He sneered, gesturing to his left and right. Maksim followed his gaze to see two landless men, on either side, aiming bows at him. The spear would barely leave his fingertips before he would be dead. "Don't think about trying to change into anything either, Warden," Scythia warned. "No bears. No wolves. No nothing. You stay just as you are and drop your weapon."

Maksim let the spear roll from his fingertips, staring past Levin at Scythia. The weapon clanked against the ground.

Wrinkles formed at the corners of Scythia's eyes. His cheekbones tightened with his smile. "The axe too. Let it loose."

Saying nothing, Maksim brought his hands down slowly and jerked the axe from its casing. He may be quick enough to kill one of the two landless holding the bows before they burrowed an arrow in his skull. He would rather bide his time for the chance to kill Scythia.

"What do you want?" Maksim said, holding the axe by the bone handle. His grandfather's femur strengthened him. He would not die this day.

"The axe," Scythia said. "Today."

Maksim ground his teeth, unblinking, and dropped the weapon. He irritably repeated his question. "What do you want?"

Scythia pulled himself to his feet, using the spear sticking through Levin to leverage his weight. The toothless smile stayed on his face. "I am going to Anaerfell. And you will come with me. Peacefully."

Maksim's scoffed. "Why would I do that?"

"To learn the truth of Wolos's death," Scythia said. "I think the temple would be very interested in knowing whether the rumors are true. And you will be able to tell them."

"You do not know anything about the temple and their interests," Maksim said.

"I know the Khagan sent you to kill us. I have been expecting you, actually," Scythia responded, smacking his lips together in amusement. He eyed the bowmen on either side of Maksim to ascertain his safety, and then took a step around Levin. "Sadly, the Vulkodlak have made quick work of my poor men. The landless are no match for the mighty wolf-men of Valarun."

"So, you want me to protect you from them," Maksim reasoned. "That is what this is about. You cannot make it to Anaerfell without me. You have probably been hiding in a cave nearby waiting for someone to clear the path ahead."

Scythia's smile disappeared, pressing his thin lips together. He warily eyed him, giving away that Maksim had guessed at the landless man's inability to move forward alone. Only three remained from more than a dozen.

No wonder the Vulkodlak had been recently quiet. Their bellies were full.

Scythia scooted closer. A few steps more and Maksim could use him for a shield against the bowmen. Maybe. "You cannot get to Anaerfell without us either," Scythia said.

Maksim frowned. "You only think I want to go to Anaerfell."

"I know you do!" Scythia shouted. "Do not lie to me!"

Maksim tensed. He wanted to go to Anaerfell, but he hardly believed he needed three landless holding weapons at his throat to get there.

The scuffle of boots behind Maksim was soon followed by a terrified gasp. "What happened to Levin? By the gods, Scythia?" Jana edged around Maksim, staying an arm's length away. She covered her mouth with her hand at the gruesome sight, twisting to see the two bowmen with their weapons raised.

"Jana?" Scythia reeled back in equal shock. His tongue darted between the gaps where his teeth should have been as though he were trying to spit out words.

Her round, brown eyes were momentarily spellbound on Levin and the pool of blood beneath him. "What have you done?" She swiftly reexamined the bowmen before fixating her gaze on Scythia. "Where is my brother?"

Scythia pointed his finger at Maksim, finding a place to direct his words. "He killed your brother." He growled at Levin's mangled corpse, curling his lip for emphasis. "They both did. They were sent here to kill us too."

"Wha—" Jana choked. "You killed Rorik? But you said..." She scooped Levin's spear from the ground, holding it awkwardly at Maksim. "You killed him!"

"Jana, no!" Scythia yelled, reaching for her, and then stepping back again when realizing he drew too close to Maksim for his own comfort.

Her uncontrollable sobbing started before Maksim could form a response. The spear wobbled in her hands, the point waving near his midsection.

Maksim tilted his head toward her, reminding himself that she was landless. He never could have been allowed to touch those pretty freckles. He should have killed her. "Yes. I killed him," he said, burying all emotion. He may as well have been frozen in ice.

She lifted her eyes and screamed at him. Her bared teeth quaked with her howl. The spear tip suddenly became unmoving in her firm grasp.

"Stop, Jana," Scythia nearly pleaded. "Do not kill him. We need him to reach Anaerfell. We must have proof."

"You would have had better luck convincing Levin to take you," Maksim said. He whispered to Jana, hoping she would do what he could not. "Kill me."

He scarcely finished saying the words before the spear twisted in Jana's hands. Her swiftness surprised him as the base cracked against his skull.

The world faded into a haze and then darkened. Shadows swept across his vision, the voices around him muffled as he dropped to his hands and knees. He could not make out the words being said, but moments later, he was kicked to the ground and his hands were twisted behind him, knotted in twine.

He groaned, too stunned to react to the landless wrestling him to the ground. Scythia would not kill him until they reached Anaerfell.

If Jana did not kill him, he had plenty of time for revenge.

Chapter VI

The first night with the landless was spent in the grove, eating the reddish-orange fruit and drinking fresh spring water. Maksim somehow fell asleep after the meal with his thoughts on Levin. He did not wake until the middle of the following day, feeling groggy and disoriented. When offered water, he eagerly drank the liquid only to fall back asleep for the gods knew how long.

The second time he woke, the stars were fading from the sky with the morning light and Scythia was kneeling near him with a spear pointed at his throat. Jana and the other two landless were gathering what little gear they carried, talking in whispers.

"We will be at Anaerfell in under an hour. Would you like to walk, or do I need Diri and Aavan to drag you around again today?" Scythia bared his broken teeth, lifting the spearhead to Maksim's cheek.

The green brush and trees lining the mountains on either side of him swirled, giving a clear sign they may have been traveling for days. The terrain seemed to have completely changed. The air was much cooler than he remembered.

The soreness in his muscles and the throbbing in his head suggested he was likely covered in bumps and bruises from being pulled along the ground while unconscious. He strained to sit upright with Scythia's spear firmly pressed against the side of his face. By the gods, his head ached. "What did you do to me?" Maksim said hoarsely feeling the dryness in his throat.

"*Felpoppies*," Scythia smiled, slowly lifting his tunic with a free hand showing a small pouch hanging from his belt next to a waterskin. "I cut them into little flakes and put it in your drink. Amazing what a few scattered leaves can do. Sure, you woke a few times, but they work quick. Kept you quite tame for our little walk."

Maksim sputtered, his tongue swollen in his mouth from thirst. His stomach growled. "How long?"

"Days. I am not like you nobles. I have no care for counting how many times the sun rises and falls."

He moved his jaw back and forth, feeling the tension to his ears and down his neck. He scanned the dark eyes of the landless man. "And how did you expect me to fight off the Vulkodlak if I was subdued?"

"Fight them?" Scythia threw his head back with a laugh, his greying hair whipping back and forth. "I would be a fool to let you switch skins with the blood in your veins. Jana told me you have the sacred *bies* blood. No, no. If it would have come to it, I would have fed you to the Vulkodlak piece-by-piece, while we made our escape."

"Nine Lands," Maksim swallowed a mouthful of air. He was nothing but a decoy to be used. "I take it you saw no wolf-men?"

"Fortunately, for you, no." Scythia smacked his lips together. "But who knows what we will find on the way back to Ayral. If you behave yourself, you might make it back with us."

"You will not keep me alive." Maksim coughed, trying to build up enough saliva in his mouth to swallow.

Scythia lifted his shoulders and winked. "I might. I have not decided yet. Depends on what we find at Anaerfell." He slowly lowered the spear and removed the waterskin from his belt. "You want a real drink of water."

Maksim rubbed his tongue against the inside of his cheek and finally nodded. Scythia warily eyed him while unstrapping the waterskin. He lifted the end to Maksim's lips and tilted the back. The fresh liquid rushed over his lips and down his chin; he gulped without restraint.

When he was done, Scythia grabbed the spear and motioned for Maksim to stand upright. "Let us go see whatever there is to see, eh?"

Less than an hour passed as they traipsed through the mountains to Anaerfell. Pine trees thickened on either side of a worn path, decorating Valarun with more green than Maksim saw on the outskirts of Ayral. Any sign of winter's snow against the mountain had faded, leaving piles of brush and debris scattered like mulch for a garden.

He kept his eyes on the edge of the path, away from Scythia, and far from Jana, who had maintained a scowl on her face all morning. He understood her hate. He felt the same toward Scythia for taking Levin from him.

The difference was he was a noble, and he was acting in accordance with the Khagan and the temple.

The landless were beyond the law. These four with him were truly no better than the Reds across the sea.

Levin had understood duty better than him, but now, Maksim began to grasp—fully—why Khagan Rhirgwe sent them to slaughter these ruthless, landless scum. They would bring the entire civilization to its knees for their own self-worth and indulgence. They lacked faith and were all the weaker for it.

"This does not look promising for the Khagan," Jana said bitterly from behind him as they stepped into a clearing. She hit him with her shoulder as she passed, striking one of the many bruises on his back.

He stood rigid, attempting to mask the sharp pain. The moment was fleeting as he focused on what caused Jana's biting dictum.

Brush and broken vines stretched over the clearing among the few pine trees still standing. Much of the vegetation was brown or black, however, as though it were surviving from some fire. The thicket was quiet. Dead.

"What is that smell?" The bowman with darker hair and bushy eyebrows asked, covering his nose. Maksim believed his name was Aavan.

The shorter one, Diri, shrugged his shoulders, keeping an arrow nocked in his bow at Maksim's side.

Maksim clenched his teeth, unable to protect himself from the overwhelming stench of rot. He sluggishly examined the valley. The faded, stone ruins of Anaerfell were crumbling against the mountain edge almost six-hundred paces to the right. The monumental structure had been built into the side of the mountain in a long-forgotten age, reaching forty or fifty feet toward the heavens. Several columns had collapsed from the temple, overtaken by what vegetation remained. Though, the worst of the scene lay nowhere near the temple called Anaerfell.

Several hundred feet more feet in the other direction, up the rise of the mountain on Maksim's left was evidence of a terrible battle. Whatever trees or rocks once existed in the area had wholly been swept away by some great magic, tossed or hurled, in immeasurable clumps against the mountain edge, forming an unnatural clearing. The tops of what trees remained scraped the ground, while the roots pointed to the sky; and then, misplaced, dented holes lined the mountainside as though they had been struck with a god's hammer. Stones, half as large as the temple, were shattered and spread over the ground. And, even more, broken arrows and burn marks painted the landscape beneath a green haze—a disgusting, miasma—hanging inches over the ground like a discolored, sick fog.

Amidst the haze, Maksim could see something, once living, corroding in the sun's heat.

"Nine Lands," Scythia's voice trembled, gagging as the wind whistled from the incline and carried the reeking scent down to them. He inched closer and stopped in awe of the monstrous, decaying creature ahead of him.

"There is the cause of the smell." Jana retched, stepping back with Levin's spear in her hands as though the dead beast beneath the fog might spring up to attack.

"Is that a dragon?" Diri asked in a nasally tone, moving his weapon from Maksim to the green-colored spectacle sprawled across the ground.

"Hm." Scythia peered, moving a bit more toward the beast to see it better. "That is Wolos, the Wolf God, and Protector of the Eternal Spring."

"He is dead." Jana said wondrously, as though she had not believed the rumors herself.

Maksim's stomach stirred, daring to advance more than the other four and breath the fumes. The jade-colored scales covering the dragon were dull from the hooked tail to the stretched snout. The beast may have been almost sixty-foot in length, weighing more than a mountain. The crystalline eyes were opened, staring at nothing, holding no life in them. The inside of the mouth looked black and putrid, despite the off-white teeth lining the top and bottom gums. One leathery wing was folded back, while the other was stretched and withering.

He stepped into the acidic fog. The fumes were nauseating. He touched the tail of the beast with his boots, tightening his hands in the knots behind his back.

"How can you be certain it is Wolos and not an ordinary dragon?" Aavan asked.

"The single head," Maksim answered. "Wolos's offspring, dragons of this world, all have three heads. They each have a name and a purpose. Not this one."

"You see the God of the Dead is *dead*," Scythia cried from behind Maksim. "Khagan Rhirgwe lied to us to protect his lands and titles, as I said. If Wolos is dead, the Ash Tree will soon perish with him."

"Your words are blasphemous and dangerous, Scythia Gergo," Maksim said. "We have a culture of law and order and purpose. You would destroy our people. You would be no better than the Reds."

"You have a serpent's tongue, Warden," Scythia said, lifting his hand and smacking his lips. "None should be forced to live in a society of lies. The Ash Tree will die, and what will happen to us then?"

"It will only wither if we fail to protect it," Maksim said, turning around to face the landless scum. "A dead god does not free us of our duty. He blessed us with his blood to protect the Ash Tree. We will not abandon our charge!"

"The nobles blood, you mean!" Scythia spat, tilting his chin to the dead dragon. "The landless do not have the power of the *bies*; we cannot save the Ash Tree."

"You have your place," Maksim said.

"My place?" Scythia's fury came quick. His voice echoed to the temple of Anaerfell and back again. "To serve the nobles? No! We will not be slaves to our own people."

"You would see the world crumble," Maksim hissed.

"I would see it liberated," Scythia replied.

Jana clicked her tongue. "I would too."

Before either of the bowman could cast their vote, a series of high-pitched screeches sounded from the temple behind them.

Maksim instinctively ducked down, taking a knee, watching Aavan spin around with his bow and arrow. Diri did the same, nearly loosing the one he already had nocked.

"By the gods," Jana cowered back until she was shoulder to shoulder with Maksim. "What was that?"

The answer came without a word as a three-headed white dragon crawled from the open ceiling of the temple. The thin, yet large wings, opened on either side of its coiled body. The white beast rose over the worn structure, tucking the two large feet to its belly. Three cone-shaped heads whipped around on the end of long necks before the center noticed them across the enclave. It soared toward them,

"*Lahmia*," Maksim said. "You better untie me if you wish to defeat the beast."

"No." Scythia smacked his lips, raising his hands with the spear dangling from his fingertips. "We are Wolos's chosen people. The dragon will not attack us."

The dragon swooped closer with incalculable speed.

"Unless *Lahmia* heard what you said about abandoning the Ash Tree. The Vulkodlak were cursed for failing Wolos; what do you think the punishment is for denying him altogether?" Maksim hissed.

"We are doomed," Diri shouted.

Scythia reached for the shorter Vucari, but he was too slow. Diri fired an arrow at *Lahmia*. The projectile flew by the left head and bounced off the wing as though it had hit a mountain. Aavan loosed his arrow, too, and watched it snap in half upon striking *Lahmia's* scaled chest.

The white dragon smoothly dived, snagging Diri and Aavan in her mighty jaws with the left and right heads, and then swooped back to the clear skies. The center head screeched again, silencing the screams of the two landless men. Maksim ignored the bones snapping and blood gushing from the dragon's maw.

His odds had improved considerably.

With a grunt, he sprang to his feet and hit Jana with his shoulder, knocking her back into the acidic fog. She cried out with surprise, flailing to the ground.

Her choking and coughing bespoke of the poison hanging in the air, and its deathly effects if inhaled too strongly.

Maksim did not wait to see the outcome. Her death would not please him nearly as much as Scythia's.

The older man was slow to take his eyes from the circling dragon, despite Jana's sudden bawl. He twisted with his spear held awkwardly against his chest. Maksim leapt onto him, straining against the bindings on his wrist, wrapping his legs around Scythia's midsection.

Scythia fell to his back with Maksim's weight heavy on his chest. The shaft of the spear crushed against Scythia's chest, threatening to steal his breath. Yet he cried out, "Stop this, please! We must flee."

Maksim called on the blood of the *bies* with aim to crush the traitor beneath him. The horns angled from his skull, his legs thickened, and his muscles grew tenfold. The tunic tore from his brawny chest and beefy arms; his bindings snapped away from his wrists.

Scythia struggled. "Oh! By the—"

Maksim slammed his fist into the side of Scythia's face, crushing flesh into bone, and tearing tendons in a single, fell punch. Grey hair flittered over his face, blood spilling from his mouth with a few of his remaining teeth.

The landless would understand the power of the nobles.

He hit Scythia again with a right fist, inciting a low warble to emit from the man's jugular—as though he may have been begging for Maksim to stop. He followed the viscous blow with a left fist to the temple, caving in the eye socket. Brains oozed from Scythia's head.

Lifeless eyes were frozen to the heavens.

Lahmia roared, whipping over his head, but not bothering to attack. The wind from her wings whipped the mane on Maksim's *bies* form. With satisfaction, he twisted his neck to follow the path of the dragon's flight. *Lahmia* would recognize him in this form as the blood of Wolos. He would be safe as long—

Jana's perfect, freckled face clipped the edge of his vision, gasping for air. She crouched behind him with the spear at his back, lined perfectly with his heart. Her round, brown eyes were full of water.

Maksim dropped his chin to see the mutilated body of Scythia Gergo. He had his vengeance and Jana meant to have hers too.

Despite the quiver of her voice, she spoke with the imperious tone of a noble. "Our people will know the truth of Wolos's death."

The dragon's call diminished as it returned to the temple.

Her spear was sharp, breaking his heart.

UNDERSUNG

Thrice Nine Legends

Month of the Sickle

Sixth of Warmth

174 CE

Undersung

In sweetness and suffering, in misery and mirth, we should honor all living things as we honor our own self.

Sahar smiled quietly, watching his sister twist and turn her head to and fro like a snake obeying the flute of a charmer. Her movements were not so graceful, often snapping her attention in one direction as if hearing a sound, while her cerulean eyes drifted along a divergent path, seemingly unaware of her own movements. The smallest curl on her lips told of some inner joy to which she alone was privy.

"Soraya." Sahar reached out his rough three-fingered hand to gently touch her shoulder, hidden by her bright, multihued robes. When her large eyes briefly met his in opposition to the turn of her head, he asked, "Are you ready?"

"Ah," she smiled, "well—yes. Of course—I—ah—was just waiting on you, broth—brother." Her chirping voice was sweet and undulated like a warm spring breeze, though gusting and redounding so that nothing she said ever came with a single breath.

He knew no other Arkono who moved as she did, or talked as she did, or exuded such tenderness with each look and smile. Their parents had coddled her—

and he did as well, despite being of an age—though it was impossible to say that she seemed ruined by it, nor that he felt his coddling somehow made him feel in any way superior to her. Indeed, his inferiority to her kindness and effortless consideration of the well-being of others was a thought eternal to his mind.

"Good. I am glad you have not decided to turn back." Sahar nodded grimly. "Amma and Appa would be pleased to see their daughter return for the ritual, though my journey and my life would be joyless." He stood, his long legs unbending so that his ostrich-like talons could grip the soft earth. He turned out his scaly hand to his sister.

Elsewise, He thought she seemed as any other of their kind, birdlike in structure and appearance. Her rounded jawline made her appear precious and petite, as if she might break at a touch. Similar to a bird, her mouth was beak-like in shape with the barest semblance of a flattened nose, but with thin black lips forming the opening of the mouth instead of the hardened beak of a bird. Fine blue-green feathers covered her face, and atop her head a flaring crest of indigo rose more than a foot in height.

Soraya's chin dipped low so that the blue-green feathers framing her round face shadowed her eyes, which continued to stare up at him from beneath the downy veil. "Well, I—ah—wouldn't want—that." She took his hand and he pulled hard so that her talons lifted from the ground before she landed with a grin, displaying wide, flat teeth.

Of the same clutch of eggs, Sahar could not imagine Soraya apart from him, and it was for her that he had abandoned home and the hope of return.

"Do you think we will be—safe?" Soraya tittered, looking off into the shadow of the forest floor, the barest glimpses of light eking through the layered canopy above.

"I will do everything I can to protect you, sister." Sahar tightened his jaw, pecking along with her at his side. "We just need to travel far enough that no one will look for us."

"But—I was chosen. I am the sacri—sacrifice our people need to—need to appease Lesh." Her head lifted slightly, but her eyes drifted away so that she did not meet her brother's gaze. "They will never—never stop looking."

"And Lesh is never appeased, else our people would not need to throw our sisters and daughters at his feet." Sahar snarled with more ferocity than he intended. Taken aback by himself, he blinked, pausing.

To his surprise, Soraya chittered merrily. "Ah—you do not want—do not nee—ah—should not be so angry." Her gaze found him again. "After all, I am—well—sort of free."

He nodded, forcing himself to smile, despite the quaking in his bones that told him *freedom* was yet some ways off. "Yes, you are free."

"And—ah—you will stay with me?" she inquired sweetly.

He chuckled warmly. "Of course, my dear sister. Where would I go?" He shrugged at a sudden realization, hunching his shoulders with the same motion. "After all, I cannot go home."

The idea of never seeing their amma or appa again, of never seeing neighbors or friends seemed to weigh upon both of them in that instant, and Sahar knew he was to blame. If their parents found them, Soraya would be dead anyway. He shook his head with a grimace, reminding himself that he should not be so dour, or his sister would come to blame herself for their predicament.

"But so long as I have you beside me, what do I need from our people who set themselves against us?" He struggled to keep his tone light. "Our concern is no longer for what we have left behind, but what awaits us in a world unexplored."

A wide smile split her lips, though her eyes did not find his. "I want to—I want to see what Aenar has to—ah—offer."

"It will be a fine life!" He reached out to pull her into a side hug. "Adventure and excitement, seeing sights that no Arkono has seen before."

"But—ah—is it the life you—want?" Soraya muttered.

Sahar was glad that he did not pause in his response, knowing that it was neither a lie nor the truth, but somewhere in between. He loved his home, but he loved his sister too, and if he could not have both, he must choose. "More than anything else."

"You can never find a—ah—mate." She twisted her head slightly. "Will you accept that? Did you want hatchlings—ah—fledglings?"

Sahar paused for a moment, considering the question, as—he supposed—he had never really done before. Soraya turned her head to look at him while he considered, slowly drifting away, only to return her gaze time and again. He certainly assumed he would have young someday, but never really reflected on whether or not he ever actually *wanted* them. Eventually, he said, "I don't know."

"Oh."

"Well, I mean, I suppose I do, but maybe I don't. It depends, I guess, whether or not I decide that I do, but I am not certain whether I should or not."

Soraya met his eyes for a moment before her head began to tilt and eventually pulled her eyes away, tittering. "You are always so—decisive."

"I decided I wanted to save you, didn't I?"

"Did you?"

He frowned at her, sputtering, suddenly remembering their conversation in which she told him she would not stay to die if her lot was drawn. Finally, he ruffled his feathers in a huff and spat, "Maybe!"

She tittered again.

His tail feathers fanned as he wove forward, further incensed by his sister's relentless twitters.

Eventually she said, "Ah—you know I mean no harm!"

He turned his head away, unable to look at her, quite aware of her meaning but unable to ease his ire. She never meant anything by it, but he could not help how her jibes made him feel.

They continued walking forward. He could feel her amusement radiating, and as a result, he could not bring himself to chatter with her for many miles, locked in his own annoyance. The canopy slowly began to disappear. The sun became hotter on his contour feathers, and his brightly-colored robe seemed a hindrance. Finally, he cast a glance to his sister, whose head turned the wrong direction, but when it found its way back to him, a wide smile revealed her wide teeth. Any time he let the silence between them linger too long, he debated whether what he had done was right. But when he saw her smile, he knew he would have changed nothing, given the chance.

Once per season, when the moon was black and the stars were bright, the elders called to see the girls of an age in the middle of the night. Lots were drawn by each to bring favor for the season next to come, and she whose lot was drawn last must succumb to the rule of the elders. Two nights ago, the lots had grown few, and as the drawing came to an end, Sahar somehow knew Soraya's would be last. He grabbed her, in fear, unwilling to lose her. They fled into the night, hoping the dawn would be slow to come; the birth of the sun brought a weeping sky and they could do nothing but run.

They had seen their pursuers twice, led by their appa, the *Tlatoani*—the leader of their people. The first time they saw him, Sahar had hoped it was only for show, as he seemed to have let them go. But the second time, it was his spear that had flown first. Soraya did not know, and he would not tell her.

After many miles of silence, when Sahar had begun acknowledging his sister again, they began to chitter back and forth with one another.

"What—do you think we will see—ah—out in the world?"

"I dreamt about it once, and if it is half as grand as my dream, it is worth a lifetime to see." Sahar could feel his lips peel back in a smile he could not contain. "As if ten thousand birds in the forest were chirping and singing as one, so too were the thousands of people joined together in hope, a dream within the dream of life itself, calling each other brother and sister as you and I do." His mind drifted to the dream. "And together they rose up—we among them—and we sang a song of life in which we brought harm to none and none brought harm to us."

Soraya smiled at him, and he could not say if the look in her eyes was glad at the thought or whether she was glad only at his own reverie. "It is a—song I hope to hear—someday."

The reverie had captured him, though. "No sisters or daughters are cast to the waiting maw of Lesh. Our only thoughts of blood are when the quickening of our song causes it to flow within our veins. Our only thoughts of pain are when old age steals us from one another after a lifetime filled with love and laughter. And our only thoughts..." he paused, his eyes briefly focusing on his sister, and he sighed, "are of hope and peace."

Her smile was bright, and for a moment she was motionless, eyes locked to his. "I will help you find this world."

Sudden shouts and cries carried in the wind from behind them, interrupting their exchange. Sahar shared a wide-eyed look of wonder with Soraya before he pushed her ahead of him. "Run, Soraya, run! Do not let them catch us."

Her talons gripped the earth, sending her springing forward at a rapid pace. Their long avian legs carried them swiftly through the jungle, Sahar gasping behind Soraya to speed her along, the sound of their pursuers in his ears. The bright colors of their homeland declined into the sahel, the vine-laced canopy replaced with sparse, stumpy trees and patches of tall, yellowish grasses.

In the distance, barely beyond the grasp of the deep shadow of the great trees and at the bottom of the long slope marred by grey and blue sandstone, a mass of figures struggled, locked in bloody contest. Many lay unmoving among the sward and stones or lay writhing, crying out. Others stumbled away from the fray, bumbling about in search of lost limbs or trying to contain leaking lifeblood. A dozen voices joined together to whimper and wail, the dissonant crescendo of wordless screams filling the blistering vale.

Sahar stumbled to a stop alongside his sister, beak-like mouth agape. "What is it?" he asked no one, a gut-wrenching nausea already closing his throat.

"War," Soraya said in a whisper. "I never—ah—thought it would be so horrible."

He could only nod his head. A cry arose from behind him, and he twisted to see several of his kind erupt from the parting vegetation, their multihued crests marking them clearly against the vivid greens. He recognized a few of them, even from this distance. Their appa, Abhay, led two of his friends, Jai and Kamal, along with three others he could not make out from such a distance. All of their pursuers were scanning but were clearly distracted by the battle below.

Sahar dropped to the ground, dragging his sister down beside him with a hiss. "Soraya!" She followed him, scrambling through the tall grasses as they tried to find cover behind a stone or earthy outcropping.

"What should we do?" He gasped, stopping behind a cluster of thorny shrubs.

"Will they—ah—help us?" Soraya asked, pointing to the warriors.

Despite Sahar's initial assessment of a full battle of hundreds being fought before them, it was now clear that the conflict was nearly over and there were no more than a few score. A couple groups of four or five warriors wearing baggy trousers and lengths of dull-colored cloth bound about their heads dealt decisively with scrawny, desiccated creatures in tattered clothes, reminiscent of their executors, while others walked about with axes or swords, ending any movement from the bodies of their enemies on the ground.

"The Uvil?"

She nodded.

He licked his lips. "They may just turn us over to our own people." He shook his head. "No. We can keep running. They will lose us in the sahel or get tired of chasing us."

Before the words had finished falling from his lips, one of the Uvil cried out, pointing to them. They were, perhaps, hidden from their kin, but in their bright robes with their bright plumage, they were easy to spot against the brown and yellow terrain.

Sahar sprang to his feet, clasping Soraya's hand, but before they had taken a couple of steps, the Uvil spread into a wide arc, blocking their escape, even as their kin closed to fully surround them upon seeing their movement. The two were left clutching each other in the milling mass of blood-stained Uvil warriors.

Abhay, the ruler of the Arkono, pushed forward among the half dozen or so Arkono he led, his green feathers ruffling and yellow plume making him seem twice as tall, already towering nearly two feet over the Uvil. In his hand, he clasped a flint-tipped spear. "I am the Tlatoani. I am the One Who Speaks."

Soraya's eyes widened, her head twisting abruptly away from Sahar. "Appa?"

He seemed to pay no heed to her, continuing as if she had not spoken. "You have stopped our runaways, Uvil, and you have our gratitude. We will take them from here and will see you recompensed for your efforts."

Sahar pulled his sister tightly to him, exchanging a brief, fear-filled look with her before turning to one of the Uvil whose arm hung limply at his side. He seemed to stand apart from the others, though his face was uncovered by the cloth bound about his head, the same as his brethren. "Please protect us. They mean to kill my sister. You cannot let this happen!"

The Uvil blinked at him emotionlessly with grey, almost colorless eyes before turning his gaze to Tlatoani Abhay. "I am Goli, son of Goshtasp, son of Farshid, and I am the *Spahbed* of the *Kara* you see before you, Arkono." His voice was cavernous, as emotionless as his expression, except for the deeper inflection that clearly identified his intentional disregard for Abhay's title. "In absence of our courts, in the field I am designated the authority of the *Databdara*, our law bearers. You are in our lands now, and in our lands our laws abide. What crime warrants the death of this girl?"

The Arkono surrounding their Tlatoani ruffled their feathers, their multihued plumes rising in unison before Abhay broke words. "You would pass judgment on our laws? You have no authority to speak against what we deem necessary for our people. It does not matter whether we are in our own lands or a thousand leagues from our borders—by claiming the right to question our laws, you claim sovereignty over all our people."

Goli's warriors fidgeted, gripping the weapons in their hands a little tighter, still wet with the brackish blood of the strange dead things in their wake. "And by denying the laws of our lands, you do the same, Arkono. Regardless, as I see it, you do not possess the—" he glanced over the six Arkono purposefully "—*ability* to resist our ruling. Though you are free to try."

Abhay's eyes flitted over the Uvil, outnumbering them ten to one, before raising his chin so that he could look down upon Goli more than he did already. "So it would seem. Suffice it to say that the life of the girl is forfeit and the boy has abetted in her escape. What do *your* laws say are punishment for these crimes?"

Sahar could take no more of his appa's aloofness. "We are your children! Do you care nothing for us?"

Their appa looked at him with disdain. "You are criminals."

The Uvil blinked again, his affect unreadable. He turned his gaze to Soraya. "Girl, your Tlatoani seems incapable of answering questions, but I expect better from you. What crime have you committed to warrant your death?"

Soraya twitched, her glaze flitting to Abhay. She pulled herself free from Sahar's grasp to answer the Uvil. "None."

"Then why does he seek your life?"

"Be—because my lot was drawn for—ah—sacrifice to Lesh." Her last words came rushed, expelled with breathless urgency. "My people kill their—kill their daughters."

"Sacrifice," the Uvil mused.

"Not crime," Sahar offered, again clutching his sister, who seemed to be trying to look in every direction at once.

"Not sacrifice!" Abhay said harshly, sneering at them. "Her lot was drawn, but it was not the last. You did not stay long enough to see that, did you Soraya? No, you fled from your people and your responsibility to Lesh. And what is worse—you took your brother with you, giving him equal part in your crime. It was *not* your fate to die, but you have made it the doom of both you and your brother."

Sahar stared at his appa, mouth agape, unable to comprehend the words he spoke. His sister shook her head, slowly beginning to sink toward the ground as sobs began to slowly wrack her body.

Goli nodded, looking down at Soraya, where she had sunk. "So you abandoned your duty." There was no question in his voice. "Though my people have no need for sacrifice and I find the practice foolish, duty is something we take seriously. Loyalty to your people is vital." He turned back to Abhay. "Among the Uvil, as among the Arkono, the sentence is death. Though our laws require that a life never be given or stolen, life must be wrested from the guilty."

Sahar worked his mouth, finding no moisture there but speaking nonetheless. "You will kill us because we refused to stay and die?"

"No, boy," the Uvil said monotonously. "Firstly, we will kill no one. We have no reason to claim either of your lives. Secondly, the life must be *taken*, which means that one of your brethren must be willing to chance his life in the pursuit. And thirdly, your life is not up for the taking. You were forced to choose between the loyalty to your sister and your loyalty to your people, and such a decision is *dvandva bhajana*, a dilemma that offers no right action."

"You steal justice!" Abhay snapped, his plumage ruffling.

Soraya looked up, her head tilting slightly and tears wetting the feathers on her face. "You will not let my—broth—brother die for my—my crime?"

"That matter is between you and your brother," the Uvil said.

"What do you mean?" Sahar asked, fervently.

The Uvil shook his head as if the matter should have been evident. "The crime demands a life. Our law says that one life is equal to another. If someone else wishes to pay the debt, then the debt is paid all the same."

"I will pay it!" Sahar cried, his tongue tripping over itself to get the words out.

"No!" Soraya screeched, her head flitting to the side and tears bursting anew.

He fell beside her, whispering fervently, even as he heard Abhay arguing with Goli. "Please, sister, you must let me do this."

She shook her head stubbornly, the movement continuing despite her speech. "I will not ask you to—ah—die for me. I could not bear it."

"It is not certain!" He put out a hand to direct her gaze at him and stop her from shaking her head. "They must take my life. I can fight. I stand a better chance than you!"

"What?" she asked, confusion etched on her face.

He looked up to the Uvil, interrupting whatever he was saying to Abhay. "You said the life must be taken. I can fight? If I win, I am free? My sister is free?"

The Uvil did not seem to be upset at the string of questions, turning his gaze to Sahar and nodding. "Yes, the law is clear. Other bylaws would apply in other situations, but for this situation your defense is sufficient. They have claim to only one life."

Sahar turned back to his sister. "It is our best chance. Let me fight," he pleaded. "Let me do this so that we can be free together. I cannot bear to see blood staining your hands. I must protect you."

A small smile etched her lips. "I do not—ah— need prote—protection, brother."

"I know. I know that." He licked his lips. "But *I* need to protect *you*."

A sigh with the slightest descent of her head sent Sahar to his feet, facing Goli. "I will do it. I will fight."

The Uvil nodded and looked to Abhay. "Who will chance their life in the pursuit of his?"

Abhay did not even turn to look at the others. "It is my duty to pursue whatever justice can be found, limited though it may be." He fixed his gaze upon Goli. "But know this, Uvil, you have damaged the peace between our people. No longer will you hunt for meat or search for fruit in our lands."

The Uvil did not blink. "Such is the price of justice among the lawless." Without pause, he continued. "What is your weapon, Arkono?"

Abhay lifted the weapon in his hand slightly. "The spear."

"And you, boy?"

Sahar licked his lips, the reality of the situation beginning to weigh on his mind—the understanding that he would be forced to fight one of his parents to the death. "I would choose the same, though I bear no weapon with me."

Abhay reached back. "Jai, your spear." The young Arkono, of an age with Sahar and Soraya, relinquished his weapon, which was quickly passed to Sahar.

The Uvil backed away to form a ring around the two and the Arkono followed soon after, speaking words of encouragement to their Tlatoani.

Soraya stood slowly, letting the others filter away. Abruptly, she hugged Sahar close and whispered in his ear, "I—ah—love you, brother."

Sahar nodded, his eyes focused on Abhay, unable to look to his sister, unable to reconcile himself to the task before him. "I love you too."

She walked away, taking her place among the Uvil, avoiding the Arkono. As she moved away, Sahar spoke. "You would kill your son, Appa?"

"You would kill your appa, son?" Abhay rejoined.

Goli spoke from the edge of the ring. "A claim of justice has been brought forward, and the claim demands a life. You both enter a contest to see the claim answered. All present will remain until a life has been taken." He paused, his grey eyes sweeping over the gathered Uvil and Arkono. "Begin."

His appa was a blur of color, striking at him before he could lift the spear in his right hand. Abhay's weapon swept forward in a wide arc, the flint tip sweeping across Sahar's chest, tearing his robes with a puff of bloody blue feathers that wafted gently to the ground. The sting of the strike sent him stumbling away, but the Tlatoani did not pause, lurching forward and stabbing him in the left shoulder. Sahar's free hand instinctively reached out to grab the haft of Abhay's spear as he fell. A cry of pain escaped his lips, pulling the weapon and Abhay toward himself. His appa did not break momentum, adjusting his grip and kicking with one of his long legs. He caught Sahar in the stomach, sending him tumbling away.

Sahar rolled head over heels, his spear flying from his right hand and the flint tip of Abhay's spear tearing chunks of flesh from his left as it was torn from his grasp. The thick grasses of the sahel were sharp, finding gaps in his feathers to act like razors, cutting him in a dozen places. He withered for a moment, his mind on Soraya. The wetness in his eyes came without invitation. He coughed, scrambling to get to his feet while forcibly trying to blink the tears away. His nostrils were laced with dust; the taste of copper filled his mouth. He needed to ignore the pain and find his weapon, but Abhay was already upon him again.

The elder Arkono's spear struck with surety and years of practice, haunting Sahar's slowed movements. His appa left no room for counter or breath. He did not gloat and did not preen, nor did he pause to relish in the task of murdering his son. He seemed intent to finish the task as quickly as he could as if speed would allow him to avoid the unpleasantness set before him.

Among the Arkono a breach of duty warranted the Death by a Dozen Warriors. The guilty party would be sent to the Ring with a mock weapon against a dozen well-trained Arkono soldiers to inevitably die, seen as part of their destiny with no hope of success. It seemed to Sahar, in the moment in which his appa's spear struck him in the abdomen for the third time, it was his appa's intent to replicate that ritual death alone, to ensure that it was clear to the other Arkono that his son never had a chance to live, and death was his destiny.

Sahar finally tumbled away, bleeding, never having found, let alone touched, his spear again. He crumpled, gasping, with blood filling his lungs. He was unable to move, a cloud of red staining the sky as his sister's face suddenly shadowed his own.

"Stop!" Her voice was fierce, something he had never heard before. "Have you no—you no heart? He is your son!"

"And I have made his death as quick as I could." The voice sounded cold and distant.

Soraya's head tilted, her eyes finding Sahar's. "I will not let you—not let your death go unanswered."

"You cannot," Sahar rasped, blood spurting from his lips. "You will damage your *Mihiyo*."

"Your death will—ah—damage my spirit." Soraya turned her head, tears falling steadily now. "I can kill," she sputtered. "But I cannot let you—cannot let your death remain unanswered. There must be a consequence."

"No!" he pled, reaching toward her desperately, the blood on his hands staining the vibrancy of the feathers covering her arms. "Not for me. Live for me, don't kill for me." His heart raced, and his thoughts grew cloudy. He could barely see her face. "Remember the dream. Go find my dream."

She squeezed his hand tightly; her voice was distant. "It is not my dream."

His words were barely audible through a gurgling sob. "My sister, you must find peace."

"Without you, brother, I—ah—I have no reason to."

He tried to find the saliva to speak, but only had blood to wet his tongue, giving voice to his final thoughts. "Then I haven't saved you at all. I am sorry."

A SONG AND SILVER

Thrice Nine Legends

Month of Birch

First of Warmth

214 CE

Chapter I

Waves of saltwater swelled and heaved, slapping alongside the edge of the Lilitu galley as they sailed southward.

"What is our depth, Marziah?" Jaffar Arjmand shouted against the northern squall. He popped his bulbous head over the railing above her.

Marziah balanced steadily in the *chains*, a small platform built on the side of the hull of the ship. With one arm wrapped around a pully, she towed the lead line through her thin fingers as her mother taught her years ago. Water from above and below splashed against her thin frame, soaking her blue garments.

No ordinary Lilitu dared cross the wide inlet called the Anusund, especially during springtime storms. While the Lilitu were natural explorers, the eternal promise of coin found with current trade regions regularly won the contest against what might be found by exploring uncharted waters. Marziah, who was known for her adventurous spirit, was thankful the captain, her friend, convinced the empress to sail southward. Then again, she would be more thankful if they survived the journey.

Jaffar yelled again. "Marziah Corran! Are you alive down there?"

"You can see me well enough." She exhaled, readjusting her grip on the pully rope. Every Lilitu, from a simple commoner to the empress, could see at night as well as day, and the unyielding storm was not so thick as to blind Jaffar. Marziah knew the years since his last voyage were many, but his over-the-top antics were becoming ridiculous. It was like he never sailed before. With a shake of her head, she loosened the plummet and counted the leather marks that slipped through her grasp. "Tell the captain, by the deep four."

"Four," he repeated. "The galley cannot go much farther. The storm is forcing us into the rocks." After stating the obvious, he scanned the choppy waves with his round, unblinking eyes. They swelled as large as two fists pushed together, with a circular black center and an azure-colored orb. Like any Lilitu, his eyes were the most prominent feature on his oversized head.

Her friend's voice, Captain Niki Karimi, thundered from the deck. "Land lies ahead! Steady as she goes!"

Marziah saw Jaffar disappear from the rail to shout over his shoulder. "Captain, wait!"

She hurried, casting out the lead line again. The raindrops thickened as the water beneath them lessened. "By the mark three!"

"By the mark three, Captain Karimi!" Jaffar echoed her own with a bit more trepidation in his voice.

Marziah took another breath before Captain Karimi was changing up her orders. Her voice was markedly less confident. "Turn the steering oar and row portside! Hard!"

Jaffar echoed the command. Directly beneath Marziah, half the rowers inside the hollow of the ship—with their backs toward the bow—pushed the long oars from the squared gaps and began to move as one.

Jaffar's voice boomed overhead somewhere on the galley. "Starboard side, hold. The rest of you row! Row! Row!"

The dark waters of Anusund stirred and crashed as the oars vigorously plunged beneath the surface to alter their heading. Despite the cruising speed, the galley quickly maneuvered through the sound to keep them from the shallower waters.

Lightning lit the grey clouds above them, pulling Marziah's attention. She kept her grip, squinting through the rain to see far-reaching hardwoods blanketing the coastline. Never in her lifetime had she seen so many trees.

"Row!" Jaffar's voice resounded. His head appeared above her again, his black hair matted against his head. "Check our depth."

Marziah tossed the line a third time. "By the mark seven."

"We are clear," Jaffar said with relief.

The blue of Captain Karimi's oilcloth mantle flashed beyond the railing. Her poise returned. "Of course we are. Now bring Marziah back on board before she is swept away."

"Yes, Captain." Jaffar held his hand in a salute longer than necessary.

Marziah had already begun ascending the knotted ropes and was stretching her leg toward the deck before Jaffar turned around to offer his hand.

He frowned, dropping his hand. Droplets of rain rolled off his cheek. "You have a knack for seafaring."

She leaped onto the deck, lifting her nose at his compliment. "We all best or we should not be here."

Jaffar scrunched his face and then looked over his shoulder. He shouted at the oarsmen beneath them, directing the second set on the starboard side to begin rowing. He then said, "I am still not convinced we should be out here."

"No? Then why did you come?" Marziah crossed her arms. "This excursion is necessary for our people to prosper."

"I am here because I belong at the sea." Jaffar lifted an eyebrow. The rain poured around them. "As for being necessary, the Lilitu get along well enough."

Marziah wrinkled her nose, wondering why he would say something so stupid. "*Well enough* is not good enough. If I were your captain I would ask you to have a bit more faith."

Jaffar grunted, squeezing by her. "I am returning to my post. Stand ready."

She pushed her hair from her eyes and surveyed the eighty-foot vessel from the horizontal stern to curved bow and noticed Niki perched near the fore, beyond the single mast in the center of the ship. She could see Niki's dark eyes focusing on the landmass to the south, yet she was guiding them westward.

Despite the lurching boat, Marziah maintained her balance on the few centerboards assembled around the mast, above the belly of the galley. The platform was elevated above the primary crew—exactly fifty Lilitu, a mix of males and females—who sat in the hull of the ship; their heads were level with her feet.

Some wore red cloth wrapped around their waists and tied at the back, identifying them as Rudhira, or warriors, among her kind. The rest of the sailors wore blue to mark them as Nili, or merchants, like Marziah and Jaffar.

Somewhere among the Rudhira was their own commander, Farhad de Zand.

Rudhira did not always accompany merchants when sailing but neither did Nili frequently explore new lands. While the galley was limited to the two caste types, larger settlements gave all Lilitu assigned stations, many of which were unlike those who mastered the sword or managed coin and trade.

"Row. Row." Jaffar returned to his place as deck officer near the mast in the center—the sails already reefed—where he could receive orders from the captain and impart them to the oarsmen. As instructed, the Lilitu beneath them churned the oars in a fluid motion at his direction.

The sky rumbled again and again as they bobbed in the water, fighting against the harsh waves smashing against them. The galley rocked, threatening to be taken back to the shallow waters. The captain ordered them to push the galley farther away from land.

Despite the cold droplets splashing over her face, Marziah could feel the heat in her ears. Niki was steering them in the wrong direction. The adventure they wanted was on land.

Marziah made her way down the centerboards, stopping Jaffar's rowing chant. He did not budge, blocking her path. "You should be at your post. The captain may need another reading."

"I know my duty," Marziah said, having no desire to exchange words with Jaffar again. She tilted her chin to see the few remaining sailors, who were not manning the oars, clinging to whatever rail they could find. "We are far enough removed from the rocks for now."

Jaffar grimaced, his reddish-brown skin glistened in the rain. He may have been the deck officer, but he was also a male, meaning he had little authority over what Marziah chose to do, even on the galley. The bluish color in his large eyes flashed, revealing a spark of irritation. "You cannot know that, Marziah. No Lilitu has sailed this far south."

She pointed at the sound they sailed across. "I know Anusund."

Jaffar dismissed her with a snort, moving out of her way and shouting at the rowers once more. Her words were true and not true at the same time; while she had sailed Anusund more than any other on the galley, including the captain, the current waters were equally foreign to her.

Lightning flashed again, dancing over the thick canopy of leafy branches. She hurried past Jaffar.

"Niki," Marziah took notice of the increasing rainfall, "we need to take the galley closer to shore and drop anchor. The storm is worsening."

"For the last time, I told you to call me captain. We are not young girls skipping through the market any longer." Captain Karimi pulled back the blue-colored hood of her mantle and faced Marziah. The boat rocked against the wave, slipping back toward the shallow waters. Fear welled up in Niki's eyes behind her black curls. She and Marziah both grabbed a rail as Jaffar yelled at the oarsmen to keep them sailing into the wind and waves.

"Staying out here is suicide," Marziah hurried to say. "I promised you I would help you out here. You must listen to me."

"We do not know what lies on shore," Niki shouted over the wind. "We can weather the storm. We have done it many times."

"We might, but shelter and our survival are certain on land," Marziah said. Rain or not, she wanted to see this new world up close. "Nothing is promised out here; a hundred victories mean nothing when compared to a single defeat. If we capsize, the excursion will have been wasted."

A large wave pushed them back farther from deeper waters.

"We cannot take the longboats out in this and we would lose the silver." Niki's round eyes darted to the landmass again as thunder rolled overhead. The waves crashed under them. The waters sounded as much a beast as the heavens.

Marziah had almost forgotten about the silver they carried below the deck in case a new trade route was discovered. She was certain they could come back for it once they explored a bit. "If we are lucky, the anchor will hold. We can come back for the silver."

The galley rocked sharply, triggering Jaffar to spit more orders at the oarsmen. "Row harder unless you want to be taken by Lilith! Get us back out there. Row away from the shallows."

Marziah put weight onto the balls of her toes as the boat pitched against the waves. She had no wish to meet the creator, Lilith, this day. If the oarsmen let a wave strike the galley at the wrong angle, they would overturn and be towed below the surface.

The boat leveled for a moment. She realized Niki was speaking again, detailing her thoughts, more to herself than Marziah. "We should not travel into strange lands shrouded beneath a veil of blackened skies and rainfall. Getting permission from the empress to sail here was hard enough with my little experience. She shares our hope of finding a new people and a new trade route. If we do cross another culture, we want a good first impression. We cannot risk asking for aid in our first moments. Such weakness would not depict the Lilitu well."

Marziah reached out and grabbed her friend's clothing, pulling her close. She was losing this argument. "Nor would drowning a few hundred feet from shore, *Captain*. Not everyone sees asking for help as being weak."

"This is Haemos Mons. You are either strong or dead." Niki tightened her jaw and turned her eyes again, signifying that despite her robust reply, she would eventually acquiesce.

"Captain!" Jaffar screamed, but his warning was too late.

The boat jarred to a halt, striking a sandbar near the beach. Marziah flew sideways, smashing into a side rail; Niki landed next to her with a grunt and a thud. The galley creaked and cracked from the impact as the seawater threatened to wash over the edges.

Marziah shook her head to regain her senses, glad she did not hit her head. She saw Niki already pulling herself to her feet. Behind them, the oarsmen shouted at one another as they slipped from their seats into a muddled mess with Jaffar sprawled among their number.

Niki shouted frantically as she stood, "Jaffar, are you alright?"

"Fine, Captain," Jaffar replied from the depths. "Give us a moment and we will shove off."

"We do not know the damage," Marziah shouted as the thunder clapped overhead. "We are already near shore. We can find shelter."

"No," Jaffar yelled back, pulling himself to the center. The many Lilitu beneath him scrambled to regain hold of their oars. "We mustn't abandon the ship."

Niki turned to examine the coast about a hundred yards away and shook her head with force. "Marziah is right. Even if we free ourselves from the sandbar, we do not have the strength to outmatch the waves."

"We cannot abandon the galley," Jaffar cried.

A substantial wave crashed into the boat, splashing seawater over them and soaking the oarsmen on their parallel benches.

"We cannot stay here!" Niki shouted. "Take us into shore. Ready the longboats."

"Captain, the longboats are no match for the waves! We will all die!" Jaffar gaped, glaring at Marziah momentarily. "We would have better luck pushing off and lying ahull."

"You would have the boat fare for itself?" Marziah belted, glaring at Jaffar. She would not let him steal this adventure from her. "I am glad you are not the captain! The trek to shore is not far. We will certainly die out here. The storm will worsen!"

"We will withstand it like we always do," Jaffar said.

"He has not been on the Anusund in over a decade, Niki. We need to get to shore," Marziah hissed under her breath before turning on Jaffar again. "We did not travel the whole of Anusund to fail now."

"Quiet!" Niki shouted, stepping away from the fore to look down on the rowmen beneath the main deck. "I have made my decision. Leave the silver. We are going to shore."

Jaffar dipped his head to the rowers, his face like stone. "You heard your captain!"

Chapter II

"I wonder if it has a name." A Nili sailor wiped the water from his forehead and cheek with a single hand before hovering over Marziah. His chin nearly rested on her shoulder as he peered at the coast ahead. "Do you think we will name it?"

Marziah clutched the side of the longboat as it was flung forward by another wave, propelling it toward the sand. In truth, taking the longboats to the coast was as suicidal as staying on the galley, but she wanted her adventure.

Pikes belonging to the warriors bounced in the base of their boat. The eight Lilitu, some of whom were Rudhira, sat with them in the craft rotating their oars in a smooth motion to keep them drifting toward land as best as they could.

"No," she finally said to the sailor. Her heart pounded in her chest in anticipation. She had an entire new land to explore. "If we find it to be uninhabited, the empress will name it. Until then, it is Haemus Mons like everything else."

His throat buzzed with sound as though he were mulling over her words. "Something must be beyond Haemus Mons."

"And the Lilitu will be the ones who find it." She kneeled at the front, waves splashing over her hands, watching the other longboat in front of them skate onto the beach.

The longboats had been taken back and forth to bring the Nili and Rudhira from the galley to the coast many times. Several more trips were needed to empty the galley, but almost half their numbers were already ashore.

"Come on," Marziah said to the sailor, springing into the shallow water. He splashed behind her with the others, spraying cold water across garments. The lot of them stomped along together advancing to the beach, while a couple stayed back and began rowing to the ship.

She had only gone a few steps when two Lilitu pushed the other longboat by them toward the galley to collect more sailors. The waves pushed against them, causing every step in the water to be a battle.

"Set a perimeter. Stay alert," Niki shouted from farther down the beach. She waved at Marziah and the other sailors to join them. Marziah stomped beyond the reach of the roiling waves toward Niki. She stepped through the merchants who held the inner circle around the captain. Their blue clothes nearly hid their red-brown skin.

The Rudhira, on the other hand, moved beyond the merchants. They stationed themselves in an arc facing the trees with their pikes in hand.

"Fall in!" the commander, Farhad de Zand, yelled at his troops. He had come to shore with Niki on the first longboat.

Niki directed the Lilitu. "No one wander away until we have all disembarked from the ship. We will all arrive safely and find shelter together."

Marziah scanned the vacant beach, realizing the forest was actually a dense jungle. Like any Lilitu, the nightfall had no effect on her vision. Besides the scurrying sailors and the pouring rain, nothing moved. Marziah reached Niki, feeling the weight of her wet clothes. She tried to mask the excitement in her voice; she wanted to plunge into the jungle. "What do you think?"

"I don't know yet. The storm is—" Niki started.

A rumble reverberated from the jungle, cutting off the captain. The sound was so deep Marziah's bones rattled; even the rain seemed to slant away toward Anusund behind her. The throaty growl ended with a *thwok* of jaws clapping shut.

She lifted her chin to the maze of shrubs, vines, and broad-leaved trees. Whatever stirred within the jungle was beyond the threshold where plant met sand.

"Front face!" Farhad shouted.

A dozen and a half Rudhira rustled in front of the captain, forming a barrier with their pikes. They were the true warriors among the sailors. The rest, including Marziah, had not trained a single day in the art of combat. It was not their place.

The heavy rainfall, an endless song, showered against the leaves and sand.

"What was that?" Niki spluttered.

Marziah did not answer, straining to see through the stream of water. The heavens thundered, nearly masking the budding growl and heavy footsteps of the two-toed hulking beast that emerged from the brushwood. Sharpened teeth protruded from thin, ash-colored lips. The creature snarled, twisting its oblong head to view them. Two ivory tusks, as long as Marziah's arm, extended from the cheekbones, belting back and forth over the pointed tips of the pikes.

Marziah squinted to see the white bone, as clear as the tusks, at its shoulders, ribs, and knees, where the rind of the beast had either been ripped aside or rotted away.

"It isn't living." Marziah bit her tongue, reactively moving backwards. Her shoulder brushed against Niki's.

"Defend at the ready!" Farhad cried. The soldiers did not hesitate, pointing their pikes at the monster.

The yelling Lilitu triggered the yellow-eyed beast to unleash a feral roar, unlike anything Marziah had ever heard before. Something between the spine-chilling cry of a speckled cat and the trumpeting olyfaunt back home.

With its knees slightly bent, it took a large step forward to reach the smaller Lilitu.

"Attack!" Niki frantically shouted.

Farhad twisted his neck to shoot a hollow glare at the captain. It was not her place to command Rudhira, no matter whether they sailed on her ship. He curled his lip and turned back, echoing the captain. "Attack!"

Nine spear tips were suddenly buried in the torso of the monster, rotated a quarter of a degree, and pulled free again. With grimy, black-hued liquefied guts oozing from the wounds, each member of the small Lilitu army gave a unified grunt and stepped back as though they expected the beast to fall.

The monster did not react, save a growl that sounded in unison with another crack of thunder and flash of lightning.

Niki retreated from Marziah's side.

Farhad glanced over his shoulder at the withdrawing captain, as though he were checking to see if she was safe. Water glistened off his bare chest, his muscles rigid. He craned his neck back to the beast and shouted again. "Attack!"

As though they were one, the Rudhira shuffled forward again and lodged their pikes into beast. The spoiled insides again seeped from the wounds, pouring out over the frayed film of skin.

As though the beast only now realized they were shredding its insides, it moved. With an unearthly snarl, a clawed hand raked at the Lilitu, but the pikes kept the beast at bay. Marziah turned to grab Niki and hurry her toward the waves. In two large steps, she reached her friend, spinning on her foot once more to keep an eye on the battle.

"Hold!" Farhad shouted, dipping down and lowering the base of his pike. Several other warriors matched his example. "Company two—ready—attack!"

Half of the Rudhira pulled their pikes free.

Twock! The monster clamped its jaws down and swiped its left arm across the longspears still wedged in its side and chest. Several of the pikes ripped clear of its torso with the momentum, knocking a handful of Lilitu from their feet.

Company two stabbed the beast a third time as the beast rotated back. The creature scooped his forearm under the edge of the pikes. With a raucous gurgle, the beast heaved the weapons upward, causing many warriors to hastily release their weapon and skitter away. The few who did not were lifted from the ground.

"Run!" Jaffar screamed from behind Marziah, only now reaching the beach with another longboat. The din of the sailors turned to cries of fear. A couple of Rudhira who accompanied them ran to join their brethren.

"Keep your position!" Farhad shouted at the warriors, disregarding Jaffar's outburst. "Gather your weapons and hold!"

Footsteps stomped through the waves, yet Marziah did not move her eyes from the beast. With several pikes dangling from its body, the monster advanced on the Lilitu, who fought to follow their orders and regain their formation.

The monster took a lumbering step, its entrails sloshing out of the multiple lesions, and snagged a single Lilitu from the ground. With little effort, the male warrior was thrown toward the jungle where he smashed into a tree. He fell to the ground unmoving.

The nearest Rudhira clambered for a dropped longspear. She scarcely reached for the weapon when the beast snagged her by a leg. Pulling her off the ground, the fiend twisted her around and sank its fangs into her face.

The warbling scream faded when the Rudhira passed out from the pain. The monster ripped flesh from her face, pulling sinew from bone. Blood darkened the creature's teeth and skin.

"Kill it!" Niki screamed.

Marziah averted her eyes from the dying warrior to pull at Niki again. "Keep your distance, Niki. We are many; we will be victorious."

Farhad de Zand began shouting orders again as the beast lurched from warrior to warrior, crushing them. Red cloth and blood became almost as blinding as the rain. Marziah almost did not notice when another handful of Rudhira raced by her with their pikes in hand, signaling the arrival of the other longboat.

Jaffar materialized next to Marziah and Niki. "Captain, you must return to the galley until the battle is won."

Marziah followed the captain's hesitant gaze to the galley. The ship rocked to and fro on the sandbar with every violent rebound.

"How many more remain on board?" she asked.

"A dozen at most," Jaffar answered.

"How many Rudhira?" Marziah asked.

"One or two," he said.

Niki was quick to reply. "Return with the longboats and bring them to shore."

"Captain?" Jaffar eyed the monster from the corner of his eye. "We can help them."

Niki narrowed her gaze. "No, we cannot. We are not Rudhira. Bring our warriors!"

"Yes, Captain." Jaffar dipped his chin. He walked away, ordering several more of the Nili to join him in the longboats.

Marziah could not believe Jaffar's outburst. "He wants to fight alongside the Rudhira."

Niki did not reply, echoing the death cry of another Rudhira with a shriek of her own.

Marziah twisted on her heel to examine the battlefield less than thirty paces away. Half the Rudhira remained, including Farhad de Zand, with six or more in pieces scattered over the battlefield. Arms were pulled from sockets, legs were torn from bodies, and skulls had been flattened.

The fiend held a hunk of its latest victim, possibly an arm, and chewed on it menacingly while watching the remaining Lilitu gather their pikes. As the beast feasted on the red-brown flesh, she saw the gashes in the monster's gut and chest begin to mend themselves.

"Impossible," she hissed.

"Save us, Mother," Niki prayed to Lilith. "Give us this victory. Carry us home."

Farhad was visibly unmoved by the loss of his soldiers, directing the remaining few. "Circle the beast. Strike true, Naser and Ramin. Pikes at the ready, Samira and Pouri! Fall in, Touran!"

"We should run," Niki whispered. "The empress did not order this fight."

"Rudhira do not flee unless they wish to be stripped of caste. Better to die," Marziah said, wondering how Niki could be raised in any Lilitu civilization and say as much.

Niki replied, "I know their code, but when have they ever faced a beast such as this?"

Marziah whispered her reply. "Never. But the laws of the Lilitu do not change because we face adversity."

"Attack!" Farhad cried. "Tear it apart! Piece by piece!"

Farhad thrust his pike first, the beast twisting his head to redirect the attack with his tusk. It snapped at the commander to no avail, while another Rudhira jabbed his weapon into the back of the fiend's leg and held tight. The beast swung to hit the new attacker, dropping his meal in the midst, and missed.

As though planned, a female Rudhira stepped next to the commander and forcibly stabbed her own spear into the creature's decomposing armpit, the tip piercing through the top of the shoulder. The blade stayed in place, stuck among the muscle and bone. She released the weapon and rolled to safety.

The second female advanced from the flank, spearing the back of the arm. Black blood spouted and the arm fell limp, hanging from a residual piece of stretched skin. She, too, leaped away to find another pike among the dead.

"Take its arm, Touran!" Farhad cried.

Another male stormed forward, spearing the upper bicep with his pike. Pitching his weapon to the side, he easily ripped the remainder of the arm away from the trunk.

The festering limb fell to the mud, drawing a shout of delight from Marziah. "I told you we would win."

The fiend on the battlefield, unaware of their excitement, lurched at the Rudhira called Touran. The longspear in its leg ripped free, but not before jerking the other male Rudhira along the ground for several steps.

The monster was quick to snag Touran by his bulbous head with its remaining arm. He lifted the much smaller Rudhira from the ground, snarling. Touran tried to twist his pike between himself and the beast.

Farhad and another male Lilitu hurried to stab the monster in the back, but it would not be stopped. With a growl, the monster tossed Touran up and grabbed hold of his scrawny arm. Then, with a twist of his wrist, he thrashed Touran back and forth before flinging him to the side while holding fast to the arm. After a few rotations, the bizarre strength of the creature effortlessly ripped Touran's own arm from its socket.

Touran soared from reach and crumpled to the sand. His eyes swelled, and his mouth gaped like a fish outside of water, before a scream ripped through from his throat.

To Marziah's terror, the beast took the small spindly arm and held it to its shoulder. The threads of the monster's tattered skin extended like thin vines, tangling and fusing with the shredded film of Touran's severed arm. Upon reattachment, the newly fastened arm extended and bulked up, resembling the removed arm of the monster, claws and all.

"It cannot be killed!" Niki cried as Touran's screams softened and then stopped entirely. "We must return to the galley! Run!"

Marziah pulled at Niki, suddenly having a similar mind. They were not Rudhira. They could escape and keep their honor. She could adventure another day.

From the returning longboat emerged Jaffar with the remaining sailors, including the two Rudhira. He pushed by Marziah and Niki, avoiding eye contact. As he approached the few Rudhira who readied another attack, he pulled a pike from a fallen warrior in his path.

He did not miss a step.

No one had time to say a word as he balanced the weapon over his shoulder and then hurled it at the hulking beast. The broad-pointed longspear sailed over Farhad's head, between the tusks of the undead monster, and sank into the soft skin between its yellow eyes.

It was dead before it fell.

Chapter III

Marziah rushed ahead to reach Jaffar's side. "What have you done…you are not a—" Marziah exhaled, knowing she did not know Jaffar well enough to speak against him.

"A Rudhira?" Jaffar pressed his thin lips together, turning his chin toward the dark clouds rolling through the sky. It would be hours before light would peek over the eastern horizon.

Marziah bobbed her head, noticing the rain was thinning. Uncertain whether he saw her gesture, she drifted her gaze to the galley sitting at a distance in the shallow waters. It bounced safely among the waves.

"No, I am not," he finally answered, "but my father was and taught me how to use a pike."

With a grunt, he marched toward Farhad.

Marziah matched his stride.

Farhad waved his hand to the few remaining Rudhira as they approached. They rushed to the tree line to watch for whatever else might emerge. "A warrior never throws his weapon in battle. What would possess you to pick it up in the first place?"

The commander pulled the pike from the beast's split face and speared the weapon into the muddied beach. Black blood oozed from the wound.

Marziah was glad to see the flesh stayed severed and the creature dead.

When Jaffar said nothing, Farhad gritted his teeth and leveled his eyes at the deck officer. "You could have killed any of us."

Jaffar grumbled. "As though you were not dying well enough on your own. You would all be dead if it were not for me."

Marziah pulled her shoulders back to keep herself from shaking her head in agreement. The monster would have ripped them all apart.

Niki suddenly stomped up beside her, the blue hood attached to her mantle bouncing between her shoulder blades. The rain had completely stopped; the heavens were all the brighter. She pointed at Jaffar. "You disobeyed a direct order. You are a deck officer, not a Rudhira."

Marziah's mouth dried. While she was glad they were victorious, Niki spoke in accordance with the Lilitu way.

"I know my position, Captain Karimi," Jaffar dipped his chin, suddenly showing more respect than he had for the commander, "but we were dying. The mission—"

"Was not yours to protect," Niki finished. "If Farhad de Zand and his warriors were meant to fall—or us along with them—then Lilith would have received us in the hereafter. Matters of life and death are not your charge."

"Captain—" he began.

"Do not riddle my ears with your misplaced reason," she went on. "You will be bound until we return to Dhaini, where you will be tried. You will be lucky if the Arjuna do not banish you and label you a Malinah."

Marziah bit her tongue, hearing her friend issue the threat with clear vehemence. To be brought before the white-clad Arjuna—the governing officials—meant Jaffar would certainly receive the strictest punishment. To be given the black cloth and called Malinah was the worse sentence to be had.

She glanced over her shoulder, hearing several Lilitu murmur under their breath from a distance. Some had already started to gather the dead and lay them along the water's edge. Jaffar certainly lost the respect of the crew the moment he lifted the weapon. He was lucky the Lilitu laws were not stricter, or he would be lying among the deceased.

"Marziah," Niki said, "take him away from my sight. Bind him."

"Captain," Farhad interjected unsteadily. His bitterness all but disappeared. "We have not stepped foot in these strange jungles. Whatever dangers lie ahead may be better faced with Jaffar's hands freed."

"You would allow him to commit another transgression? To lift a pike with those deserving of the right?" Niki's voice was ice. "Do not insult your own Rudhira, Commander."

Farhad spoke without emotion, holding his gaze to the captain. "We have few Rudhira remaining to protect the expedition—"

"Pray to the Mother that they are your best," Niki interjected. "I suggest you see to them and prepare them for whatever lies ahead."

"All the same," Farhad said the moment she stopped to take a breath, "do you plan to keep him detained on the galley while we traipse through the jungle? Nili should not be guarding him and I cannot spare the Rudhira. He must come with us. You told our empress that you hoped to find an indigenous people to expand our trade routes. Will you meet them with one of our own held as a prisoner?"

Niki drew in her cheeks. "Then he will stay on the galley until morning. You can spare one Rudhira for the remainder of the evening. He can help unload the silver from the ship and bring it to shore. Without the weight, we might break away from the sand bar."

"I will watch him myself, Captain," Farhad said.

She looked over her shoulder at Marziah. "Take him from my sight."

Marziah beckoned for Jaffar to follow her. She could not say she enjoyed the man or his company, but she had no doubts he was honorable. If Niki had demanded he be restrained, Marziah knew he would slit his own throat before rejecting his captain's order.

"A wise decision, Captain," Farhad said as the two of them worked their way back to the crew.

"We may need you on shore, Farhad. Send one of your other Rudhira to watch him. Samira, maybe."

Farhad nodded in agreement. "I am willing to make the accommodation, if you would refrain from ordering my troops in battle. *That* is not your place."

Niki must have gestured to him. Marziah heard her change the topic. "What do you make of this *thing?*"

"I don't know." Farhad's voice trailed off.

Marziah looked to Jaffar from the corner of her eye, no longer able to hear the conversation. He was unreadable, staring beyond the onlookers on the beach.

"You saved us," she managed to whisper. "You condemned yourself, but you saved us. We are now free to explore this land."

"I am not a hero." He turned on her, his spherical eyes holding as much life as his flat expression. "We would not be in this situation if you had not swayed the captain to bring us ashore. We were safe on the *Valiant*." He pointed at the bodies being lined up along the shore. "Do you not see what death you wrought?"

Marziah gaped, following his extended finger. She could not believe she tried to praise him. "I did not kill them. That creature did."

"A creature we could have eluded if we had stayed on the ship," Jaffar said.

The reality of his words washed over her. "You cannot pin this on me. Their duty is to defend us. Death is a natural outcome of battle," she said weakly. She struggled to keep her eyes off the dead being piled up, looking at Jaffar. She wondered at the extent of his blame. "You think I am liable for you too? You raised a weapon."

He squinted his eyes at her. "You must see that your actions, no matter how slight, have consequences. Your adventure-lust brought us to this shore, and now our brethren are dead. Are you so eager to rush into the blackwood now?"

"I could not have known what would happen once we reached the shore," she said, "but I knew the danger of staying on the galley."

"You inflated the threat so the captain would direct us to come ashore. You wanted to quench your curiosity," Jaffar said. "You could not wait a few more hours. We have survived worse storms."

"We hit the sandbar," she said.

"Because you left your post," he retorted. "May I also point out, the galley remains safe. We did not need to abandon the ship."

Marziah knew his words were as true now as they had been while on the galley, but she would not give in to the accusations. "We had no reason to risk staying on the boat with the shoreline so close."

He scoffed. "Do not think me the fool. You have the reputation of being a fine sailor. In any other instance, your advice would be to brave the storm."

"Am I interrupting something?" a feminine voice spoke from behind Marziah.

Marziah looked over her shoulder to see one of the Rudhira, Samira, standing with her pike fastened between her fingers. She flexed her muscles slightly as though keeping her tongue from saying more took effort.

"No," Marziah said.

Samira winced, her dark eyes incapable of hiding her doubt. She adjusted the red cloth wrapped around her waist, then brushed her hand through the dark-colored topknot in the center of her scalp. Marziah could not help but think the hair looked like grass sprouting from a barren field.

"Good," Samira said. "I was instructed to take you back to the galley and wait for daybreak before returning."

Jaffar dipped his chin. "Very well."

"Both of you," Samira clarified.

"What?" Marziah huffed. "Why me?"

"The captain wishes to have the silver brought to shore in the morning. She has chosen you to see it done."

Marziah gaped, swiftly looking for Niki. Her friend made eye contact with her for a split second. She provided a half-nod as though she heard the conversation from a distance.

"Come along," Samira said. "We do not have all night."

Chapter IV

After little sleep, she was awake again. Standing in the belly of the galley, Marziah lifted another small chest of silver to Jaffar.

"Is this the last of it?" he asked.

"Clearly," Marziah said, motioning to the oars strewn about the bowl of the galley with her open hands. She cocked her head hoping Jaffar would catch the crossness of her tone. Since waking, he had acted as though they had not been arguing hours ago.

"I am glad we are finished. I know you were excited to explore the jungle. I wonder what we will find," he said.

Marziah eyed Jaffar. The thin grey clouds behind him held a yellowish glow, moving at a steady pace across the sky. The cool wind that carried them whipped over the galley, rustling her hair and blue cloak.

She clicked her tongue on the roof of her mouth to keep herself from ripping into him. "You want to give that to Samira so we can get out of here."

"Yes." Jaffar took no action to move. "I hate dragging these to shore before we explore the land. Might not be anything living here besides the beasts."

"We need to lighten the galley anyway." Marziah gritted her teeth, shooing him with her hand. He took a single step back onto a plank but moved no closer to Samira on the opposite side of the galley. Marziah pulled herself up on the main deck. She wondered if she would have to carry the chest to the Rudhira herself. "Besides, the captain is optimistic."

"After last night? I think any emotion beyond desperation is a stretch," Jaffar joked. "She needs to discover something worthwhile before returning to Dhaini. Half the crew is dead."

She pulled herself to her feet in time to glare at him.

"Sorry," he squirmed, hoisting the chest up to his midsection. He tried to sound more positive. "I am certain we will find someone. Let us hope they are more pleasant than the Uvil."

She rubbed her nose, wondering if she needed to push him to the edge of the galley herself.

The Uvil were a strange, rugged race who lived in the western reaches of Haemos Mons among the desert and mountains. The relationship between them and the Lilitu wavered between peace and war depending on the Uvil's so-called *prophecy*. In the past century, the Uvil initiated a war against them twice and lost. For now, peace reigned, but it was only a matter of time before they crossed iron again.

She tensed her jaw at Jaffar. "Can we go?"

"Marziah! Jaffar! Come on. Something has happened!" Samira shouted. "Let's go."

Marziah snapped her attention to the Rudhira who waved at them to hurry.

"What are you talking about?" Jaffar blurted, finally stumbling along the centerboard with the heavy chest gripped in his hands. Marziah trailed his footsteps.

"The beach is empty. The captain, commander...they are all gone," Samira said.

"What?!" Marziah exclaimed. Stumbling behind Jaffar was almost painful, waiting to get to the fore of the boat so she might better examine the shore.

The jungle looked no different than it had during the night, painted with brilliant colors of lesser flora and shaded trees. The brown sands, however, that separated Anusund from the jungle were completely desolate.

"Where did they go?" Jaffar asked.

"They left?" Marziah's stomach sank. "Why would they head out without us?"

"No telling what has happened. Come on," Samira said. She took the chest of silver from Jaffar with ease and then started down a side ladder on the galley toward the longboat. Marziah followed after her with Jaffar right behind her. Moments later, the three of them were tucked in the longboat and rowing to shore.

The journey took too long with Marziah looking over her shoulder every other turn of the oars to comb the sands with her eyes. She could see indentions in the sand leading toward the tree line where something may have been dragged, but nothing more.

"Everyone is gone." Jaffar bounded into the water. Samira jumped into the shallow waters behind him. "Our dead, too. This does not make any sense. Neither Farhad nor the captain would leave without us."

"Maybe Niki thought it best to bury them in the jungle instead of bringing them back to Dhaini for burial," Marziah offered, joining them in the water. "The journey was not too far, but depending on how long we explore this land, the bodies would certainly rot away."

Jaffar winced, holding the edge of the longboat behind Samira. "When would they have left? Samira, you stayed awake through the night, right? Did you see or hear anything?"

"Nothing. Though I cannot say I was watching the shore, either. My charge was to watch you." She reached into the longboat and retrieved her pike before stepping onto the beach. She lifted her finger to the tree line. "Look at all those long marks in the sand. The bodies were dragged."

"We lost a lot of our own last night during the fight against that creature," Jaffar asserted, scratching his head, "but not this many. It looks like the entire company was dragged off the beach."

With a final heave, he finished pulling the longboat onto the sand.

Marziah looked into the longboat to see the several chests of silver and then moved to join Samira, who was already advancing closer to the tree line.

Samira turned around. "Do you see the compressions in the sand?" She pointed to numerous spots as she moved forward. "It looks as though several of them fell to the ground before being dragged, but there are no signs of a struggle."

"You think they were really attacked?" Jaffar wondered. "Surely we would have heard the battle."

"Maybe there was not much of a fight. If nothing else, we know the creature did not return to life," Marziah said, pointing to the corpse. The rotting hunk of meat and bone had not moved since the night prior.

Jaffar frowned. "Let's hope there was not more than one." He ventured closer to the jungle several feet away from them. "How do almost a hundred Lilitu disappear in a few hours? This could not have been done by one creature."

"The plants are flattened over here," Samira rushed forward. Jaffar moved to join Marziah and Samira.

Marziah nodded, kneeling to touch the trail of compacted grass and plants. She was not a tracker of any sort, but it made her feel more useful. "We need to follow the trail."

"We are not Rudhira. We might find our deaths at the end of it. Your need for adventure will get us all killed," Jaffar said. Marziah kept herself from rolling her eyes. Since being reprimanded by the captain and commander, he suddenly seemed to lose interest in showing any signs of bravery. Marziah could not understand why; he was already condemned.

Before anyone could respond, a wind-like silvery song, delicate and sweet, suddenly sprang from the jungle. A high timbre mixed with low notes melodiously flowed, delicate and graceful.

"Fall back!" Jaffar cried.

Samira took the lead while the other three of them stepped away from the blackwood trees and green leaves. Samira swelled her chest and bent her knees, carrying herself as though she were a thousand Rudhira.

The tune did not waver. It was shrill then light, forceful then delicate. After several notes, Marziah realized a secondary and tertiary sound whistled beneath the first like the sweet singing of birds, agreeable with the melody.

"It sounds nice," she muttered.

"Show yourself!" Samira shouted over her.

A glimpse of blue and yellow wavered in the sea of green, and then the music stopped. A wave of whistles and chirps resounded, echoing back through the jungle as though a thousand birds were repeating the same message to the ends of the earth.

Marziah took a step closer to Samira. "I am Marziah Corran of the *Valiant*." She pointed back at the galley. More colors flashed between the leaves— violet, crimson, orange—indicating several creatures were moving swiftly through the trees. Yet the only response was chirping.

"Lower your weapons, Samira," Marziah whispered. "If these are the natives, we do not want to threaten them."

"They may have taken the others," Samira hissed under her breath.

More whistles and peeps came from the jungle.

"I am not sure anything sounding so sweet could be so cruel," she said.

Samira look to Jaffar for a moment, who signaled for her to lower the pike.

"I hope you know what you are doing, Marziah," Jaffar said. "I am no less cautious than Samira."

She elevated her voice again. "We do not wish you any harm. We are looking for our friends."

The dark shadow of an avian creature standing on two taloned toes on each of its two legs emerged from the abruptly hushed jungle. Standing nearly seven feet tall, the humanoid frame was wrapped in a brightly colored silken cloth from neck to waist. With its flat chest and neutral characteristics, Marziah could not say whether the creature was male or female. It cocked its head, stretching out its long avian legs to balance on the sand. The strange form completely overshadowed the long black-tipped spear in its hand.

"Hail, Marziah Corran. Welcome to the Masura Jungle. You will not be able to say my name with your words," the creature cooed, ruffling the green and blue feathers of its plumage.

She took note of the name of the place while gawking at the creature, who seemingly spoke her language with ease. Its facial features seemed to be a combination of bird and most humanoid creatures she had met. It had narrow eyes and its nose was so wide and flat, it seemed almost a pair of nostrils in its face. Soft downy feathers faded into the rough leathery skin of its lips and eyes, while the barest hint of flesh was hidden beneath the rest of its face. The facial features seemed almost out of place, distracting Marziah momentarily from the brightly colored plume atop its head. The avian jerked its head sharply several times to align its eyes with her, Samira, and Jaffar. Then it said, "You may call me Akna, daughter of K'awi. I suspect we are a rather strange species to you. We are collectively known as the Arkono. Where do you come from? *Valiant*, you say?"

Marziah suddenly realized she'd placed herself in a commanding position by speaking to the Arkono. She supposed that with Jaffar being a prisoner of sorts and Samira being a Rudhira on a ship of merchants, this did demand her leadership.

As though the other two understood the natural order, Jaffar and Samira shuffled a step away in order for her to speak.

"No. The *Valiant* is our ship," Marziah said, gesturing to the galley. "We are called the Lilitu. We come from a city, Dhaini, several leagues beyond the water."

Akna flexed her talons in the sand. Her feathers rustled as she examined the galley.

"How do you speak our language?" Jaffar asked.

"We learned your language from the Uvil in the West," Akna said, unblinking. "They have spoken of the Lilitu many times before."

Marziah swallowed. The Arkono knew of the blue-skinned desert people. She wondered whether they were allies or simply tolerated one another as the Lilitu tolerated the Uvil.

"You cannot allow them into the Masura," another Arkono interrupted tersely at Akna's back. The creature revealed itself, poking its head through the leaves to examine them. It was brightly adorned in lilac cloth with yellow flowers sewn into the fabric, but again, Marziah had no indication of its gender.

Akna made a strange guttural sound in her throat like she was gurgling water.

The other Arkono pointed at Marziah with a feathered finger; its other four fingers held some sort of instrument that looked to be six or seven flutes of different lengths tied together. Beads of painted clay rattled around the Arkono's neck and wrists as it continued, "We would be unwise to let them come into the jungle. It is not safe. Not anymore."

"Not anymore? What has happened?" Jaffar asked, peering at the new Arkono. Marziah noticed several more. She could not see them distinctly, but she guessed their numbers to be around ten.

"It is not your concern, but Tepin is right." Akna side-eyed her companion. "You would be best to return to your boat and go back to Dhaini. The Masura will only bring you death."

"We cannot leave without our friends," Marziah said. "They were here last night and gone this morning."

"They killed a bagiennik," Tepin said.

Marziah looked at the corpse of the creature they fought the night before, pinning the name to the strange beast.

Akna replied to Tepin with a smile. "And yet their friends were taken by the little Likho."

Rowdy tweeting and chirping, indicative of laughter, emitted from the small flock of Arkono in the trees.

"You know who took our people?" Jaffar asked. "Where are they?"

Lifting his hand in the air, Akna silenced the voluble sounds behind him. Tepin said, "You know they are likely dead. Send them on their way."

"What would you offer if I took you to your friends?" Akna asked.

"We have silver," Marziah offered. "We have brought chests of silver that we can trade for their safe return."

Akna perked up, blinking several times with her plume standing upright. "What do you think of that, Tepin? Silver."

Tepin cooed and cocked his head. "The chieftain would be pleased."

"I cannot promise their safety, but I can take you to the Likho's nearest village," Akna said. "Are you going to fight them?"

"We do not all fight," Marziah said. "I am a trader; a sailor."

"Hm. We will help you. We agree that if you survive, you will then leave Masura." Akna gave the semblance of a smile, eyes crumpling with wild excitement. "We will take the silver."

Marziah dipped her chin. "Agreed."

Chapter V

For half a mile, they trekked through the Masura Jungle while Tepin blew air through the hollow reeds of his instrument, which Marziah learned was called a syrinx. The other half dozen Arkono whistled and tweeted along with the song, fanning out a distance away from them and carrying similar black-tipped spears like Akna. Marziah could not keep her eye on them consistently as they slipped in and out of the trees, often hidden by the thick foliage.

She could not truly determine why they kept their distance, but with their constant song, she assumed they were giving notice of their approach to any other creatures in the area. Regardless, she was stupefied by their merriment. Even when celebrating special occasions, the Lilitu were never so jovial.

She listened to the water dripping through the leaves and branches, splashing into scattered puddles on the jungle floor. The Arkono stepped to and fro through the smaller plants, twisting their long legs and fluffing their feathers. When she did see them emerge from the foliage, she noticed many would tilt their head at her or the other Lilitu, all the while continuing their rich and thin trill. To her surprise, the Arkono barely rustled the plants as they moved, whereas every step Marziah took seemed like she was determined to crush each blade of grass back into its seed.

"Are you sure this is wise?" Jaffar fell in step with her about twenty feet behind Akna. The deck officer leaned in closer from her right, whispering beneath the never-ending harmony. "We do not know anything about these people. Even in all this noise, I get the feeling they are communicating to one another."

Marziah scrunched her brow. The Arkono seemed to be singing and nothing more. "What choice do we have?" Marziah replied, eyeing the several avians stirring around them through the twisted trees.

"Plenty," Jaffar said. "We can return to our boat with our silver and go home."

Marziah shook her head in defiance. Being here among these strange creatures in this foreign land was worth all the silver in the world. Luckily for her, Jaffar no longer held the position to make decisions.

The Arkono were honestly intimidating to Marziah, standing so much taller and moving with such grace and speed. Not to mention, their bright colors sent a chill up her spine. The assortment of oranges and blues, yellows and reds, purples and black caused her to wonder how they roamed the blackwood without being noticed by creatures like the bagiennik or Likho. Since leaving the beach, however, she had seen no sign of anything more, making her wonder whether the Arkono's colors served as a warning to those with whom they shared the jungle.

Samira's rich voice carried forward between her and Jaffar. The Rudhira eyed the Arkono around them warily, using her pike as a walking stick, its tip pointing toward the sky. "For all we know, they took the others. They could be leading us into a trap. We will follow your orders, Marziah, but Jaffar's advice is sound."

"Why would they set a trap for us?" Marziah stepped to the side, feeling the woman's breath on her cheek. "They could have overcome us on the beach and taken the silver. If they took Niki and the others, they had no problem doing so, and we are but a quarter of the size. No. I believe Akna wants to help."

"The silver was given to us for trade, not as a means to rescue our brethren. If you find the captain alive, do you think she will approve?" Jaffar growled loud enough to be heard. "She scorned me on the beach for interfering with the battle against the bagiennik, stepping in between the natural roles of life and death."

"She faced a threat of death and now she might actual be dying," Marziah said plainly. "I also have not lifted a weapon to aid her. I am within my bounds as a Nili."

Jaffar whispered through gritted teeth, noticing Akna twisting her head to peer at them. "You clearly know your friend better than I would. However, I think we would do better to take the Arkono's advice and return home."

Jaffar turned away and stood up straight. She wondered if he prayed for the captain and commander to be dead, potentially saving him from his sentencing back in Dhaini.

"Pray to the Mother that they are well," Marziah said while admiring the jungle.

"Let us also pray these Likho are not large like the bagiennik or the Arkono, and while you have Lilith's ear, ask for them to die easily. May I remind you I am the only one among us permitted to cross iron?" Samira clicked her tongue. "I will do my duty, but I cannot defeat an army."

"Oh, I am certain Marziah has a plan," Jaffar said, almost mockingly.

Marziah swallowed a mouthful of air. She honestly had not considered how they would retrieve—

A dart zipped by Akna and plunged into Samira's bare chest. Marziah screeched nearly as loud as the Rudhira's startled scream. Samira crashed to the ground in a heap, gripping the long-feathered stick piercing into her flesh. While the wound looked small, Samira's cry was fixed, her body jolting violently.

Tepin's syrinx quieted, replaced with a short, high-pitched alarm. *Dee, dee, dee.* Akna repeated the sound, waving at the other Arkono.

Marziah strained to see what order the Arkono may have been given, but the effort was futile. Diving to Samira's side, she pulled free what looked like a thick feathered twig. The projectile oozed a black goop that coated the tip.

"Get down," Marziah hissed at Jaffar.

Several more darts flew overhead as Jaffar crouched to her side.

"Stay quiet, Samira," Jaffar said, arching his head in an attempt to see from where they were being attacked.

Marziah could see nothing in the brush ahead any more than she could see where the rest of the Arkono had fled.

Akna, who remained close, stepped lightly through the grass until she hovered over them.

Samira tensed under Marziah's hand, quieting considerably, despite any effort of her own to move. Her mouth opened and closed like a fish from water; her eyes glazed over.

Jaffar eyed Samira's pike where it fell among the greenery. He flexed his muscles as though he might charge the jungle ahead.

Several more darts flew by, several striking Akna's colored feathers. The few that pierced through, Akna pulled out and tossed to the ground with little concern.

"What are these?" Marziah asked.

"One of the Likho's poisons," Arkna cooed, reverberating in her chest. "It will relax her and make her think she is dying, but she will be fine as long as they do not get to her. They like to weaken their prey before eating them. I hoped they would all be gone before we arrived, but they clearly did not want to abandon their food supply."

"What? You mean to say that our friends could have been eaten by these Likho?" Marziah's throat tightened.

"Did I forget to mention they are flesh-eaters? Oh, without a doubt, yes. I would not expect to find many living," Akna replied, cocking her head sideways, "but surely some survived the night." Her plumage rustled as she scratched at the ground with a talon.

Marziah's tongue twisted in her mouth. "If you knew they were dying, why have you been singing and prancing through the forest?"

Akna stood a bit straighter as though she did not understand the question. "The world is at an unrest. The remedy is death."

"What?" Marziah asked.

Akna chirped.

Jaffar ducked lower as another dart whizzed by Akna. He glared at the Arkono with suspicion. "Why does this *poison* have no effect on you?"

Akna creased her eyes, seemingly grinning. "The plant they make their poison from is consumed by my people from infancy onward. We have quite the tolerance."

"Perfect," Jaffar said.

"You Lilitu are really a dull, puny people, aren't you?" Akna said.

As though Samira was proving her point, she sighed and slipped into unconsciousness.

Marziah held her tongue. She had no desire to either argue or understand the Arkono while under attack. Besides, Marziah saw no reason to inform the Arkono of the hundreds of thousands of Lilitu scattered across the northern realm of Haemus Mons.

"We thank you for your help," she said.

"You are welcome," Akna chirped.

Several death cries unexpectedly echoed in the distance, shadowed by the soft melody of Tepin's syrinxes. A rusty screech followed by a bell-like whistle then resounded through the jungle.

"Ah. Come along. The Likho are defeated and your friends have been found." Akna waved them forward, turning on her talon. Marziah withheld her gasp, realizing Jaffar was correct—the Arkono could communicate with each other through what sounded like song. She could not wait to learn more of their species. Akna pointed at Samira. "You might want to stay with her or bring her along before something sees her as an easy meal. No Arkono will be out here to keep her safe."

Jaffar stood up slowly, reaching for Samira. "I will carry her."

"She will wake up in a few hours," Akna assured him, turning to the continued tune of the syrinxes.

Marziah followed Akna closely for a few hundred feet while Jaffar carried Samira behind them.

When they reached the clearing ahead, Marziah was surprised to discover how natural it seemed with plants, vines, and brush drawn to the side or replanted among the jungle trees. A handful of small huts, covered with bamboo and green leaves, were built against many thick trees. Outside of the cottages, the half dozen Arkono who had come with them now strutted among dead bodies the size of Lilitu children. Their new allies held their spears at the ready as they pulled the huts apart. They hardly seemed concerned by the threat of any more Likho rushing forth, acting as though they had just waged war against insects.

Their attackers, a handful of Likho, lay sprawled out in the clearing. Bright red blood oozed from their distorted green torsos where the Arkono's black-tipped spears had found their mark time and again. Marziah glanced at one of the little beasts—no more than two feet tall—as she passed. None of them wore anything more than a loin cloth; their bamboo blowguns lying out of reach of their thin fingers.

The creature was very similar to the Lilitu with a larger cranium, lanky arms and legs, and a spindly body. She leaned closer to see that each of them had their left eye plucked from its socket.

"They remove their eye at childhood to have them focus on their other senses to survive the jungle," Akna explained as they passed. She shrugged, chirping, "I cannot say the tactic helps, but they are known to be a bit mindless."

"Marziah!" Niki exited one of the huts, shiftily eyeing the Arkono. Nearly two dozen more Nili came out behind her, ducking as they passed by the Arkono. Niki rubbed her arms under her blue mantle. She darted her eyes to Jaffar, who lowered Samira to the jungle floor. She stumbled with her words. "How?"

Stepping over a fallen Likho, Marziah examined Niki with a half-smile. "Praise to the Mother, you are okay. Akna and her people helped us track you in the jungle. I hope we are not too late. Akna suggested some of you may have been—"

"More than some," Niki interrupted, eyeing a cottage behind Marziah. Naturally, she turned to look and wished she had not. Bile burned the back of her throat, seeing the chopped limbs and splattered blood of many Lilitu piled up inside the bamboo, straw, and copious amounts of greenery. "These beasts are ravenous. They slaughtered all the Rudhira first. I am afraid very few of us remain."

"Farhad?" Jaffar asked.

Niki shook her head. "He was one of the first. We barely knew what happened on the beach. One moment we were there and the next we were here."

"Surely these few small creatures did not drag all of you back to this place," Samira said.

Akna approached to provide an answer. "Oh no, hundreds of them roam beneath the forest floor. They typically scatter when they hear our songs. Though eventually their hunger overcomes their fear.

These few were especially stupid." She gestured at the dead Likho around the clearing.

Niki gazed up at the Arkono. "We saw more than we could count."

"I suspect you did." Akna said, eyeing the two dozen Nili who stumbled from the huts and into the clearing. "I would like to return to my own home. So, as agreed, it is time you return to your ship and go home."

"We should first discuss how our people might benefit one another in the days to come," Marziah said.

Akna widened her eyes. "You would return to Masura? Your brothers and sisters would be food for the Likho." Akna chirped. "Let us be done with words. I am eager to gather the reward of silver for my people."

"Reward?" Niki lifted an eyebrow.

"Marziah traded the silver for your safety," Jaffar said. "I advised against it."

Niki scowled at him. She then looked to Marziah and grimaced. "We came here for trade. Not to give away our treasure for the life of a few Lilitu."

"The silver allowed us to trek into this marvelous place. Only a fool would think the coin was merely spent on securing your life, Captain." Marziah was quick to say. She would not lose her chance at another adventure. "Not all is lost."

"How can you say that? Look around you. Our people are dead," Jaffar barked.

"We are not all dead," Marziah said.

Niki hummed in agreement, motioning for Marziah to finalize the deal.

"We will not shield you forever," Akna said.

"Of course not." She concealed her smile, looking at the Arkono. "May we return with more silver and discuss a long-term treaty? Peace and trade? I promise we can learn much from one another."

Akna chortled, standing her plume on end. "Bring us silver and you may return as often as you like."

STRONG ARMED

Thrice Nine Legends

Month of High Grass

Third of Warmth

1158 CE

Chapter I

"Horse! Oi, horse, look here!"

Sin-sim smiled an oily smile so slick that Balvoc thought his lips would slide from his face. The merchant sauntered towards the wagon—as much as a tubby man such as himself could saunter—his jowls swaying with each lumbering step. The fat of his cheeks nearly hid his crooked teeth.

Horse? He was a Svet! Not some dull animal for men to mount as they mounted their women. The man might as well call him a goat for the horns that curled atop his head. Having the hindquarters of a horse made him no more akin to the beasts than his torso made him akin to the Anshedar.

Balvoc bared his own teeth, fangs by comparison to the Anshedar's. There was no keeping the murder from his eyes. For the moment, he did not even care that he was in the middle of the Lilitu capital of Havre.

"What is it, filth?"

The flabby man chuckled. "Oh, well that is no way to speak to me, horse." He cocked his round head and continued in a sing-song voice, "or do I need to have another finger sent for? Hmm? To remind you of your place?"

The Svet glowered at the man, incapable of speech. He felt more than capable of a few physical expressions, but he could not risk letting his wrath take hold. Instead, his fingers clenched and unclenched while he fantasized about wrapping them around the Anshedar's fleshy throat. All men were vile, but Sin-sim made the rest of their contemptuous race smell like baklava.

"You should be proud. I went to great pains to recruit you—and you have certainly lived up to your reputation." Sin-sim managed to achieve a dignified pose, chins lifted and fists on hips. "What with finding and capturing your wife to ensure your loyalty and all that unpleasant business that went along with breaking you in…Well, my dear Balvoc, I thought we had reached some understanding of your place." Sin-sim paused, always keen for the dramatic. When he spoke again, his voice had dropped to a snarl, "So, *horse*, I ask again—Do I need to remind you of your place?"

At the mention of his wife, Maruda, Balvoc fought to keep his gaze from the merchant, trying his best to look abashed and reticent. Unlike the Anshedar, he found such dramatic performances did not come easily to him. Instead, his concern was for drawing too much attention from the city's authorities. The Lilitu were notoriously unforgiving of any kind of disturbance. His eyes found the Lilitu guards marching to and fro nearby, paying little heed to the apparent argument between a merchant and his hired hand.

Sin-sim had used his connections to capture his wife and hold her prisoner so Balvoc would escort his wagon into the Lilitu lands. He had refused at first, and Sin-sim began to cut fingers from her hand. Every misstep cost another. By his count, his lovely Maruda only had four remaining. Idly, he touched the leather pouch at his side that contained those fingers he had received—all bones now.

"Do I?"

"No," Balvoc managed to choke out.

"Good." His tortuous teeth pushed past his lips, his tongue slipping between them as if to savor each word. "I have always maintained, *horse*, that you Svet are best controlled by the blood of your kin. Coin is too easily spent. Too easily lost. At the first sign of trouble, I would expect you to gallop away." He made a hand gesture which the Svet supposed was meant to represent galloping.

"But," the merchant held up a fat finger, "if I have something you want? Something you can get nowhere else?" He chortled so his stomach bounced. "Well, then, I suppose you will be keeping my skin as safe as your own."

After a moment Balvoc spoke again, as deferential as he could force himself to be. He tried to turn the greasy man's mind from Maruda. "You wanted to show me something? What is it that you have, Sin-sim?"

The Anshedar barely blinked before pulling a purse from his belt and trickled its contents out onto his palm. A dozen multi-hued gems poured out into his broad hand. "Opals!" He giggled, an odd sound for his flabby frame. "Enough to make the whole of the journey to this dismal place worth my time."

Balvoc shook his head, forgetting his anger for the briefest of moments in utter surprise. He looked about for the Lilitu guardsmen to come thundering down on them at any moment. He could see four of them standing by the gate leading out of the Seller's Quarter. Each had a red sash around their waist. "How could you afford them? How much did you pay?"

Sin-sim grunted. "Well, pay is a loose term, mind you. Perhaps 'picked' is a better one—when the Lilitu merchants came to display their wares." A mischievous grin crossed his face. "And, given such terms, we best be on our way, eh?" He poured the gems back into his purse and carefully tied it to his belt.

The Svet stepped backwards, his hindquarters bumping the side of the wagon. "You will get us killed!"

"Careful, fool," Sin-sim snapped, all joviality gone. "There is merchandise in that wagon. You will knock it loose and the price will come off of your wife's hands!"

Balvoc snarled, grabbing Sin-sim by the throat. He wanted to yell, to roar, but he forced his voice to a whisper. Harsh. Quiet. Grating through his teeth. "No one steals from the Lilitu. No one! Why do you think they lock all foreign merchants in the Seller's Quarter? They already do not trust us, which means they watch us twice as hard. We turned our weapons in at the gate. The Lilitu do not even let us bring in our own food and water."

The fat merchant's feet lifted off of the ground. Balvoc's muscles quivered. The pudgy man's lips worked, but only wheezing squeaks came forth. He could snap Sin-sim's neck with a sneeze.

"They will kill us. And if you die, then my wife dies. If she dies, I will hunt down your corpse in the

Netherworld. The tortures you face there will be petty next to those I bring you!"

Sin-sim's face had turned purple. Balvoc threw the man to the ground with an emphatic stamping of his front hooves.

The fat man gasped for air, rolling about like an upset turtle trying to get his feet beneath him. When he managed to reach his knees, his face was no less purple, but the hue came from rage. "You have just cost your whore wife her hand!"

Balvoc spent a moment in a silent fury, his blood roiling through his veins. He could kill Sin-sim. He could do it without breaking a sweat. He could be rid of Sin-sim now and forever. But his wife's face haunted his thoughts and would not let him. He could not kill the Anshedar. Not yet.

Maruda was depending on him, and he did not know where she was being held to rescue her. Sin-sim had teased him with tales of the dark torments being inflicted upon her even now, and there was nothing he could do to prevent them.

He spoke through a snarl, baring his fang-like teeth, "Sin-sim, if you have no tongue to tell them and no fingers to write it, my Maruda will not suffer by your hand or mine. The Lilitu are not kind to those who steal from them."

The fat merchant was still on his knees, staring up at the Svet's great height. Despite Sin-sim's breath still not being his own, Balvoc realized he had a pudgy hand on the small knife at his belt.

After a moment of wordless staring, the merchant labored the rest of the way to his feet. "Then, we must go! If I am held, or dead, and my friends do not hear from me, your pet horse is dead anyway." He kept a hand on the small knife, pointing a finger at Balvoc with his other. "And if I hear another word of why we must go, it will be her arm. The Lilitu have eyes and ears and you bring suspicion down upon us with your every word."

"The Lilitu are *always* suspicious of outsiders," Balvoc returned. "That is why no foreigner is allowed to travel anywhere in Havre without a Lilitu escort. You seem to think them senseless or frail, but even I know that multitudes can crush the mightiest of us." Despite knowing that his fingers would find nothing, he reached to grasp his missing axe. The Lilitu had taken his weapons at the gate when they had arrived.

"Figure that out on your own, did you? I have been to more Lilitu cities than your wife has fingers," Sin-sim snapped. "So don't lecture me about their ways! Keep silent and do as I tell you. I will not warn you again, horse."

Balvoc snorted, turning away from Sin-sim without another word. He could not risk it, though he had plenty more to say. He had taken coin for guarding merchants throughout the north, throughout Maharia, and he could not name a place he had traveled where he had not seen at least a dozen of their kind. In other cities, they bobbed their heads and smiled and leeched coin from every man, woman, and child that met their eye. Here, they did not bother. They had power and used it. The Lilitu merely forced every merchant to bleed out their coin and then sent them on their way into the desert. They had no need to pretend they were small and weak. Here, among the Lilitu, Balvoc was weak. Sin-sim was weak. The difference was the fat Anshedar seemed too stupid or willful to acknowledge it.

He retrieved their team of horses from the stable and began to hitch them while the merchant piddled in the wagon. He could not ignore the clanging of wares while Sin-sim attempted to secure his precious commodities. Though, in short time, Sin-sim meandered back into the streets to speak with a Lilitu guard about being escorted from the city. Balvoc watched from a distance, unable to keep his hindquarters from stamping with discomfort.

Chapter II

It took some time for an additional guard to be called to escort them from Havre. The interim was filled with no shortage of suspicious looks from the red-sashed Lilitu, who watched the Anshedar and his Svet companion.

The Lilitu were suspicious of outsiders, but more so of those choosing to leave in the middle of the day when the desert sun was hottest. Balvoc grimaced at the sight of their too-large eyes bulging from their too-large heads. Suspicion atop of suspicion.

Sin-sim brushed away their agitations with soothing words, assuring them that he knew what he was about, blathering on in regard to early starts to avoid dealing with fellow travelers and plans to continue on into the night.

Before long, the guard announced he was ready to take them from the city. Sin-sim managed to drag his chubby frame into the driver's seat, and they were underway.

The street was a single, narrow passageway which lead directly from the Seller's Quarter to the Seller's Gate at the edge of Havre. The street had no intersections with other streets and only the buildings backing the street could be seen. Being the middle of the day, the street was deserted, as most merchants had already arrived at their destinations and would not travel under a risen sun.

Sin-sim's breathing, the creak of the wagon, the clop of his own hooves and those of the two horses were the only sounds that met his ears. The added anxiety of making it out of the city with Sin-sim's stolen gems simply made the desolate march all the more worrying.

Looking back down the street, Balvoc could catch glimpses of the city proper, where towers rose above the more meagre builds lining the street to the Seller's Quarter. Havre was as grand a city as any that Balvoc had ever seen. He had heard a few of the Lilitu call Havre the Golden City, and in the right light, it was evident why.

Many buildings were made of brick and clay and sandstone, but when the sun glinted off of the yellowish rock, they seemed to shine like gold. Standing nearly twice as high as any Anshedar building he had even seen, the great domes and piercing pinnacles of Havre dwarfed the cities of the northern lands. Each home and tower in Havre was interconnected with covered walkways to protect from sandstorms that swept across the desert. Indeed, the entire city seemed to be one massive structure, a hive bustling with uncounted Lilitu.

In the villages of his people, there was almost never more than a floor or two above the first. The Svet were not fond of being off of the ground.

They reached the Seller's Gate in short order. A half a dozen guards stood at attention, armored with pikes slanted across their chests just so and red sashes about their waists. The colors had something to do with their position in the Lilitu world, which Balvoc did not even pretend to understand. What he did understand was that any Lilitu wearing red meant they knew how to use a weapon. Beyond that much, he did not particularly care if the Lilitu were nude.

A Lilitu with a blue sash across his chest stepped up to meet Sin-sim when they approached. "Sin-sim Gadinu, Anshedar of Eldhaft and Merchant traveling with Balvoc Beledarva, Svet of Sidwohl and personal guard, yes?"

Sin-sim grunted, trying to climb down from the wagon. "Yes, yes. Sounds all in order. I will just sign the papers and be off then."

The Lilitu did not blink. "Please present receipts of all purchases made while within the Golden City of Havre."

The Anshedar had managed to make it down to the ground, gasping heavily from the exertion. A breathy giggle escaped his thick lips. "Oh, my, yes, of course. Give me just a moment."

While Sin-sim produced a few slips of paper for small items he had bought to keep up appearances, Balvoc had only had eyes for his weapons.

He nearly snatched his great double-headed axe from the Lilitu guard handing it to him. Once the labrys was secured, he paid heed to the guard attempting to hand him his bow and knife. Balvoc felt some of the tension go out of his shoulders when he had his weapons back in his possession. At least when things went sideways—and they always did—he would be prepared.

"You do not seem to have purchased much since you arrived." Dark, searching eyes lifted from the receipts. "Did you find everything to your liking?"

Sin-sim nodded vigorously, his jowls rippling from the movement. "Yes, yes, of course."

Balvoc could not help but smile at how agreeable the Anshedar suddenly became while dissembling. The clinking sound of the chain coming from inside the large sandstone guardrooms on either side of the gate preceded its slow rise.

"I would hardly think that such a long trip from" the Lilitu paused, seeming to make a show of checking his notes, "*Eldhaft* would be worth such a long and arduous trek to our great city."

Sin-sim had started turning red, starting at his neck, the color quickly began rising through his cheeks.

Beyond the portcullis, Balvoc could see road to the Seller's Gate intersected with the main thoroughfare that led away from the city and towards the Lilitu town of Khonjra. If they could make it that far, they might stand a chance of avoiding a Lilitu prison cell.

The gate had nearly risen fully when Balvoc heard the sound of running feet from behind him. From the direction of the Seller's Quarter, a red-sashed Lilitu sprinted down the street.

Balvoc plucked at Sin-sim's sleeve. "Perhaps it is time to be underway…"

The fat merchant ruffled, turning furiously towards Balvoc, but his words seemed to die on his lips when he caught sight of the running guard. It was too late.

"Hold! Hold them! Do not let them leave the city! There has been a theft!" The red-sashed Lilitu cried.

Before the guard nearest to Balvoc could turn his pike towards him, the Svet's hand darted down and caught him by the face. Balvoc snarled, throwing the small, red-brown figure into the sandstone wall. The Lilitu had no more than crashed to the ground before Balvoc took Sin-sim by the collar and flung him up onto the seat of the wagon. The fat merchant landed like a sack of flour—albeit a rather corpulent sack of flour.

The Lilitu were obviously well-trained, immediately springing to action. A cry rose up to shut the portcullis and half a dozen pikes were pointed at Balvoc. The Svet did not pause to consider their numbers. He could not afford to be trapped by the Lilitu. Maruda could not afford for him to be trapped.

With a hand nearly the size of the Lilitu's head, Balvoc clasped the nearest pike, just below the blade. His throaty roar filled the street as he used his superior weight and strength to swing the pike—and the attached Lilitu—into the other guardsmen. The guard let go of the pike, falling on his fellow warriors. But Balvoc had not forgotten the guard who had started it all approaching from the rear. The soldier barely had enough time to draw a curved sword before Balvoc's rear hooves sent him sailing back down the street towards the Seller's Quarter.

Inside of three strides, Balvoc was in a dead gallop, his hand slapping the rump of one of the horses pulling the wagon. The portcullis crashed down behind them and cries erupted from the wall and towers. Horns and bells resounded across the desert landscape.

Balvoc could hear the sound of arrows tinging off of the sandstone road, clunking unto the wagon, and thumping into the sandy ground. At first, he tried to weave back and forth to avoid giving too stead of a target, but a piercing pain in his hindquarters nearly made him lose his stride and crash to the ground. After the initial shock, he was able to ignore the pain. He knew that it hurt. Yet the sting was a distant thought, the pounding of his heart helped hide it away in another part of his mind.

The wagon thundered along beside him, Sin-sim cowering, slumped down on the buckboard and letting the horses have their heads. The mindless beasts screamed, trying to run in two different directions.

Balvoc strained to reach the front of the wagon where he could grab the fat man's collar. "Hold them straight, you fool! Follow the road!"

It was all he could do to get the words out. But the merchant seemed to regain some measure of his wits and took the reins in his pudgy fists.

With his free hand, Balvoc retrieved his helm and settled it around his horns. The last thing he needed was a well-shot arrow through the head.

Ahead, a sandstone lookout tower rose on the northern side of the broad road that led from the city. Balvoc hastily glanced around to see if he had any way to avoid going near the mighty structure, but the sandy, rocky terrain would tear the wagon apart before they could make it a dozen strides. He growled. One last fight and he could turn off the road, where they could lose themselves in the Kalinov Desert.

Lilitu guards stormed from the base of the tower, forming rank and file with more pikes. The soldiers atop the structure rapidly strung their bows and nocked arrows.

No doubt the commotion from Havre was enough to alert the watchtower guards, and seeing foreigners racing from the city certainly could not have helped their case.

Balvoc turned to Sin-sim again. Talking and galloping was not easy. "Hold them steady. Follow me. I will lead."

A shaky, wide-eyed nod was the only response he got from the merchant.

The guards held their pikes at the ready, calling for the merchant and the Svet to halt, but Balvoc merely slapped his hand on the rump of the horse again.

He balanced the pike he had taken from the Lilitu guard at the gate firmly in his grasp. Rearing mid-gallop, Balvoc threw the weapon and struck one of the soldiers in the middle of the formation who blocked the road. The guard fell away and the Svet cast one more glance to Sin-sim before galloping ahead of the wagon.

Unlimbering his double-headed axe, he let out a steady roar, certain he would die. He hoped his sacrifice would convince Sin-sim to free his wife. Surely the Anshedar would grant him that kindness.

To their credit, they barely flinched when he charged into their ranks.

Balvoc's axe crushed through bone and sinew of the first rank of soldiers, sweeping aside both the weapons aimed against him and the bodies of the soldiers who bore them. He galloped with such speed, he had no hope of reversing the swing to sweep aside the second rank.

He could feel the horses pressing on either side of him and the evening which joined them against his hindquarters, pushing him forward. A few of the Lilitu seemed to hesitate, attempting to move their pikes to stop the horses and wagons—killing Balvoc would not stop them from being crushed by the wagon.

For all he tried to reverse his swing, their piercing polearms struck home multiple times. He did not even need to look down to know that blood was pouring from his chest and abdomen.

And he was through. The wagon just behind him

Balvoc let the horses continue to push him forward down the road, using his weight to slow the wagon slightly. With heavy hands, heedless of the Lilitu blood staining his axe, he strapped the weapon back over his shoulder.

He was not trying to kill the Lilitu, or even fight them. Balvoc simply wanted to make it past them. He shook his head, trying not to dwell on how he had murdered and maimed multiple men and women to help a thief escape justice.

He was so sickened by the thought; he could not bear to look at the merchant. A snarl wretched his mouth as he grabbed the bridle of one of the team leading the wagon and began to drag it forward with him.

Balvoc winced at the sight of blood dribbling through the punctured holes of his thick, leathern armor. He did not want to think about the depth of his wounds, relieved they were not immediately fatal. Still, he could feel his life leaking away, and the exertion of galloping under the heat of the desert sun was devastating.

His chest heaved. Balvoc could not find enough air, restricted by his armor as he was. His knees felt weak, threatening to fail at each hoof-fall. He could not stop, though. If he did and Sin-sim or he died, his wife would soon follow.

He was not certain how long he ran, but he knew he could not let the Lilitu catch them. The Svet half-expected to hear complaints from Sin-sim, but the man was silent, and Balvoc did not have the energy to give the man any attention. It was not until he noticed the white lather coming from the horses pulling the wagon that he slowed and glanced at the fat merchant.

When he did, his breath caught in his throat. The fat man was pierced by several arrows, slumped to the side. Blood oozed from his lips.

Chapter III

Balvoc's hands shook. He reached to touch the fat man slouching in the seat of the wagon. In an attempt to steady his hands, he clenched his fists, and reached out again. To think he could be dead? Well, it was unthinkable. If Sin-sim was dead then, what would that mean for him? For his wife? If Sin-sim's contacts did not hear from him, then they would kill his wife before he could possibly reach her. He knew the Anshedar were weak, but surely not *this* weak. What were a few arrows? He had to be alive.

His fingers hovered over the man's lips, but he felt no breath stir the air. A hand on his chest told no tale of a beating heart. For a moment he could only stare at him. Nostrils flared. Eyes watered. Teeth bared.

Balvoc's heart was in his throat and he could not breathe. With a rising cry of frustration, his fingers tangled in his hair. Tearing at his mane, he screamed wildly at the sun.

With a wordless roar, his open palm caught the chubby Anshedar across the face. Before he could close his fist for a second blow, Sin-sim started. Balvoc was speechless.

His blow had roused the man!

The merchant blinked twice, squinting into the sun. Balvoc nearly hugged him, but when he leaned forward, an ear-piercing scream made the horses jump and nearly made the Svet leap from his own skin.

At first, Balvoc thought Sin-sim was screaming at him, but soon realized that he was staring at the three arrows in his stomach.

Before the Anshedar's scream had fully died away, he was unconscious again. A surge of emotions railed inside of Balvoc. The only response he could muster was a quaking laugh.

"Oh, you pathetic Anshedar." Balvoc muttered to himself. "Cannot stand the sight of your own blood? And I could kill you with a sneeze."

The words died on his lips at the thought of Sin-sim's death. He quickly turned his thoughts elsewhere. The portly man was not safe yet, and so long as he was not safe, neither was his Maruda.

He tried not to think of the merchant dying…yet.

Trying to shake the thoughts from his head, Balvoc looked to his own wounds. The excitement of battle could often cause pain to go unnoticed, he knew. Once he had a sword stuck in one of his rear legs and did not notice until his employer had pointed it out to him.

The arrow in his rump was just within reach, for which he was thankful. He did not think he could get Sin-sim to help him with the wound. His torso was his main concern, and more than a few deep gauges would take a long time to heal. Luckily, some of his injury had been reduced by his armor but did little against the sharp tips of the polearms. None seemed to be deadly if treated properly, at least.

A more rational glance back at Sin-sim made Balvoc wince at his reaction earlier. The man was so flabby that the arrows did not seem to make it much past the layer of fat that covered his body. No doubt that the pain was intense, and healing would be arduous, but it was likely the man's organs were undamaged.

Balvoc cast an eye to the sky with a sigh. The sun was barely past its apex, which meant the cool night air was still some time away. He wanted to set a camp to tend to their wounds—each horse seemed to have taken a few arrows as well—but to do so would mean that the Lilitu could easily catch up to them.

But traveling much further in the sun would be tantamount to returning to the Lilitu. Sin-sim had condemned them no matter which direction Balvoc happened to lead them. Although, he supposed that he should be thankful the merchant was not awake to add in his unhelpful opinion.

He looked back at the Anshedar. "You just lie there like the bag of meat you are, Sin-sim. Let those more capable make decisions for once."

Determined as he was to keep moving, Balvoc could not bring himself to do so without some rest. He watered the horses and himself—even going so far as to try and get Sin-sim to drink something. He snapped the shafts of the various arrows—a total of eight all told—and splashed some water to clean the wounds. With torn strips of cloth, he bound each shaft as best he could to keep the arrow from moving and to hide the wound. His own wounds from the pikes he dealt similarly, covering his midriff with cloth to stop the bleeding and setoff at a slow pace toward Khonjra, paralleling the road out of Havre.

The Lilitu had undoubtedly sent word of their travel ahead as fast as they could, but there was no sense wandering off into the desert to die. If Sin-sim was well enough upon reaching Khonjra, he might be able to sneak in for supplies. The Svet were not common in the area, but if the Lilitu were anything like he was, all Anshedar looked nearly the same and there were plenty of merchants in Lilitu lands.

Despite having attended to his wounds, the pain was still distracting. His thoughts dwelt on stopping to rest and drink a bit of Sin-sim's liquor to take the edge off.

Balvoc found himself muttering at the horses, at Sin-sim, and even at rocks and desert plants, just to keep his mind off of the pain.

"I tell you, horses, I wish I were as dumb and useless as you. That my greatest worry was whether or not my driver was too handy with a whip." He chuckled, "Oh, no great warrior here. No, just a dumb horse that pulls a wagon. No need to capture his wife and force him to fight and protect you. He is a horse. Doesn't have a wife. Doesn't know what in the Netherworld love is. Just walks around shitting where he likes. Why? Because he is a horse."

Balvoc kept his waterskin handy and did his best to drink regularly. The journey to Havre had been enough to convince him of the wisdom of not letting his body go too long without water.

Luckily, he knew where Sin-sim stored the water— a series of large barrels on the underside of the wagon—and used some pots from the back of the wagon to water the horses as well.

"I could kill you now, Sin-sim." Balvoc muttered, pouring water over Sin-sim thick, dry lips. He sighed,

"But I could always kill you. You know it as well as I do. But my hands are tied, so you spit in my face each chance you get and laugh, because my hands are tied, and I cannot wipe it away."

He dampened a rag and threw it over the man's face to keep the sun off. "When this is all over, you must know that I will kill you. As soon as my Maruda is safe, I will hunt you down and skin you alive." Balvoc paused, a stunning realization stilling his tongue. His eyes darted back to Sin-sim. "We will never be done, will we? You will keep me bound until I am dead or my wife is in a million pieces." His mouth was dry, and not from the heat of the Kalinov Desert. "How many warriors, like me, have you forced to an honorless death?"

A persistent breeze blew from the south, for which Balvoc was grateful. Not only did it help to cool him slightly, but it also served to shift the sands over the tracks left behind. It was a small blessing, but one he believed would at least slow the Lilitu if they were tracking them. Though rare, he also picked any scraps of wood or dead plant and began to stack it on the buckboard beside Sin-sim. They would need a fire when they eventually stopped.

He looked hard at a distant mesa, blue and gold in the dying light. "Why would anyone live here? I, for one, am sick to death of deserts, sand, and stone. I miss the cold, the rain, the snow." He could not help but smile, his eyes scanning the stubby trees and bushes that dotted the landscape. "Ah, snow. Have you even seen snow? Or, by the gods, rain? Or do you just know the sun and moon? How you must want to live where the winds are refreshing and doesn't only serve to stir up the sand, biting and stinging away at you. How every stone must envy those trundling creatures that bring noise and life but leave when the sun is too hot and the wind too biting."

Balvoc did not halt the wagon even when the sun finally began to sink in the sky so that long shadows were cast by the aping dunes. His voice was tired, his legs were tired, and his skin felt parched of all moisture. But he traveled on, letting the night hide them and get them as far from the Lilitu city of Havre as they could. When he felt as weary as the horses looked, he finally stopped, the waning gibbous moon well past its zenith.

He left Sin-sim where he was and started a small fire at the base of a dune. The last thing they needed was for the Lilitu to catch sight of that light. While the nights in the Kalinov desert certainly became cool, Balvoc had more utilitarian purposes in mind for the fire.

The mighty Svet was a warrior and knew his way around an arrow wound fairly well. Unlike the Anshedar, who had confusing practices, to say the least. Among the Anshedar it was common practice to leave an arrow lodged in the flesh long enough for it start forming puss. The men argued that it made the extracting process easier. Afterwards, they often cauterized the wound with boiling water or oil.

Balvoc had never considered the practice to be— wise. His own people had a method which, albeit painful, removed the arrow without the long wait.

After setting the fire, the Svet watered the horses before putting a pot to boil over the fire. He then dug to find some of Sin-sim's clothing to make bandages. Among the Anshedar's belongings was a sword he doubted had ever been used. He put the tip of the blade in the fire.

Balvoc did not bother to unharness the horses, but he did hobble them and brake the wagon—the last thing he wanted to do was chase a wagon through the desert at night. When the water had begun boiling he placed his belt knife and what looked to be a pair of shears with an egg-shaped portion where the blades should be—known as an arrow scoop among the Svet—in the water.

After a moment, and a long pull from his waterskin, he retrieved the exposed hilt of the knife from the water and set to work. The process was awkward, Balvoc being forced to turn around so he could see himself and make the necessary cuts. He had performed the operation to remove arrows more times than he could recall, and a number of those on himself, but it never made the process any easier.

With a sharp intake of breath, he made two identical cuts on either side of the arrow, lengthening the wound in his hindquarters. The worst of the process was always ensuring the cuts were as deep as the tip of the arrow itself. The wound, which had nearly finished bleeding itself out, began anew.

Tossing the knife back into the boiling water, he shuddered, trying to shut away the pain. His hind leg over the wound shuddered and tried to kick. He took another drink of water to calm himself. What he would not give for something stronger. Now came the difficult part.

Balvoc carefully angled the arrow scoop into the modified wound as near to the shaft as he could manage. The oval head stretched open the injury causing blood to well forth. Spreading his hand, the egg opened, spreading the wound wider still so that it could cover the arrowhead. He bit off a cry, forcing the egg as wide as he could manage and thrusting it over the sharp spurs of the iron tip. With a gasp, he pulled the remainder of the arrow free. Before he could give himself a chance to think over the coming pain, Balvoc took the sword from the fire and pressed it into the wound to cauterize it. This time, he could not bite back his scream.

Chapter VI

The morning caught Balvoc unaware, wiping drool-adhered sand from the side of his face. He had spent much of the night tending to wounds and, coupled with the exhaustion of the day's events, was tired enough to fall into a dreamless sleep. The sleep had been deep, and the Svet did not remember having lain down at all.

After licking his dry lips with an even drier tongue, he struggled to stand, looking for water. It was still early. A glow appeared on the eastern horizon, though the sun had yet to make its entrance. Sin-sim was slumped on the wagon seat where Balvoc had left him. The pudgy Anshedar's eyes were open, and more than a little strained.

"What happened?" The fat toad croaked.

Balvoc attempted to respond but found that his mouth was too dry to even speak. Catching up his waterskin, he gulped heavily before tossing it to the merchant. Sin-sim made an attempt to catch it, but his wounds resulted in an immediate retraction of his extended hands and a bark of pain. The waterskin hit him in the face.

"You nearly got us killed for a few jewels." Balvoc's voice was deep from sleep and came out as a snarl that even he thought was fierce.

"Bah, I did no such thing," Sin-sim gasped, bending to pick up the waterskin from the buckboard where it had fallen. His crooked teeth were clenched in painful triumph as his thick fingers clasped his prize. "I could have talked us free if you weren't so bent on bloodshed."

Balvoc's jaw worked for a moment while Sin-sim drank. Finally, he said, "What?"

"You heard me." The Anshedar's voice was renewed, if still strained. "I could have talked to the Lilitu. I could have smoothed the way, but you are a savage brute who has no notion of the efficacy of language." His pinched eyes gazed down his flat nose, voice hissing through his warped teeth. "You horses are all the same. It is why we Anshedar are superior. You only have two thoughts in your thick heads: sex and violence." He took another long pull from the skin. "I am lucky that you had a mind for the latter rather than the former, or I could not say what state I would be in. It is no wonder we have nearly wiped your pathetic people from the face of Aenar."

How Sin-sim could rationalize such madness. "I saved your life, you worthless sack of lard!"

"After you nearly killed me." Sin-sim did not miss a beat, as if he knew how the Svet would respond. "Do not pretend that you did me a favor in keeping me breathing. You know as well as I that my death means the death of your mare. You are lucky I don't ask for her hooves in payment for your blunder." The merchant seemed to try and appear noble, his many chins rising so that he could look further down his flat nose. "I am nothing if not forgiving."

Balvoc could do it. He could kill Sin-sim. It would be easy. Like killing a child. A fat and terrible child.

To keep from doing so, he turned away from the merchant to see to the camp. He moved efficiently, covering the remnants of the fire, feeding and watering the horses, ensuring the wagon was prepared to move. All the while, he daydreamed of the many ways he would kill Sin-sim. He finally settled on a slow and tortuous death in which he would consume him little by little, starting with his fingers.

It was once common practice among the Svet to eat their foes. Time had lessened the practice, not for lack of wanting, but lack of availability. The Svet were cornered away in Maharia, and the slightest hint of violence saw an army of Anshedar marching toward their lands.

"Horse!"

The Svet shook his head, realizing that Sin-sim had been attempting to get his attention for some time.

"What?" He murmured, turning to him.

The merchant was on his feet. "Help me into the wagon. Unlike your livestock, we Anshedar prefer not to spend the day covered in our own filth. Your foolishness has already caused me enough pain."

Balvoc's grinded his teeth.

Getting the merchant into the back of his own wagon should have been an easy task, but his constant whining and grimacing at his injuries turned it into an ordeal. When Sin-sim finally stood inside the door, he was flushed with exertion, likely from screaming profanities and insults rather than the pain or labor of lifting his tubby frame two feet from the sandy ground.

He managed to look down his nose once more, despite his heavy breathing and the fact that the stumpy Anshedar still was not even eye-level with Balvoc. "I will remain here today. Lead the horses forward and do not jostle me. I will be *healing*."

"Khonjra?" Balvoc asked, unable to keep the irritation from his voice.

"Of course, fool. I highly doubt we will make it through the gates, but we will try. Luckily for you, I secured enough opals to pay for this journey ten times over and have supplies enough to feed myself to the edge of the Kalinov."

"What of the horses? What of me?" he growled. His stomach mimicked the sound, reminding him that he had not eaten since the morning before.

The Anshedar waved his hand. "Bah! Must I think of every little thing? Pray to your savage gods we can make it into Khonjra or hunt something with that foolish bow of yours."

Before Balvoc could respond, Sin-sim slammed the door to the wagon closed. He could hear him bustling and cursing as he moved about whatever task he had a mind to. The Svet glared at the door for a time, his mind a fury with thoughts of how to deal with the merchant. Finally, he stamped his hooves and left the man to himself.

A last look around the camp revealed little except the sword he had used to seal wounds. He took it and slid it through one of the straps on his back so that the hilt rose above his left shoulder, opposite the handle of his labrys. No telling when he would need another blade.

After a few tugs on the riggings for the horses, he set out. A small smile crossed his lips when he heard something heavy crash in the wagon and a string of curses follow from his tormentor. He longed for those curses to come from his hand directly, but any pain or discomfort brought him some measure of satisfaction.

Balvoc paralleled the road as best he could over the coming days. He tried to avoid coming too near to be seen, while trying to remain near enough not to become entirely lost in the massive expanse that was the Kalinov Desert. Yet he and his tormentor slowly made their way to Khonjra.

Sin-sim remained in his wagon, hiding from the heat of the sun, much as he had done throughout the journey to the Lilitu lands. Balvoc preferred the merchant out of sight. He could not stand the sight of him.

He occupied himself with thoughts of Maruda. Balvoc knew his daydreaming was meaningless—she suffered each day he was away with the merchant—but it helped to soothe his spirit.

He pretended that she would come galloping over one of the craggy hills or around a rocky outcropping. She would laugh and smile, as he remembered her, telling how Sin-sim had lied and had never harmed her or how she had escaped his bondage. But each time—every time—her hands and fingers were whole. Her smile was pure and the only pain she had experienced was missing Balvoc.

During the day, he could keep such thoughts at the forefront of his mind. The nights were what terrified him.

In the dark, when his dreams were not his to control, she would come to him still, but maimed and tortured. Fingers, hands, arms, hooves gone. Blood-soaked bandages covered her face and chest. Maruda, his sweet Maruda, would cry to him—bruised and abused—questioning him. Why had he not saved her? And then, only then, would he realize that she had not been returned to him. She was gone. Dead. A corpse in the Netherworld, never to be his again.

And so, he looked at the sun, hot and dry and unforgiving, and pretended she was still his and Sin-sim was merely a liar.

Smoke rising ahead, barely glimpsed as it rose over the craggy mesa's before him, pulled him from his reverie. His heavy fist fell against the side of the wagon.

"What!" Sin-sim's muffled growl sounded.

Balvoc swallowed. "Khonjra is under attack."

Chapter V

Sin-sim trundled out of the wagon, his pudge-encased eyes popping. The man was obviously still in pain, each step gingerly taken and each breath a shudder that caused his thick rolls to undulate tremulously.

Balvoc glanced back at him but did not bother to help him down the steps onto the semi-sandy ground.

"Under attack, you say?" The Anshedar gasped, no doubt winded from his short walk.

The Svet grunted.

"By whom?"

"I could hazard a guess," he muttered, "but I can't see through rock."

The merchant looked up at him. The man's head did not even reach the Svet's chest. "What are you looking at, then?"

"The smoke and the towers, Anshedar," Balvoc spat. "The smoke is coming from the north end of Khonjra. I can see enough of the towers to know that the Uvil have not yet made it any further into the city."

"Uvil? What makes you say it is the Uvil?"

He turned to look at Sin-sim, hoping the gravity of his features would impart upon the man just how ridiculous his question was. "Because I am not a fool. Only the Uvil would dare to attack the Lilitu."

Sin-sim's chins quivered. "Well, it is no matter who is attacking. Now is your chance to sneak in and get what supplies we need."

Balvoc felt he should not be surprised by Sin-sim's suggestion, as often as the Anshedar proposed preposterous notions, but he could not keep his jaw from his chest.

The merchant was nearly back inside the wagon before he could manage a response. "Are you mad?"

"Eh?"

"Mad? Are you mad?" He turned to face Sin-sim, whose round face was poking around the corner of the wagon. "You want me, a Svet—a mighty warrior that dwarfs both the Lilitu and the Uvil—to *sneak* into a city that is currently under siege."

A flabby sigh exhumed from the man's tuberous lips. "Is there any chance we can get our supplies after the battle?"

"Of course not. The city will either be locked up tight by the victor or ransacked."

Sin-sim stepped down from the steps he had already begun to climb and advanced slowly towards Balvoc, his voice as dry as the desert air. "Then, yes, I do expect you to *sneak* into the city, you filthy, crossbred savage. I am weary of having this conversation with you and I refuse to have it again. You may either travel into that war-infested city to procure anything that isn't nailed down, or you can wait here while I send off to add more pieces of your wife to that sorry collection you carry at your belt."

Balvoc's hands twitched furiously while he watched the Anshedar turn around and climb into his wagon. He stared at the wagon for a long time after the merchant was gone from sight. Anger and fear seemed to be the only things he could feel anymore. The two emotions tripped over themselves, trying to lead his thoughts. His actions.

He struggled against his helplessness. His wrath was great enough to utterly destroy Sin-sim, but his terror for the safety of his wife kept him bound. His rage at his helplessness made him want to take action, but his dread at the prospect of entering a war-torn city for trinkets paralyzed him. No matter what he chose, he could not succeed.

If he stayed, his wife would die. If he killed Sin-sim, his wife would die. If he entered the city and failed, his wife would die.

For now, his only hope of keeping Maruda alive lay in Khonjra. His chances of living through the battle were slim. But the thin, almost intangible sliver of hope spurred him to action.

A focused haze fueled Balvoc's movements. He only half-saw what his hands did, his thoughts almost entirely focused on Maruda's face. When he knew battle was coming, it is how his mind worked—efficient and resolved.

Swift hands checked his weapons, the labrys on his back over his right shoulder, the sword he had taken from Sin-sim's wagon over his left. The now-strung bow strapped to his right side and the quiver on his left. Knife sheathed where his back met his hindquarters, hilt facing downwards and accessible by either hand. His armor, patched from the wounds he had received in Havre, snug over his chest and abdomen.

With a decisive snort, the Svet trotted towards the Khonjra. He quickly found the road. Danger or no, he was a warrior and he was tired of the sneaking. But since meeting Sin-sim, all he had done was skulk about like some lowly vermin. If he was going into battle, he would do it without the deceit of the filthy Anshedar.

A small rise brought him within sight of the walls, reddish-gray like much of the Lilitu structures. A great iron portcullis blocked the eastern road into Khonjra, but it was clear the Uvil forces were already within the city. Balvoc could see the short, squat figures moving beyond the latticed metal barrier, bereft of a sally port. The cries of the dying and the clang of battle reached his ears.

The Svet hoped that the Uvil presence meant that the Lilitu would not notice his approach. At a glance, the eastern facing entrance into Khonjra appeared to be unmanned. He increased his steady trot to a canter, still unnoticed for all that he could tell. As he drew closer, his hand instinctively went to his labrys, though the bow was likely the better choice.

The portcullis suddenly began to rise. Balvoc slowed, uncertain what this new development meant. Certainly the gate would not be raised on his account, whether to permit entry or to sally forth. A lone archer on the twenty-foot wall could deal with a lone warrior easily enough—Svet or no.

He trotted to the side of the entrance and pulled his labrys from his back, the heavy axe filling his hands. The weapon felt good. Solid. Real. Too much of Balvoc's mind had been a panic lately, a surreal battle between the demands of the merchant and the love of his wife. War was tangible, though, a gritty and material landscape that he did not have to think about.

When the portcullis had risen nearly six feet, a heavy clunk announced that it had been locked into place. A red-sashed Lilitu darted beneath the heavy iron barrier, blood dribbling down his chin. A gash on the soldier's cheek allowed too many teeth to show along the left side of his face.

He had met the sharp end of an Uvil's sword to make it outside the walls.

The soldier had barely made it beyond the portcullis when he spotted the Svet and stopped, his rent face making him appear all the grimmer. Without a word, he drew a thin blade from his hip and shrugged a shield into his opposite hand.

Balvoc realized he had his axe in his hands. He moved as if to put it away but did not remove his hands. "I am not here to fight you, Lilitu. Be on your way. You no doubt have reports to make to your Empress."

The soldier glanced at the road and then back to the Svet. He visibly swallowed, but his voice was calm, the words as clipped as if he were reading from a ledger. "If you come armed into a city of the Empress, you are my enemy."

No cry filled his lips, but he advanced as if there were. His sword lifted over his shoulder, no doubt intent to end the Svet with a single, mighty blow.

Balvoc brought his double-headed axe to purpose with one, smooth and decisive blow. Despite a quickly raised shield by the thin Lilitu, the great weapon ended the soldier's advance as assuredly as a wall.

Using a hoof to pull the labrys free of cloven shield and bloody remains, the Svet sighed and shook his head at the waste. The Lilitu should have listened to him.

He ducked under the half-raised portcullis to enter the city. After advancing a mere fifty feet, the cries of battle suddenly seemed louder. Balvoc hoped the Uvil did not react towards him the same way the Lilitu did, or he stood no chance of escaping Khonjra alive.

Chapter VI

Balvoc had only made it to the end of the first street when he saw a force of long-armed Uvil clashing with rank upon rank of red-skinned Lilitu. The Svet could not help himself from stopping and watching. He was not like the finicky Anshedar, fascinated by shiny objects and coin. Rather, Balvoc appreciated war and battle in all of its forms.

The Lilitu fought in a set, dense formation—shields interlocked and spears jabbing forward, the back lines supporting the front lines to make a veritable wall. The spear wall would incrementally push forward, polearms in the too-large hands of the thin-armed Lilitu jabbing into the ranks of the Uvil soldiers. At a glance, there appeared to be no means of getting past the red-sashed soldiers, their line extending the width of the street, despite how small they appeared to be.

But Balvoc knew something about the spear walls. Oh, they were certainly mighty, but a strong enough push against the right flank sent the whole thing toppling. The shields the soldiers used were more for the man to their left than for themselves, which meant the soldier on the far right was only half-covered by his shield.

The Uvil, however, did not appear to want past the Lilitu. Unlike the rather stagnant Lilitu, the Uvil rotated their formation almost continuously. Soldiers continuously moved forward and back, keeping fresh warriors engaged with the Lilitu line. The retreating warrior would use a hooked axe or sword the catch the shield of a foe and pull backwards, allowing his replacement to rapidly stab the Lilitu when the defense was weakened.

The result was a mulling of Uvil lines that looked to be disorganized and haphazard, but ultimately picked away at the Lilitu lines faster than they could replace their fallen comrades. The Lilitu defense was too focused on being pushed backwards, but the Uvil were pulling rather than pushing.

All and all, Balvoc could not help but be impressed by the Uvil's superior tactics, despite remaining assured that a charge of Svet warriors would break their lines with little effort. Certainly the Uvil could tear apart an enemy who seemed to approach tactics from a defensive point of view, but the Svet were aggressive fighters, and not easily pushed—or pulled—about.

Balvoc was not certain how long he had watched the battle, but the Uvil had come much nearer to him. The desert warriors slowly gave ground to the Lilitu, but gave far fewer lives than their counterparts, pulling the small, red-skinned people forward and decimating their forces. Even when a Lilitu managed to strike a blow against the Uvil, their silvery armor repelled the thrust as if the weapon were made of wood.

The idea of possessing a labrys made of that metal made Balvoc salivate.

Lost in reverie, it took Balvoc a moment to realize the officer commanding the Uvil from the rear had turned. When their eyes met, he backed away slowly, hands raised as the blood drain from his face. He had spent too long here, and now it would cost him his life.

But the officer merely watched him, his face all but hidden behind his tannish veil, a cap of the shiny metal on top of his head, making it so that only the glint of his eyes was visible at this distance. The Svet had seen one or two Uvil before, but they nearly always had those veils drawn so that their features were hidden. The one thing he could say about them is that they had bluish skin and hard eyes.

When Balvoc had retreated a dozen or so feet, the officer turned his gaze back to the battle with the Lilitu. The Svet sighed and felt blood flow return. He was not Lilitu and, therefore, not the enemy. He hoped all of the Uvil felt that way.

And the Lilitu.

Turning, he trotted down the street, desperate to find some evidence of a marketplace where he could get needed supplies and be gone.

Coming to a crossroads, he hesitated. Slowly, he peered one way as far as he could before he hugged the opposite building to poke his head around and look the other direction. With a quick backward glance, he moved on. He was not going to make it very far if he had to keep stopping to peek around corners.

Most of the fighting appeared to have moved deeper into Khonjra. While not as large as most of the other Lilitu cities, it was still larger than most northern cities. He had heard tales of how the Lilitu built extensive networks of tunnels running beneath their cities. How each city was two or three times larger than it appeared on the surface. If such tales were even half-true, there was no telling when another legion of soldiers might appear from seemingly nowhere.

Coming upon what appeared to be a stable, he darted inside as quickly as he could move his bulky frame. These tiny Lilitu did not make entrances easily accessible to a Svet. Even their stable entries were built for their short, desert livestock.

Such a specimen of desert livestock stood snorting and stamping in its...stall? Whatever they were called. Casting a quick eye over the place, he found a sizeable bag of grain and various tack that he was certain would be useful. He had nearly made it back to the stable entrance, when he cast an eye back at the small horse.

A smile came to his lips, quickly turning into a chuckle he couldn't suppress. He had spent too much time among the Anshedar. Why should he travel through the city looking for food, when a perfectively fine source stood not twenty feet from him? Sure, he would have to make Sin-sim stop for a short while, so he could slaughter and dry the meat, but the desert sun would be more than enough to do most of the work for him. And the inevitable buzzards would give him even more sustenance if he was quick with his bow.

He quickly harnessed the horse and drew it behind him to the stable door. Now he needed to find his way back out of the city again.

Balvoc had not gone more than twenty feet before he heard the sound of someone coughing to his left. A growl preceded more coughing.

"No! I will not fail," a gravelly voice choked. "to be *preta* is not my fate. Guide me, my fathers, guide me to my destiny at your side."

More coughing ensued.

The Svet edged forward to peek around the corner of the building to his left. A distance down the narrow alleyway lay an Uvil warrior, broken and bleeding. His veil was down, revealing pale, bluish features.

He sighted Balvoc at once. "Do not end me yet, warrior." The Uvil struggled to sit up, but wounds to his arms and torso left him nearly immobile. "Please, grant me an honorable death. Retrieve my *quoin*."

Balvoc frowned. "Your what?"

The Uvil attempted to motion with a useless arm, finally nodding his head to the side. His voice was breathless. Desperate. "My token. My birthright. My deathright."

Peering about to ensure no other Uvil were present and no Lilitu soldiers would swarm upon him, he pulled his horse down the alley behind him. When Balvoc reached the Uvil, he towered over him. Small and broken as he was, he wondered how such a creature could ever be a threat to his people. Of course, his people had never thought the Anshedar would be a threat either, but they had nearly destroyed the Svet. Now they were confined to a small corner of the world, ignominious and defeated.

"You want an honorable death, Uvil?" Balvoc asked, leaning down. "You are wounded on a battlefield. You could not ask for a better death than this."

Red-rimmed eyes met his. "Yes. Yes, I will die well, but not with honor. *Not* without my *quoin*." He turned his gaze to the side where Balvoc finally caught sight of the item the Uvil was so concerned with.

Reaching down, he picked it up, lying but a few feet from the Uvil's hand. The token hung on a leathern cord, now broken. Made of iron, it was, perhaps, the plainest ornament that he had ever seen. No gold gilding, no jewels, and no ornate workmanship to speak of. On one side, an inverted V was punched into the surface.

How like the Uvil was Balvoc? What he wanted most was within reach, if only he could make his arms to work. He could strangle the merchant, if he so chose, but then what he wanted most would be denied to him. No matter what he did, he could not return his Maruda to his arms any more than this warrior could reach his little token.

"Please. Give it me."

Balvoc shook his head, clearing his thoughts. "You cannot grasp it."

The Uvil's eyes were set upon the token. "Remove the cord and place it in my mouth." He choked, blood oozing from his thin lips. "Please. I *cannot* die without it."

The Svet had the distinct sense that the Uvil meant his words in the same way that he himself would claim he could not live without his wife. Quickly, he did as the warrior asked.

The Uvil took several tries to swallow the token, but persevered with a large outburst of air, which

Balvoc was certain announced his death. But before Balvoc could turn, he spoke.

"I am Saraf, son of Hash, son of Duman. I will make certain my people know of your kindness." Saraf seemed at ease, the breathlessness now gone from his voice.

Balvoc chuckled, "You will be dead soon, and no one will know what I have done here."

"Dead, yes, but we Uvil do not pass on. My *quoin* ensures that I will join my ancestors in the world between worlds rather than becoming a *preta*." His turned his head slightly, stifling a cough as he considered Balvoc, "You truly have no idea what you have saved me from, do you?"

The Svet frowned. "An honorless death."

Saraf smiled, an odd expression, given the copious amounts of blood on his thin lips and narrow chin. "Without the *quoin*, I am doomed to be *preta*—a false life. Can you imagine your body continuing on, your spirit trapped inside, yearning to eat, to drink, to hold that which you can never have?" He coughed again, blood spewing onto his already spattered armor. "You would hunt your kith and kin. You would be locked behind your own eyes, forced to watch as you slowly killed everyone you have loved. Everything you honored." He shook his head, coughing again. "I would no longer be Uvil. I would be *preta*."

Balvoc said nothing. *Preta*. A false life. His life was a false life, ruled by Sin-sim. He looked back at the small horse. Was this how he would spend the remainder of his years? Bound to that fat Anshedar? Doing his bidding until he found a shallow grave?

He turned his gaze back to Saraf. "I must go."

Chapter VII

Khonjra had erupted.

From beneath the city proper, Lilitu warriors surged forth to battle the Uvil. Every corner saw skirmishes between the troops. No longer the organized tip for tap Balvoc had witnessed upon first entering the city.

No, Khonjra was a mess of Lilitu soldiers moving in ranks, groups of two or three, or individuals looking for their brethren to stand beside with the Uvil doing much the same.

Balvoc had drawn the sword from his back, his other hand pulling the small horse along behind him. More than once, a Lilitu warrior had stood before him, attempting to stop his mad gallop for the city gates, and he had either charged the warrior down or slew him outright with the weapon.

The first time an Uvil had done the same, he had hesitated for respect of Saraf. That respect, that hesitation, had cost him a deep gash on his left arm. Now, each time the horse pulled, blood welled from the wound and Balvoc could only grit his teeth.

Now, he killed anything in his path, Lilitu or Uvil.

Some distance ahead, Balvoc could make out three red-sashed Lilitu confronting an Uvil warrior in the middle of the dusky, brown brick street. The Uvil, for his part, appeared to show no fear. Before they reached him, he merely snapped the cord at his neck and placed his *quoin* in his mouth. The Lilitu surrounded the warrior, and despite his deft shield work, he was outmatched quickly.

Just as they laid eyes on Balvoc, half a dozen Uvil turned the bend behind the Lilitu and charged forward. Balvoc did not waste any time in turning down an alleyway to find a war around the skirmish.

As luck would have it, he quickly realized that few Lilitu or Uvil soldiers went through the backways. If he could have made his way back to the gate through the alleyways, he never would have left them. But he became lost when he spent too much time meandering along and would eventually have to find a main road.

He thought his superior height would allow him to place landmarks and navigate, but too many of the Lilitu structures soared skyward. Coupled with the narrowness of the back passageways, he could make out the walls of the buildings on either side and little else.

Eventually he would come upon a street and dart across to a new series of alleyways and begin making his way towards the gate, or as near as he could tell. The sound of battle constantly echoed into the alleyway from all directions, making it impossible to tell where the fighting was actually occurring. Though he would occasionally catch glances of Uvil or Lilitu warriors marching up and down the streets or clashing with indiscernible battle cries.

When he finally caught sight of the gatehouse, he paused to catch his breath. He felt as though he had been galloping about the city for hours, and by the height of the sun, he did not think he was far off. His left arm was stiff from his wound, but the bleeding had stopped.

He retrieved his waterskin to take a long pull. He had lost track of the time long ago, but the rising desert heat told him that morning had passed some time ago. He was from the north, and he was lucky to see one day in ten years get as hot as it was on a daily basis here.

He hoped the gate was clear.

When Balvoc finally made it to the gate, he found his hope was misplaced. A force of Lilitu soldiers stood five ranks deep and at least as many across faced towards the city proper.

He pulled back to keep from being seen, but could already hear the footfalls of approaching troops coming from inside the city. The Lilitu officer began issuing commands to his warriors.

Balvoc frowned, issuing a low growl.

Leaning heavily against the wall, he looked for his opportunity to get to the portcullis. The clanging of weapons resounded as the armies clashed. It was the same battle he had witnessed before, the Lilitu pushed, and the Uvil pulled. Only, this time, the Uvil were not fairing as well.

Balvoc watched intently, gritting his teeth. He had once chance to make his move.

Once the armies moved past the alleyway, he bolted for the gatehouse yanking the smaller horse behind him. Not a single enemy soldier had glanced in his direction. Once he stepped into the gatehouse, he understood why. The portcullis was down, and the chain dismantled.

Balvoc held back a roar, clenching his fingers around the reins until his knuckles ached.

Turning from the gatehouse, he returned to the street to see the Uvil in full retreat. A dozen or so Lilitu pursued, but their officer held back a few of his soldiers, who had not been killed or wounded. No doubt to man the gate he was now exiting.

The officer faced Balvoc, who, for his part, tried to look as non-threatening as possible.

"Let me leave," the Svet called. "I only want to be away from the fighting."

"No doubt you would, thief," the officer replied. "However, that is a Lilitu horse and, war or no, justice will be administered."

Without a word, the Lilitu officer motioned toward the Svet and the four remaining soldiers advanced. Each bore a spear nearly ten feet long and a shield.

Balvoc sneered. Damnable livestock. He would not die for a *horse*. Tossing aside the sword that had brought him this far and the lead line for the horse, he freed his labrys. He hoped the grimace of pain for his injured arm served to make him appear more threatening.

From the blanching face of the soldier on the far left, he had been successful.

"You will all die here today," Balvoc snarled, showing his fangs. A little intimidation could go a long way in a fight. Warriors could feel fear, and if they felt none from him with such uneven odds, well, maybe they would hesitate and give him the break he needed to come out of this thing alive.

He was convinced of such thoughts and rather pleased and with his performance to boot. That is, until he realized his little stunt had inspired the officer to draw his sword and join his men.

Bloody glorious.

Rising on his hind legs, Balvoc roared, twisting his double-headed axe over his head. He hoped the resulting grimace from the reopening of the wound looked more like anger than pain.

Their advance paused and he leapt forward, weapon coming to cause. As long as their spears were, they had to balance them, which meant they were not reaching the full length of their weapons. Rather, their reach actually came out shorter than the Balvoc's.

He swung on the right flank. He had watched the Uvil fight the Lilitu and, like all phalanx the right flank was always the weakest.

His axe crashed into the half-raised shield of the Lilitu soldier, the weight of the weapon along with the power Balvoc put behind the swing was enough to splinter the shield. The red-sashed Lilitu crumpled under the blow, his piercing cry filling Balvoc's ears.

Falling into his fellow soldiers, they stumbled to the side, trying to catch their footing from the powerful strike. With another roar, Balvoc brought the axe back around for another swing from their right, catching the next soldier in line with a like blow.

Before he could try for a third, something struck him in the hindquarters. The Svet reeled to the side from the weight of the weapon, stumbling in pain. The officer had thrown his sword!

It had not been a direct strike, but the blade had certainly done its work. A chunk of Balvoc had gone with the weapon after it collided with his unprotected posterior and dark, red blood oozed from the wound.

Trying to stamp down the surprise at having had a sword thrown at him, he adjusted his grip on the haft of his labrys. Filling his lungs, he bellowed away the pain.

The interruption, however, was enough for the two remaining soldiers to regain themselves and bring their spears to the ready. They divided now, left and right instead of trying to come at him together, likely realizing that multiple small targets together were the same as one big target to the Svet.

Balvoc did not try to follow both, turning to follow the one who came to his left with his axe. When the Svet used his weapon to prod at the soldier, testing the man's defenses, the one to his right immediately drove his spear home, catching him in the ribs from behind. Although the armor and bone were enough to keep the weapon from going any deeper.

With a grunt, he took one hand from his axe, seized the spear, lifted his rear hooves and kicked the Lilitu all in one smooth motion. The small, red-skinned soldier flew backward to strike one of the brown-brick buildings and not to rise again.

As soon as he pulled the spear free, the other Lilitu soldier struck with his own, his weapon gouging into Balvoc's lower abdomen. He growled from the bite of the spear, blood flowing freely from the wound almost immediately.

Again, he took hold of the spear, using his superior strength to toss the soldier aside when he refused to let go of his weapon. Stumbling from the movement, the soldier fell to the ground in a heap over the first two of his comrades to fall, finally releasing his hold on the spear.

Before Balvoc could be rid of the spear to use his axe again, the officer advanced, having taken the spear of one of his soldiers. Unlike his soldiers, however, he did not appear concerned with killing the Svet so much as wounding him.

The officer kept as much distance as he could manage, and with no shield, used both hands to make quick and powerful jabs with the spear. Again and again, he stabbed Balvoc in the hindquarters, the blade of the weapon sinking deeply into his flesh.

Trying to reach the Lilitu officer was impossible. He continuously moved back and forth, always staying to Balvoc's side so that the Svet could not get a decent swing with his labrys. Now behind him, he heard the sound of the last Lilitu soldier running away down the street. Reinforcements would be coming soon! Balvoc let out a cry of frustration, stamping his hooves.

For whatever reason, the horse started and leapt forward down the street, knocking the officer down as it ran past. Balvoc could not decide whether he should curse the loss of his source of meat or rejoice at being able to finally catch the wily Lilitu. Determining that rejoicing was the more prudent of the two options, he abandoned his axe.

With one large hand, he clasped the officer by the neck and lifted him from the ground. With the other, he discarded of the spear, ripping it from the Lilitu's grasp.

"Now," the Svet snarled, "You are going to tell me how to leave this blasted city, or I am going to start peeling your flesh off, one long strip at a time."

Chapter VIII

Wounded and still bleeding, Balvoc stumbled back into the camp, just as the sun was falling beyond the distant horizon. The only thing he had to show for his venture into the city was a sack of grain, the tack he had secured had left with the horse.

Sin-sim sat in the sand at a fire, leaning against a red sandstone block as large as he. In his hand he held a jug, which Balvoc could smell the contents of long before he had entered the camp. Turning his gaze up at the Svet's approach, the man smiled readily, his crooked teeth appearing decidedly demonic in the firelight.

"Eh? So the dear *horse* returns to his master after being long afoot and wearied traveled by. Blood and turmoil scored into his flesh and bone." The liquor had clearly put the chubby merchant in a poetic mood.

Balvoc said nothing. Every movement was agony and the only poetry he wanted to think of would be written in the Anshedar's blood.

Sin-sim took a drink from his jug before bringing it back to rest on his rotund belly with a satisfied grin on his thick lips. "So, dear horse, what have you brought me, eh? A bag of gems? A golden trinket?"

He lowered his voice with dramatic effect, "A sack of coins?"

"A sack of grain," The Svet growled, reaching back to retrieve it from where he had lashed it to his hindquarters. When he felt the empty sack, he could not help but laugh. A great bellowing sound that seemed to fill the desert.

He had nearly died and had nothing to show but a feed sack torn by Lilitu spears. It was the story of his existence since he had met the filthy merchant. Month after month of tireless work, only to be repaid with rubbish.

Sin-sim's merriment seemed to have diffused. "What are you braying at?" He sat the jug in the sand and struggled to his feet. "Are you telling me that you have wasted a full day and have nothing to show for it? Two gems? No gold? Not even feed for the damned horses?"

The Svet's laughter was far from joyous at the outset, and he had little trouble turning his ire on the Anshedar. His voice was low. "If you want gold, then feel free to go to Khonjra and pull it from the pockets of the dead. I was not drinking the day away as you were."

"You waste a day of my time, I will have a day's worth of your wife's hide whipped away." The merchant belched.

Balvoc sneered. "Your time? You are evil, selfish creatures, you Anshedar. You take away days— weeks—months—of my time with your selfishness. And for what? For trinkets? For gold?"

Sin-sim snorted. "I am the selfish one, am I? Maybe so, but you are the worse by far. Are you really so stupid? Or do you care nothing for the well-being of your wife." His eyes bulged, reddened with liquor. "If I am so evil, so selfish…then why do you push me, hm? You *know* who I am. You *know* what I will do. You *know* that your beloved wife is at my mercy. But *you* continue to question me, badger me, defy me, and then *blame* me when I act in the exact manner in which you *know* I will act."

He laughed incredulously, his jowls swaying and his tone jovial. "I tell you I will cut off a finger if you speak, and you ask *why*. I tell you I will cut off another if you move, and you *dance*. I tell you I will *slit her throat* if you fail to protect me, and you strike me yourself." He spread his flabby arms wide, cocking his head. "I ask you: Who is evil? Hmm? Who is selfish? You think only of yourself. You think only of the moment. Of *your* anger. You never stop to consider how *your* behavior is the reason you have a bag of your wife's fingers.

"Do you blame the fire when it burns you?" His voice dropped, grating and harsh, flecks of spit flying past his crooked teeth. "Do not pretend you are better than me—that you are somehow superior just because I am the fire. You are the one who casts your wife into the flames over and over again then call the fire evil and selfish when it tries to consume her and she comes away with scars."

The desert air had never seemed so dry, until now.

Sin-sim was right.

Each time Maruda had been injured, it was because he, Balvoc, had pushed the Anshedar. He could not let the fat merchant be and do as he was told—merely travel with him and protect him. If he could just keep his mouth closed—keep his fists at his sides—his dear wife would still be whole.

He looked at his hands. How cruel he had been to her—how relentless in his pursuit of what *he* considered right. He never thought how much pain she had experienced at his hands. How many months had she been forced to wait for the next time one of Sin-sim's henchman would come to take another finger? And she knew—she *knew*—it was because her husband had failed her again. Her husband could stop her pain, her suffering. Balvoc could have prevented it all.

Saraf's words came back to him: *Can you imagine your body continuing on, your spirit trapped inside, yearning to eat, to drink, to hold that which you can never have."* He *coughed again, blood spewing onto his already spattered armor. "You would hunt your kith and kin. You would be locked behind your own eyes, forced to watch as you slowly killed everyone you have loved. Everything you honored."*

He approached the merchant and placed his hands around his neck.

"What are you doing, you fool?" Sin-sim snarled. "Your wife will suffer for this!"

"My wife will finally know peace." His voice was quiet.

When Balvoc was finished, he walked into the desert.

WHEN BLOOD FALLS

Thrice Nine Legends

Month of Rutting

Second of Frost

1347 CE

Chapter I

Tyr's body crashed against the frozen rock, his chest cracking with the impact, slipping and sliding as he snatched Maruda's thin wrist in his desperate grasp. The six fingers on his right hand held fast, while he skated with his sister along the ice-laden rock.

"No!" Tyr cried as she plummeted over the edge of the suspended cliff, vanishing from sight. He flailed, digging his toes into the frost, and grabbing at the ground with his free hand to stop his momentum.

He slowed to a stop, moments before plummeting over the threshold with his sister. He felt her thin fingers clawing at his wrist in desperation.

With a wheeze that ached his innards, he stretched his neck to peer over the edge at his older sister. She hung suspended for a second, and then swung up to clasp his forearm with her other hand. His muscles threatened to give way as she dangled beneath him, kicking frantically above the frozen sea hundreds of feet below. He strained, looking across the landscape of wintry islands and freezing waters stretching as far as the eye could see.

Digging deep for newfound strength, he tightened his hold on Maruda's wrist. If anyone were to die today, it would be him. He was more deserving than she.

"Pull me up." She inhaled with a frosty breath, whipping her head toward him. Strands of her blood-red hair clung to her wide cheeks, down to the white fur that layered her lengthy body. "Hurry."

Tyr flattened his body, balancing her weight. His long frame—over seven-foot—stretched across the perimeter of the overhang. His raspy breath billowed small bursts of fogged air with each exhalation. He tried to soothe himself, knowing with every exasperated breath he was dehydrating himself further.

"Tyr?" Her grip on his forearm slipped in her meshed gloves.

He hastily held fast. "Don't move." Tyr bawled, hampering down with his weight to keep her as steady as possible. His wide torso and expanded ribcage, which helped keep his vital organs insulated when the islands turned mysteriously cold, throbbed with soreness against the solid ground. The fall would most assuredly leave bruising across his chest.

Maruda stabilized her movement, her blue irises wide with terror, "Don't let me die—"

Tyr glared at his older sister, silencing her. His eyes burned in the dry air. "Bah! I won't let you die," he growled.

She changed her tone, nearly whimpering. "Please." She tore her gaze away from him to stare at the deathbed awaiting her. The icy waters, patched with small glaciers, surrounding the islands of Tundris Mor were never forgiving during the winter. One plunge promised death.

"Keep your eyes on me, Maruda," Tyr said.

He did not wait for her nod. With a grunt, Tyr scooted backward with his free hand. Inch by inch, he felt her body move toward the solid uprising. Despite the frigid cold, he could feel warm drops of sweat sliding down the back of his neck. His long, crimson hair stuck to him like wet cloth.

Maruda clawed at the ice-covered rock with her hand as she was lifted to solid ground. Her granular face, burdened with red scars from her infancy—a memory of her own sacrifice for Tyr against the demonic Witiko—faced him as she rose over the cliff side. Tyr only glanced at her for an instant, her shoulders emerging from the overhang.

Her scream stopped his heartbeat, instantly reminding him of what had caused Maruda to fall in the first place.

Tyr turned his head enough to see the monstrous white bear, as large as any Ispolini, looming over him. The sweat that had etched down the base of his neck was nothing more than the massive creature's gelatinous slobber. In horror, Tyr let loose of his sister and flipped to his back to defend against the clawed attack.

Maruda screamed again as she slid back over the crag.

"No!" Tyr howled, realizing his mistake. He lurched for the fingertips of his beloved sister but was struck by the long claws of the beast. The white bear cut through his forearm like flame through ice.

Maruda's scream was long. Haunting.

The wound burned, blood splattering, but Tyr had no time to tend to it. Hastily, he pulled his legs back and propelled them into the chest and shoulder of the white bear. The beast rumbled, tumbling to the side and landing on all fours.

"Maruda!"

Tyr scampered to his feet, having no time to check on his sister before the bear charged at him. Tyr pulled the crescent-bladed axe from his belt loop and met the bear head-on.

The roars of ferocity were equally matched.

His eyes locked with the bear's, taking measure of every step. At the last moment, Tyr sprung off his right leg, twisted in mid-air, and enfolded his body around the bear's back. His hands worked quickly, wrapping the axe handle around the bear's neck. It served as an anchor as the white beast thrashed its claws and head uselessly at Tyr.

Tyr skimmed the edge of the cliff while struggling with the bear. *Nothing.*

He would kill the animal!

"Die, beast." Tyr screamed, pulling tighter. His muscles rippled under the soft glow of the distant sun. Blood dripped down past his elbow. He ignored it, bending his knees slightly for more leverage. The bear's weight was impressive, pushing against him, but the Ispolini were as strong as they were ancient.

Tyr bawled out in fury, pulling his arms back all the more. He did not stop until he heard the cracking of the white bear's neck. The animal's body went limp.

"Maruda!"

Silence answered Tyr.

Dropping his weapon next to the bear, Tyr slid once more to the edge of the mountain side. Claw marks were visible in the ice mapping a path to the edge of the cliff.

Swallowing hard, Tyr peered over the threshold, already knowing what sight awaited him. Painted against the pasty glaciers floating in the far-reaching, frozen sea were the pulverized remains of Maruda.

He felt faint, his stomach reeling with realization. He wrapped his massive hands around himself and fell back away from the bluff. Holding back the urge to vomit, he scooted back until he had passed several feet beyond the bear's carcass.

His sister was dead. His chest heaved. Warm tears welled from the corners of his eyes and rolled down his cheeks.

His first thought was to lunge off the cliff to meet the same fate, but instead his memory trailed.

Two decades ago, when Tyr was a child, the demonic Witiko had assaulted Almdalir from the Deep. The monsters had slaughtered hundreds, including his mother, scouring through the city for any living, breathing Ispolini. Tyr would have been killed too if Maruda had not protected him until their father had arrived.

And now, Tyr had failed to save her.

An hour passed before Tyr found the will to start the trek back home, to Almdalir, in the hollow of Mount Dvargen. Alone.

The northwestern coast of Tundris Mor towered above the ocean. The body of islets were more like mountains erupting from the sea than islands. To the northeast, even in the pale light, Tyr could see the mainland of Saudis Dar looming across the expanse of water. The scaling Shade Fells on the horizon were brush strokes between the sea and sky, dwindling all else. The tallest mountain amongst them is what the Stuhia, the dragon people of the north, called Mount

Zyem. Beyond the darkest of mountains sat the Stuhian capital, Lairhein.

Tyr had said long ago that if he ever ventured as far as Lairhein, he would discover a worthy death. Almdalir had gifted him with misery since his birthing. His mother had died when he was young, and now his only sister. At this rate, his father might be dead before he returned home. He suspected something between here and Lairhein would give life and death purpose.

The muscles in his arm flexed against the weight of the white bear that he dragged behind him. The little warmth that the sun provided during the shortened days would soon be absent. He had no interest in sleeping in a hollow tonight, but night was coming.

Without a doubt, dragging the carcass of the bear had largely slowed Tyr down. He had considered leaving the bear on the cliffside or tossing it to the sea after Maruda. He had not been sent to the western coast with his sister to hunt and had no direct obligation to bring back food for his people, but meat was meat.

Flurries started to fall as he trekked onward with heavy feet, the glowing bulb sinking beyond the skyline. In Tundris Mor, the winters were bizarrely long and filled with snowfall. The irregularity of the weather had long been blamed on the magic of the dragon people in the north.

A sound much like steam billowing from fissures of the caves of Almdalir sounded in the sky above him. Tyr suddenly stopped to scan the dark blues and grays of the world above, feeling his heart pound in his chest.

"A wyrm," Tyr rustled, dropping the bear carcass. He would invite death from the dragon rather than return home to explain his sister's death to his father.

As if on cue, the world above seemed to open, bringing heavier snowfall with the ominous enemy. The flapping of leathery wings could be heard against the wind gusts. The wyrm snaked through the sky far above him, white scales shimmering, wriggling through the air currents like a serpent. Its two thick legs were tucked up against its cylinder-shaped body—a body three times longer than an Ispolini. It twisted in the sky, using its large wings to direct its course with its three crescent heads swaying menacingly.

"Lahmia." Tyr acknowledged the white dragon with a snarl, loosening the weapon from his belt loop.

The beast from the Shade Fells screeched, taking sight of Tyr below. Curling its long tail, Lahmia hovered momentarily before diving toward him. Tyr was filled with fury, more than willing to take his anger out on this unsightly monster. Tyr rushed forward to intercept Lahmia, bracing himself against the frozen ground.

Ignoring the pain in his injured arm, Tyr raised his axe and roared.

The clever dragon disregarded him, swooping several feet over him without concern. Tyr spun to follow the dragon's descent, helplessly seeing the dragon snatch up the hide of the white bear in its talons, and then continue its route back into the sky.

Tyr huffed, defeated, as the dragon disappeared into the dark.

Chapter II

Tyr tottered toward the handful of sentries standing outside the base of Mount Dvargen. The double iron doors behind them remained open, marking the entrance to his home city, Almdalir. The burrows beneath Mount Dvargen stretched for miles, snaking below the sea, uniting the Ispolini cities across the multiple islands of Tundris Mor. Some tunnels branched further down into the Deep, the domicile of demons.

He had no need to announce himself to the guards, who stood with arms folded disapprovingly under layers of animal fur and iron armor. Already, he could hear their whispers; though he could not hear their words.

"Tyr," one stifled a chuckle once he was in earshot, "did you find the Blood Cascade? Did you bring glory to your father's name?"

Tyr's tongue twitched with sarcasm, keeping his eyes from the brash Ispolini. "You are brave, Gharkis, to insult my father when he is not here to defend himself. Do you forget he is an Elder?"

"What?" Gharkis raised his hands with a smirk, mocking innocence. "You cannot shield your father's madness? The Blood Cascade does not exist. You should know as much; how many winters has he sent you out looking for the fiery aura of souls?"

Tyr held his tongue, walking by the shorter man.

"Your family was not the only ones to lose loved ones during the Witiko raid," Gharkis went on. "When will he accept that your mother is dead? There is no magical light to bring her back from the grave. Nothing brings the dead back from the grave."

Another sentry, Vaghor, snorted with amusement, stepping into Tyr's path to stop him. "The Ispolini should not be wasting time searching for a child's tale. We should be preparing to keep the Witiko within the Deep where they belong."

Tyr halted. Vaghor had come close enough to Tyr that their noses nearly touched. "What in the Nine Lands is this?" Tyr twisted his head. The remaining four guards snickered but kept their distance. "The lot of you bored with guarding the snow? Mocking my loss will not end well for you." Tyr swallowed, unable to keep the threat from his tone. "Not today."

Vaghor did not budge. He pushed his tangled, red hair from his eyes. "Your mother is dead, and your father is a madman. We all know it. Why can you not accept it?"

"What of your father, Vaghor Fhar?" Tyr rolled the name off his tongue venomously. His voice carried further than he intended. "Your entire family is nothing but a legacy of half-wits and drunkards. Best hold your tongue unless you welcome death."

He noticed the other sentries shuffle backward as he bellowed.

Tyr felt Gharkis close the distance from behind him with a single step. The man attempted to pull

Tyr's attention from Vaghor's glaring gaze. "Where is your sister, Tyr? She had gone with you, did she not?"

"I bet she is dead, too," Vaghor flared his nostrils, his eyes darkened with hate.

Tyr's chest tightened. His deep voice rattled from his lips. "She is dead. Killed by a bear." Gharkis grated from behind him with a sense of sympathy. His footsteps crunched against the ground as he moved away.

"Let him be," Gharkis said.

Vaghor puffed his chest, inching closer. "Mother killed by a Witiko. Sister killed by a bear." Vaghor cocked his chin and clicked his tongue. "Where is the bear? We need food and resources."

Tyr explained with a single word. "Taken."

"Taken?" Vaghor echoed.

"Vaghor," Gharkis warned.

"No," Vaghor pressed. His breath was hot against Tyr's frozen cheek. "We should expect better from Tyr Og, the son of an Elder."

Tyr's muscles instinctively flexed, causing his injured arm to throb from shoulder to wrist. "Bah! You haven't been outside of Almdalir for three months. Try to provide before demanding from those who keep your belly filled."

Vaghor growled, balling his fists. Gharkis reached past Tyr to calm the giant, only to have his hand swatted away by Vaghor. The Ispolini sneered. "Are you wishing to join your sister and mother?"

"I welcome it!" Tyr's left hand clamped onto the jugular of Vaghor seconds before his fist connected with the giant's nose and upper lip. Bones crunched. Blood gushed.

It was not enough.

Gharkis shouted something unintelligible. Tyr disregarded the smaller sentry, striking Vaghor a second and third time. The nose flattened and crumpled under his massive fist. Vaghor thrashed back in surprise, trying to yell or break free. His feet kicked at nothing. Tyr's vision turned dark, a clouded haze, stifling the giant's voice with his powerful grip. And hit him again, and again. Vaghor might have well been a rabbit beneath a boulder.

Vaghor buckled to the ground, and Tyr followed, crushing the little bones in the guard's throat. He felt the meaty arms of Gharkis wrap around his chest. The four other guards were soon on top of him. Their attempts to stifle his ire only enticed him to further maddening. Perhaps, he was also as mad as they claimed his father to be.

Forgetting his shredded arm, injured by the white bear, Tyr turned on the men who attempted to bring an end to the onslaught. He threw them back, standing upright with a beastly roar. His axe entered his hand without thought, twisting to face those he would call brethren.

"No—" the first sentry cried. Tyr grabbed him by a tuft of hair, tearing his head back and ripping his iron blade across the man's throat.

He crushed the back of the axe into the temple of the second before the first guard's body hit the dirt. His skull caved under the impact. Blood danced through the air, splattering Gharkis, who reach for the long axe over his shoulder. Screams resounded behind him into the tunnel toward Almdalir. He barely heard the pleas of the other two, cutting through them as easily as the bear had sliced through the flesh of his bicep.

"Tyr—" Gharkis tried.

He saw the Ispolini's lips moving but could not hear the rest of the words. His ears were deafened, overwhelmed with bloodlust.

Seconds later, Tyr found himself kneeling in the crimson pool of Gharkis's entrails, his own hands laden with blood. His mind was disquieted with thoughts of Maruda and his mother.

And he felt nothing. Yet he was still alive.

Chapter III

Tyr kneeled on the smooth cave floor, his legs aching against the hard rock. His arms were spread wide with two Ispolini guards on either side, holding him in place. His hands had already gone numb, looking swollen under their tight grip. Twenty more sentries lined the circular room in preparation for his anticipated revolt.

Tyr did not move, staying as still as the stone columns strategically carved out throughout room. He averted his eyes from those he had once called friend and brethren. He especially kept his eyes from the judging faces of the proceeding Council on their stone seats. Six of the seven Elders watched him with bafflement.

The lava pools bubbled behind him while the Council considered him. The heat was nearly nauseating in the underground furnace, compared to the chilled winds of the surface world. Yet the sweat that etched Tyr's brow was not from the heat.

"You have admitted your guilt, Tyr Og, and have brought shame upon your family name—what little family you have left." The old Elder shook his head.

"If your father were here with us, he would likely cast you into the pit of fire behind you."

Tyr kept his stone poise. His father was more likely to have done the same if given the chance. Tyr licked his lips, eyeing the blood on his fingers, still moist from the giants he had slaughtered. "Where is my father?"

His eyes briefly skated across the empty chair again before falling on the Elders.

Jastrab, the eldest of the Elders, found the capacity to answer him. "He left on errand a day's past to meet with the Uvil, so he said. He will not return soon enough to see you, but he will know of your fate."

A man called Dag began speaking before Jastrab had finished. "Do you not understand your crime? Do you not understand what you have threatened? No Ispolini has killed another of their own kind in my lifetime!" His voice echoed throughout the chamber.

Tyr choked, where he meant to speak boldly. His words were muffled. "I was defending the honor of my family."

"Left little witnesses to say otherwise, didn't you?" Dag sneered. His red beard bounced with every word. "Do you forget why a Council resides in this city?"

"They threatened my life." His voice was stronger this time.

"Verbal threats do not give sanction to kill!"

"They would not let me pass into Almdalir," Tyr mumbled. "They insulted my father, my sister…my mother."

"What?" Jastrab asked with sympathy, his timeworn ears likely faltering.

"The bastards insulted my family." Tyr screamed, feeling madness tug at his wits. He jerked against the Ispolini that held him.

A giant, taller than the rest, stormed forward from his rock chair towards Tyr. His march was thunderous as he made his advance.

Jastrab called out hesitantly, "Mork'ash!"

Mork'ash jabbed Tyr in the stomach, where he kneeled, with full strength, and then plowed his fist upwards into his jaw. Tyr grunted, his head snapping back from the impact. "Vaghor was my son! He was no bastard, you motherless bastard!"

Tyr gasped for air, having no strength to retaliate. He hung his head.

Mork'ash raised his fist again.

"Enough, Mork'ash." Jastrab pleaded, suggesting the compassion the old man might possess for the brutality Tyr had displayed.

Mork'ash answered. "He deserves death!"

"I second that," Dag growled. "Be done with this murderer. Fling him into the fire."

The Ispolini guard jerked Tyr to his feet to do as they were instructed, as though two out of six Elders were enough to forward the sentencing.

"No," Jastrab said. "He can be of better service to us alive than dead. An immediate sentence of death is hardly acceptable without his father present."

"Bah!" Dag threw up his hand. "You obviously have an affinity for the boy, Jastrab, despite his deranged behavior. He is no better than his father."

Jastrab frowned. "Speak well, Dag."

Another Elder asked. "What are you proposing?"

Mork'ash interrupted, "The only sentence that he deserves is death. Death for death. That is the law."

Tyr attempted to lift his head and failed. The room spun.

"I know the law, Mork'ash," Jastrab said evenly, licking his aged lips. "I would not dare bring further blasphemy to our people. Yet sometimes a life of suffering is worse than an immediate death."

"The suffering he will have in the lava pit will suit me just fine," Mork'ash sneered, balling his fist up again.

"And," Jastrab spoke firmly, "it will bring the Ispolini no reprieve. His actions require sacrifice, not death."

There was silence among the Elders as they considered these words.

It was Dag that finally spoke. "Very well. You have captured our intrigue, old man. Tell us already what you are suggesting."

Tyr lifted his head slowly, making eye contact with the eldest Elder. The words left him breathless.

"Send him to the Deep."

Chapter IV

Tyr had no knowledge of any Ispolini venturing into the Deep and surviving. For certain, none had ever returned to Tundris Mor alive. The Deep was said to be an unforgiving place, chockfull of demons, likely the footpath to the Netherworld itself.

This history of Almdalir, as Tyr knew it, said the Ispolini had sealed the Deep to keep the demons buried in the endless concave beneath Mount Dvargen. When the Witiko had cut through the mountain twenty years ago, invading Almdalir, they had barely been pushed back by the Ispolini. Since that time, the way had stayed shut.

Tyr was uncertain why Jastrab would be motivated to open the tunnel again. If he were to die, he should be thrown to the fire pit as the law instructed. Tyr did not fear the Deep any more than he did the pit of fire. But the pit of fire would have been deemed mercy, considering Tyr was bound to face the murdering demons of his mother.

But not a single Ispolini pleaded on Tyr's behalf, or said another word in respect to the law. The sentries at his rear remained as silent as the adjacent Elders.

The rock blocking the abysmal darkness rolled aside.

"Wait for my father. Let him say his goodbyes," Tyr said. "Jastrab?"

"You gave no such option to our sons in your bloodlust," Mork'ash said. "Be gone."

Tyr nodded his head in acceptance. Images of Maruda's scarred face filled his visage momentarily as he turned to look at each of the men from the Council, the sentencers of his inevitable death. He had no interest in intervening with their mandate. After slaughtering his brethren, no life in Almdalir remained.

The all-powerful Council had governed over the Ispolini people for millennia and more. Nothing Tyr could say would fall on their ears, nor sway their hearts. He was likely as broken as his father.

He clutched his axe against his thigh, twisting back to glower at the tunnel ahead of him. His mouth was dry, but his hand stayed clear of the animal skin that held drink at his belt. The Council had given him enough water for a few days, his weapon, and his white fur cloak.

It would be enough until his death. He stepped into the darkness opposite side of the boulder.

The path ahead, covered in dust and indistinguishable debris, stretched into the depths of the mountain. The torch that he held only illuminated a small portion of the darkened underpass. The path angled at a sheer decline towards the center of the world, its radius over fifteen feet. There were no sounds except whooshing of air funneling through the cavernous abyss.

"Move the stone back into place," Jastrab bade in a hollowed whisper.

The Ispolini guard began to roll the massive boulder behind Tyr, larger than ten Ispolini men stacked against each other.

Tyr turned once more. The old giant, Jastrab, turned his head away from the scene as though it would ease the pain or steal away his memory. Tyr's voice vibrated against the tremor of the rolling boulder. "Tell my father I am sorry. Tell him...I will return honor to our family."

No one spoke, but Jastrab dipped his head, keeping his eyes averted. The boulder sunk into its position.

A moment passed.

Tyr was alone.

The time Tyr stood facing the darkness was without measure. The shadows twisted and frayed, making no image and giving no suggestion. He simply stood in isolation without direction from anything above or below. His path was stretched before him. It could be argued that there was no choice but to take his first step. But, in doing so, it would be as an infant first walking toward its mother. His first step into the darkness would be a step toward his union with the Deep and his acceptance of fate.

So, Tyr stood at a standstill. His mind struggled with moving forward or remaining stagnant. The light of his torch flickered and nearly diminished many times, giving little light to the harsh jagged stone of the tunnel walls. It was true that the path was worn, covered with smut, but the walls were like the fanged teeth of horrendous beasts. To stumble would bring death. To remain would bring death.

Tyr was powerless.

Yet the dearth of options did not keep the wicked grin from forming on his face. If he were going to die, it would be in glory. He did not know what the Deep would bring, but then again, the Deep did not know what was coming.

The whispered words lastly coming from his lips were telling. "I'm coming."

Tyr steadied his feet on the path with one hand holding the torch and the other stretched outward to keep his balance. And he walked.

For half a day, he walked without any sign of life, without any sign of anything. His arm ached. His feet were sore. His mind played tricks on him, and once in a while, he thought he heard the sound of Maruda's voice.

Darkness enveloped him with only the faint torchlight to light his path. If Tyr continued in this way, he was certain he would soon be talking to himself. He would never again experience joy. He would never again find happiness. He would never know love. If anything, his solitude would be his spouse and madness would be his mistress.

His hand gently grazed alongside the jagged stone that lined the path as he maneuvered down the bleak path. He found no reason to hurry, delicately ducking and dodging, descending through the tunnel. When his destination was nowhere, he had little need to rush ahead.

Tyr sighed heavily.

If the Deep had nothing to fear but the terrain, he would only find death in starvation. There would be no glory in that.

The sound of gagging interrupted his thoughts. It reverberated, nearly gurgling, before growing silent once more.

Tyr halted, thrusting the torch forward to lighten the path ahead of him. He had only known there to be demons in the Deep, but the sound appeared more humanoid than monster.

"Hello?" he managed to keep his voice deep, intimidating. His blue eyes pierced through the fire light, looking for any sign of movement.

The gurgling sounded again. Closer.

Tyr moved the torch from his right hand to his left and reached for his belt. He loosened his axe and stepped back a couple of steps. The soreness in his ankles and knees suddenly intensified from traipsing on the uneven ground, moving continuously downhill without a break. He had not given himself proper respite since entering the Deep. He silently cursed to himself.

"Speak to me if you are able. You will not find me an easy opponent, I assure you!" Tyr bellowed into the darkness. As he finished his sentence, he noticed an ash gray, clawed hand skim by the surface of the light. It was barely a glimpse, but it was enough for him.

"Witiko," he hissed, pulling his axe completely free from its holding.

The stench of decay touched the edge of the nostrils.

The Witiko sprang into the light, its grating howl giving indication of the narrow passageway that gave life to its lungs. The eyes, level with Tyr, were sunk beneath the surface, bluish bulbs within the backs of the sockets. Its skin was shriveled, clinging to bone and muscle as though it were dried leather sewn directly to the skin. Like a skeleton from the grave, it advanced with full strength.

Tyr did not falter. He did not have the time to pull the axe back for a full swing. Pulling his torch hand back behind his head, he made a fist around the handle of his weapon and punched the demon across the cheekbone. The Witiko's face, sharpened fangs and all, jerked roughly at an appropriate angle before recoiling back into position.

The Witiko swiped a claw upward with impressive speed, cutting Tyr across his extended arm. Tyr roared in pain, pulling back his right arm.

The demon sprang for his throat. Its mouth parted, its rasping cry echoing against the cavern walls.

Tyr doubled-back, flipping his axe upward from his waist. The blade sank into the softened flesh beneath the chin, splitting the bottom of the demon's face in two.

Tyr growled. He used the lodged weapon to push the Witiko backwards, knocking it off-balance. The monster gurgled with bluish blood spilling from the gaping hole in its face. Screeching, the demon swung clawed hands at Tyr to no avail. With a final burst of strength, Tyr lifted the Witiko off its feet and flung it into the jagged rocks. The Witiko screamed an unearthly sound and juddered as it hung suspended against the stone.

Tyr bared his teeth, unleashing the fury building in him since his sentencing. With his axe freed, he hacked at the Witiko's neck until the shrieking and gurgling had stopped.

The male voice from the tunnel path ahead nearly knocked him off his feet. "You can stop. I think it's dead."

Chapter V

The Witiko's body was beyond mutilated, laying in the desolate tunnel in bloodied pieces. Tyr turned from the demon's corpse to face the red-headed man, half his size and drowning in red robes, approaching in the dim torch light.

"Stuhia?" Tyr wrinkled his head in confusion. "What are the dragon people doing in the Deep?"

His light blue eyes lit up by some inner magic. "We are readying ourselves for the end of the world. You come from Tundris Mor?"

Tyr nodded, confused by his response. He had never known anything living to traverse this far underground. Losing the strength to keep his weapon drawn, he returned the axe to his belt loop.

"You better wrap those wounds," the man said.

"We are all dead down here anyway," he replied.

Before the Stuhia could respond, another male's voice joined the conversation with a second torchlight from the depths of the tunnel. "Who are you speaking with?"

Tyr barely had time to make a sound before his father emerged from the darkness holding the torch near his head. The man's red and gray locks flowed down to his thick red beard, marching forth in his leather armor, holding a new, large battle-axe in his right hand.

"Tyr?" His father gasped in perplexity. "What are you doing down here? Where is your sister?" The old Ispolini shook his head, saying louder, "What are you doing here?"

"Father," Tyr choked, falling backwards onto his buttocks. The torch lay behind him on the filthy floor. "I have been exiled from Tundris Mor. Maruda is dead. I…I killed many defending our family name. They said you were mad…" Tyr was suddenly overcome with sadness, tears creeping from the slits of his eyes. The rest of his words were lost in muffled sobs.

The older Ispolini took his time before issuing a response. "Tyr…" Enlil started with a heavy heart, likely trying to rationalize what he was hearing, "we have long been foreigners in our own home. Nothing for us is left in Tundris Mor."

"Where were you?" Tyr wept.

"I have been keeping these passageways clear from the Witiko for a generation with the Stuhia. The Deep runs for miles in all directions with hundreds of entrances and exits. A secret I have kept from the Elders, save Jastrab." His father gave a warm smile. "I know them well. This man knows them better."

"Jastrab knew you were down here," Tyr said, his voice drifting into the darkness.

His father smiled. "The old man has done well to protect our alliance with Eisliev Kluk and the Stuhia. Us Westerners must stick together, as we did in the first wars."

"Eisliev?" Tyr said with surprise.

"A pleasure," the Stuhia said. "Enlil has said much about you, Tyr."

Tyr pulled at his red hair, attempting to gain control of his emotions. "I...I don't understand."

"The Uvil have come to war with the humans," Eisliev said, "and the vile *Kadari* are rising in strength. The world will soon break."

"Son," Enlil added, "the dead have been pouring from the Deep for millennia or more, twisted by Marheena's death magic, and a greater darkness will soon come with them. The *Kadari* cannot fend them off forever. We must go with Eisliev and prepare to face this darkness."

"What about the Blood Cascade? What of mother? Maruda?" Tyr asked.

"Eisliev says the Blood Cascade will return when the demons are sent back to the Netherworld, Tyr. For now," Enlil paused, taking a breath, "any who die in this life return as a monster in the next. None are worthy of that death."

Eisliev moved closer, eyeing Enlil and Tyr. "We have to keep moving, Enlil. More Witiko will come. They always do, and I will not waste my life away fighting them."

"Come on, Tyr," Enlil said.

Tyr lifted his gaze, feeling like a boy under his father's gaze. "Where are we going?"

"Lairhein," Eisliev answered. "We will return to Lairhein and give our children and our children's children a promising afterlife."

Standing to begin a new adventure, Tyr's thoughts hung heavy on his mind. In his ferocity, in his grief, Tyr had been earnest of dying, never considering death was not yet worthy of him.

THE NAME OF DEATH

Thrice Nine Legends

WHEN BLOOD FALLS

Month of Ripening

Fifth of Warmth

1351 CE

Chapter I

Drada Koehn's armor-clad knees sank into the soft mud on the eastern bank of the forked river. Undried by summer's heat, a hundred miles from the war and hundreds of miles more from home, the mud was cool in the far-reaching shade. Drada relaxed, balancing on her knees and toes, while carefully reattaching the veil to the bottom of her helm, hiding the lower half of her face.

The thick, tannish cloth heated her cheeks and anchored her breath while she kneeled under the canopy of the concentrated treetops. Never had she seen trees as wide and high as those in the Dyndaer Forest. The trees from her homeland, beyond the mountains in Haemus Mons, were admittedly sticks in comparison to these tall woods.

Wrylyc, the skittish Kras, had claimed the Dyndaer was unfit for travel with beasts and barbaric men to boot. His forewarning had not scared Drada, and even now, with Eryet dying, she had little concern. Kras were known to be a jittery race—afraid of their own shadow as much as they were anything else—and besides, Uvil did not fear death. In addition, no one had asked Wrylyc for his advice, let alone for him to come on this quest.

She drew in a breath, redirecting her attention, and touched the arm of her war-brother, Eryet Petrie, son of Ergred. His short, squat figure lay near the water's edge, bleeding heavily from his split gut. The stained bandages, covered with pus and remnants of healing herbs, had been unraveled to quicken his inevitable passing. Drada had uncoupled his veil from his silvery helm minutes ago, laying it to rest against his dislodged shoulder guard. His lips were swollen and bloodied beneath his wide nose. The last two days had been less than pleasant for him. She impassively stared at his beardless, blue-hued face, a shade lighter than her own. If not for his faint breaths, Drada would already think he was dead.

Birds fluttered from somewhere in the forest. She mentally noted the abrupt change in the environment, but physically ignored the sound. Wrylyc likely was returning to camp. He had gone to scout ahead an hour ago, while she stayed to watch her war-brother and fulfill her duty. She would contend with a threat if and when it emerged from the hedge.

Her training had taught her not to worry over intangible thoughts until they had fully materialized. An imminent battle did not threaten death; though, an axe lodged between her breasts might.

Eryet suddenly wheezed, straining for breath. He squeezed his eyes shut and parted his lips. "Drada..." he faintly whispered.

She leaned further over him and waited for him to find the strength to continue.

"You... cannot be afraid."

Drada's response was full of air. "I am not afraid."

"When I pass through the veil," Eryet went on, "I will go to our people and tell them how far we have come. But you must keep going."

She shook her head. "I hadn't planned on doing otherwise. Do not worry about my path, Eryet. Listen for the whispers of our ancestors. Listen for the name of death."

"I…" He stammered and groaned. He turned his head away from her, having no strength to hold himself upright.

She waited.

"It…is time." Eryet finally choked out. His insipid, blue skin was etched with black veins. Drada remained stone-faced. The poison lacing the cleaver that had split Eryet open had finally reached the full purpose of its crafting.

Surprised by her own resolve, Drada grumbled in her throat with understanding.

"My *quoin*…"

Drada wasted no time, grabbing the leather cord with the iron token with the inverted V from around Eryet's neck in her gauntlet. With a jerk, the cord snapped with ease. She slid the ornament from the cord into her hand. His quoin.

Following the sacred tradition of the Uvil, she pushed the token into Eryet's gaping mouth and into the back of his throat. Forcibly, she covered his mouth to help him swallow the round coin whole. Without consuming it, Eryet would be transformed into the hideous, undead preta, to roam the world without honor.

Eryet sputtered and convulsed against Drada's hand as the token clogged his throat. He harshly swallowed, over and over again, his tongue brushing against her hand, and in short time the token was downed. By the time she lifted her hand, he was dead.

Drada scowled under the cloth covering her face. His last breath escaped his lungs and no words with it.

"Did he tell you?" Wrylyc moved so quietly, she had not heard him approach, but his high-pitched, excitable squeak was unmistakable.

"No. Our journey continues." Drada exhaled. Scooping up her hooked sword, she stood to face the red-skinned creature. Wrylyc hunched against a thick tree under his wool cloak. The black coals of his eyes were barely visible in the dark slits on either side of his angular nose. The Kras was likely the ugliest creature she had ever seen. Changing the topic, she asked, "What lies ahead?"

"Trees. Lots of trees," Wrylyc said offhandedly, tilting his head away from the unbending bark of the tall wood. His face scrunched up with confusion. "Are you not going to bury him? Burn him, maybe?"

Drada cleared her throat. "Why? He has consumed his quoin. He is dead."

"But he fought bravely against the Anshedar."

"Fighting humans doesn't require bravery. They are weak," Drada replied, picking up her shield to examine it. A depression near the center caught her eye. The shield had been damaged a month ago during the siege at Raybin; she had meant to have it mended or replaced. Though, the Uvil recently had been in short supply of extra armaments. Some of the humans had acquired the weapons and armor of the Uvil, either from battle or while raiding supply camps, and not surprisingly, their possession of Uvil steel had balanced the odds of the war.

Humans were cunning, she admitted, but still weak. She tossed the shield to the ground and went to fetch Eryet's undented guard for herself.

"*Weak* humans killed him," Wrylyc argued with a crooked grin. "One actually."

Drada frowned. "The wanderer slew Eryet with a venom-coated cleaver. Where is the honor in poison?"

Wrylyc scooted forward, holding his smile. "Honor does not win wars."

"We were not at war with the wanderer. He was a frightened coward," Drada said, leveling him with her eyes.

Wrylyc stopped. After thinking for a moment, he shrugged, and grinned the wider.

"You *are* at war with the Anshedar, which the wanderer clearly was," he said, advancing. The spindly Kras was a head shorter than her, and with the lacking muscle, was about as intimidating as a flea on a donkey's ass. Yet when Wrylyc talked at her as though he held authority—an attribute he only aired when speaking about history, or humans, or Maharia—he appeared greater in size. Drada turned away and tried to ignore him, placing Eryet's shield on her back.

Wrylyc persisted, "How did you expect the man to act when two Uvil came parading through the forest? I mean, the Ariadneans are right south, and those from Ariadne pride themselves as being hero-warriors. Not only do they fight directly on the battlefield, but every living thing in Aenar knows the Uvil and Anshedar are at war."

"You disagree with our incursion?" Drada asked, trying to make sense of his little speech.

Wrylyc laughed out loud. "I do not have any opinion on you invading Maharia. If I had, you may have heard about it during the last many months, but opinions on armies and politics are not my peoples' way. I simply watch."

"I don't believe you can have no opinion."

Wrylyc tilted his head at the simple accusation. "The humans took Maharia from the Svet. I can only imagine the Svet took it from some other race before the humans crossed from Kalamaar. Surely, someone was destined to eventually take it from the humans," Wrylyc said. "The world must change, or we wouldn't have history."

"That is what interests you? History?" Drada asked with a shake of her head, trying to understand the strange creature. "What use is history if you never apply what you've learned?"

The Kras crumpled up his hooked nose, expanding his nostrils most unattractively. "What makes you think we Kras don't?"

"Don't the Kras stay in mountains and caves, and claim nothing?" Drada reasoned. "They *have* nothing."

"Nothing?" Wrylyc smacked his lips with delight. "The Kras do not suffer from futility, as those who seek riches, or land, or power," said Wrylyc, wriggling his eyebrows. "We all die no matter what we possess."

With a sigh, Drada latched her sword to her belt. "Why are you here, Wrylyc? I did not invite you along, and Mariek gave you no order."

"Someone should record what happens here," Wrylyc talked with his hands, moving them wide from his hips in slow motion. "General Mariek had agreed," he pointed a finger at her, "which is why he allowed me to stay at your camp." The odd Kras spun on a toe. "And like I said, the Uvil are interesting. You have traveled hundreds of miles because one of your people—"

"The Speaker—"

"Yes, yes." Wrylyc went on, still spinning. His wool cloak circled around his knobby knees. "He claimed your dead ancestors said the Uvil would defeat the Anshedar. He said a new world would be born."

Drada crossed her arms and dipped her head with acknowledgement. "He did."

"Do you not find that fascinating?" Wrylyc squealed, suddenly coming to a stop.

"No," she muttered.

His dark eyes flashed with mischief. "How does this Speaker talk to dead people?"

Drada huffed through her veil, ignoring the question. "I am not the only one who left the camp at Raybin."

"No…" Wrylyc agreed, wrinkles forming around his eyes with confusion. "You were not."

"So, why are you *here* with me? Why didn't you go with another pairing?"

Wrylyc shrugged his little shoulders. His eyes shifted to the dead body behind her before answering. "The Kras called the Dyndaer home for a long time. And I thought you might need a guide. The others went further into the desert or toward the Shade Fells. I know little about those places."

"Then stop with all your twirling and bouncing, and guide," Drada said. "I need to find the name of death."

"I don't know what that means," Wrylyc said.

"Prophecy is not meant to be known until it has already happened," Drada said, "but if we can find death, we can unearth its name. Somewhere in the Dyndaer, death must linger."

Wrylyc's mouth opened wide, revealing the rows of his crooked teeth. "Shayol Domier. I will take you to Shayol Domier. We will find plenty of death there!"

Drada let the words linger for a moment, and then nodded. "On with it."

Waving the Kras onward, Drada followed Wrylyc into the deeps of the darkened Dyndaer, never looking back at her fallen comrade. Somewhere within this ancient forest, dusky as the grave, she must find death's name. She had her duty. She had her honor. She was Uvil.

The midday sunlight barely penetrated the intertwined, dense branches of the tall woods. The foliage at their feet was abundant, slowing their progress tenfold than what they may have traversed at the southern end of the continent. Even the tropical Masura Jungle, south of Dauthaz, did not match the breadth of the Dyndaer.

Drada squinted into the murky world among the trees. A hazy fog swirled around her feet, overlaying the moss and muck. The rotten air seeped through the veil covering her face. Clearly, the mountains and desert were a distant memory.

"The forest smells like death." Drada sniffed, stumbling awkwardly behind the light-footed Kras. Wrylyc effortlessly danced over the tousled roots and strewn brushwood. "How are you moving so freely in this light?"

"I do not see the darkness like you," Wrylyc said.

"You have eyes like the Lilitu then," Drada said. "You can see always as though it is daylight."

Wrylyc nodded. "The Kras lived underground for centuries, digging for precious stones, before we were yoked by the Anshedar. The darkness is as familiar to us as breath."

The weight of her foot snapped a branch in half. The crunching sound ricocheted between the trees, countered by a heavy snort and the clacking of teeth.

Wrylyc jerked back with wide eyes. "A simargl." As quick as the words were uttered, the Kras's body evaporated into thin air. By some inexplicable magic, Wrylyc had disappeared from sight entirely.

"Wrylyc!" She hissed, spinning around in the smoky forest.

"Hide." She heard the weakling answer from an unseen place among the trees.

"Uvil do not hide," Drada replied, retrieving the shield and hooked sword. She squinted into the dark, hearing the beast rustling toward her.

Drada stood motionless as the wolf-like creature, a head taller than she, with webbed wings, black as pitch, growled and moved between the thick tall woods. The animal was massive in comparison to her stout body. Her eyes captured the protracted claws extending from a lifted-and-falling paw—as long as her forearm—and then the pinpointed teeth, twice that length, protruding from the grimy, ruddy chops.

She remained motionless. The beast was a shadow among the shadows.

The simargl narrowed its gaze on her and growled.

"Come on," she hissed through bared teeth. She crouched and balanced on her toes as the bundle of muscle and fur barreled toward her, the wings tucking against its body. Her breath remained steady behind her veil; her heart evenly beat in her chest. Without a clearing, Drada was certain she held the advantage over the oversized beast, even in the murky light.

The simargl stopped inches in front of her and snapped at her head. Calculating her movement, Drada stooped low and circled behind the closest tree, the creature clamping its jaws around nothing in the space where her head had hung. Staying on her toes, Drada skirted around the thick trunk and jutted her sword into the broad side of the animal. The blade dug into the pelt, releasing a half-whimper, half-bark from the animal's gullet.

The blow was anything but a death wound. The simargl twisted fast, ripping the sword from her hand and leaving it buried in its flesh. Drada withheld her cry, lifting the shield in time to connect with the beast's second attack.

The strength of the simargl was immeasurable, striking the shield with its snout and knocking Drada across the dampened brush. She rolled over and over, her metal armor clanging against the rutted roots.

"Run!" Wrylyc screamed, still hidden somewhere among the tall woods.

Drada was back on her toes in time to see the simargl amble toward her, whipping its head back and forth, and ignoring her sword still budding from its gut. Blood oozed from the wound, coloring the black fur. Yet the cut was not deep enough to lay loose its insides.

Keeping her shield steady, Drada stepped back, digging in her toes. She had been raised in the barren lands of the desert and the underearth of the mountains. She felt unbalanced in the grassy terrain, but the animal was injured. Even without her sword, she had the upper-hand.

Out of nowhere, a bolt whistled through the trees and was buried into the simargl's shoulder. The animal bellowed in pain.

Before Drada could react, a cavernous bellow rung unintelligible words from behind her. She barely twisted her head before a creature—half-man, half-horse—stomped next to her with heavy hooves. Drada, in shock, stumbled as the Svet raised the crossbow to fire another bolt.

The simargl whined with a muffled rumble, the projectile striking the beast in the neck.

Already, the Svet was re-arming the weapon. Behind him his companion—an Anshedar—wearing a leather tunic and carrying a *sovnya*, a five-foot wooden pole with a curved blade erected from the end, emerged from the tall wood.

The human ignored Drada, hurrying to face the simargl, eagerly jutting his blade into its throat. The simargl gurgled and fell.

As the human stepped back, Drada eyed her hooked sword still sticking from the animal's side.

The human tore the sovnya free and spoke to Drada. "I am Seigfeld Brecher, son of Stelghar, from Hleduk," the human said, cleaning his blade on the carcass. He nodded toward the Svet. "This is Farthr of Brannan. Now, why is an Uvil so far from the war, here, in the Dyndaer?"

Drada peered up at Farthr's sharp teeth nearly as threatening as that of the wolf demon. His fawn ears on either side of his long black mane twitched. He snorted air through his enlarged nostrils, as though he was picking up her scent.

"You aren't going to kill me?" Drada asked.

The man's face creased as though he were holding back a smile. "I suppose that depends on your answer. Do you plan on killing us?"

"No. I have no orders to fight you." She returned her shield to her back. She replied honestly, "I am Drada Koehn, daughter of Vrayda. I am going to Shayol Domier to discover death's name. Peacefully, if I can."

"Death's name? Alone?" Seigfeld asked. The human warrior remained strangely unruffled by her response, which sounded strange even to her. If she had not known any better, she would have thought he had expected the answer.

Drada replied, "My war-brother died on the road. And unless the Kras has disappeared for good—"

"Of course not," Wrylyc said, suddenly materializing from thin air at Drada's side. "Wrylyc Titchen, son of Gard, son of Potap." He crossed his arms with a sudden sense of entitlement, wiggling his eyebrows.

"I thought I smelled something odd," Farthr said.

"Hush, Farthr," Seigfeld ordered. He then spoke to the Kras. "And you are also looking to find *death's name?* Seems a bit far-reaching for a Kras."

Wrylyc raised his shoulders and sheepishly smiled. Drada suspected he would turn red if he were not already colored crimson. "I am here to record the plight of the Uvil."

"I suppose you will be interested to know our story as well then," Seigfeld said, a crooked smile forming on his lips. He brushed a blond strand of hair from his eye without hurry.

The Kras's offset eyes lit up, widening on either side of his hooked nose. He bobbed his head, no bigger than a child's, and said, "I might."

Seigfeld gave a knowing look. "Tales of dark spirits inhabiting ruins, including Shayol Domier, have reached the folds of the Crimson Sun in Tamarri. I have been tasked to investigate the rumors and shed some light on their truth or falseness."

"You are also heading to Shayol Domier?" Drada asked.

Siegfeld nodded. "I am."

"So, you will not kill me, although my people are at war with your own?"

Seigfeld took a step closer, his soft boot nearly soundless against the soil. "Like you, I too have no order to fight in this war. I have heard of the honor of your people, Drada, and if you had been commanded to slay the Anshedar, I suspect you would have already attempted to kill me."

"I would have," she confirmed.

Seigfeld dipped his head with respect. "I propose we travel together to Shayol Domier and see what we can see. It stands to reason that your quest for death's name and my enquiry of demons have an eerie likeness."

Chapter II

Bound by honor, Drada walked along the Anshedar enemy, Siegfeld, and his silent cohort, Farthr. Wrylyc bounced along in front of them, leading the way to Shayol Domier. The Kras made little sound as he hopped over fallen branches and through scattered brush in the dark forest, seeing the darkened path ahead.

The tree birds provided an ambience somewhere in the depths of the tall woods, fluttering and squawking, amongst the distant howls of unknown beasts.

"The forest is alive," Drada said, making the effort to step as lightly as she could behind Wrylyc. Farthr seemed less concerned, crunching the brush beneath his hooves. She kept her eyes off the towering Svet. "What other terrors lay within its fold?"

Siegfeld's hand gripped the handle of his weapon, as it had for the past hour, while he steadied his walk with his free arm. "Any dark tale of the Dyndaer holds more truth than most would readily admit. Naturally, many kinds of monsters flock to this darkness."

"How do you know these demons you seek at the ruins are not only more monsters?" Drada asked.

"I do not," Siegfeld said, "but I am told that traveling to the ruins bears necessity. You may know demons are regular on the northern island of Kalamaar and were once said to have marched on Shayol Domier over a thousand years ago."

Wrylyc piped up. "Quite true. My grandfather was among the many saved when Branimir Baran freed the Kras from the clutches of the Kadari. Of course, they were known by another name during that age. The songs are magnificent, telling the stories of how Branimir and the Highborn fought against the Bukavac of the Netherworld, guarding the Ash Tree from being destroyed."

"The Ash Tree? You mean the Tree of Life?" Drada's mouth suddenly dried with disbelief.

"The same." Wrylyc twisted his neck to flash her a crooked smile.

"Pay no attention to the Kras," Siegfeld laughed. "The creatures are full of fancy stories to stir the heart. Sadly, they are only stories. Shayol Domier was a ruin long before any human stepped across the ocean."

"No," Farthr rumbled. "The red beast speaks truth. The Svet know."

"Quiet, Farthr." Siegfeld's voice grew terse.

"If humans did not build Shayol Domier, or these Highborn," Drada cocked her head, "then who did?"

Siegfeld took a moment, and then finally shrugged his shoulders, showing his lack of interest. "Maybe the Uvil. I hear they had built Garain'l in the age before."

Drada disagreed, knowing the Uvil had not ventured as far as Shayol Domier, but held her tongue. Arguing with the human over something so trivial was pointless. She retraced the conversation. "So, why do you think demons haunt the ruins?"

The crooked smile returned to Siegfeld's lips. His blonde hair shadowed his cheeks. "The world has seen more blood as of late, notably with the Uvil arising from the sands of the South—"

"And you suspect demons bid our coming?" Drada concluded, peering at the swaggering human.

"I suspect demons sway those who are good in equal measure to those who are evil, planting ambitious seeds, without revealing their true nature," Seigfeld replied.

Drada squinted at Seigfeld, unsure if the human was attempting to compliment her or otherwise. Opposite of her, she saw Farthr twitch his ears and give Seigfeld an equal look of confusion. Likely, Siegfeld spoke for the sake of speaking, and was not saying anything really important at all.

She moved her attention to the Kras. "Wrylyc, how much further to Shayol Domier?"

"If we make camp soon," Wrylyc tapped his finger on the edge of his crooked nose, "... midday tomorrow."

Taking the suggestion, Siegfeld stopped where they stood. "Farthr, fetch some wood for a fire and hope it keeps any passing simargl at bay."

Within the hour, the four of them sat nestled around the crackling embers of the fire. Drada readjusted her veil to keep her face hidden, watching the others with careful consideration. With the dangers of the forest, they would take turns keeping watch for simargl or any other beasts that might approach the camp. Yet she was uncertain she could trust the human and his centaur. She had never known humans to hold the same honor as an Uvil. They may still cut her throat while she slept.

Wrylyc scooted closer to her, wrapping a blanket over his shoulders. The odd creature looked at her with his uneven black eyes, shining like gems in the firelight.

She asked the question as it came to her mind. "How is it that you have no purpose, Wrylyc?"

"What would I do with purpose?" He laughed.

"You would live your life."

"I am living now."

"But you are not living with any meaning," Drada muttered. She tried again, "Wrylyc, there must be something that you aim to accomplish, something you wish to prevail over…"

"Why?"

Drada faced the fire, unable to comprehend the Kras's belief. "You tarried around our camp at Raybin for months, doing nothing but watching us go to battle and return. Such a life… without ambition is…"

"Peaceful," he finished.

"I have known their kind for a long time," Seigfeld offered from across the fire. "The Kras fear to love anything too much lest they might feel something real. Surprising any have lived without masters to lead them."

"We feel," Wrylyc said softly. He scrunched up his nose, wiping his sleeve across his face. "Kras are as much a part of this world as any other living thing."

Siegfeld scoffed. "And you give nothing."

"Nothing?" Wrylyc's tone changed considerably to a familiar one of authority. "The Kras have died for others for thousands upon thousands of years. We have been hardened to think every life is worth more than ours, and thus we give ours freely as we do the knowledge we gain."

Drada remained stoned-face, but the Kras's speech touched her heart. "It sounds as though the Kras give everything and take nothing."

Siegfeld's jaw dropped, speechless.

Farthr snorted with amusement from somewhere in the trees. For the first time since meeting the two, Siegfeld did not silence the Svet.

"True." Wrylyc raised a thin finger, and added, "Mind you, no one dies for a Kras."

"Is that your purpose then?" Drada asked. "To give your life away for another to use as they see fit?"

Wrylyc grinned, displaying his row of crooked teeth. "I suppose. And for now, my purpose is to help you complete your purpose."

Drada folded her hands. She kept an eye on Seigfeld and asked Wrylyc her question. "What will you do once I discover the name of death?"

The human, again, hardly flinched at mention of her quest. The thought of discovering death's name was peculiar enough to her, she would expect any to inquire as to her purpose. Yet Siegfeld stayed quiet.

Wrylyc shrugged, speaking at a whisper. "If I survive to see the day, I will tell you. Until then, I could not know. I do not know the future."

In the distance, the rumble of bestial growls resounded from the forest. Drada turned her ear, gazing into the pitch and then upward to the equally dark canopy of feathered limbs, blocking all view of the moon and stars.

"Worry not," Farthr said. "The beasts are far removed from our location. If they come closer, I would let you know."

Wrylyc twisted his hands, staring at the centaur. Drada noticed his eyes widened with a thought that had likely been looming on his mind for the course of the day. Suddenly, without easing into the conversation, he blurted, "Are you a slave, Farthr?"

The Svet, taken by surprise, snorted through his enlarged nostrils, and bared his sharp teeth at the Kras.

Seigfeld answered swiftly, lifting a hand to ease the beast. "No. Farthr is not enslaved like many of his poor brethren. Though he may pretend from time to time when we pass through uncivilized *civilizations*, he is a free mercenary among the Crimson Sun."

Wrylyc rocked back on his buttocks, unaware of the dangerous glare Drada noticed in Farthr's eye. "Amazing. I have never met a free Svet. How did you come to meet?"

Farthr growled in his throat.

"Calm yourself, Farthr. Check the area and I will tell the story," Siegfeld said. Farthr snorted and disappeared into the darkness. Seigfeld smiled at Drada and Wrylyc. "He is not fond of this story."

"I got the hint," Drada muttered. "You do not have to tell it."

Wrylyc shook his head in disagreement. "I am most interested. If I am going to tell the tale of this adventure, I must know all the details."

Seigfeld chuckled, rubbing his knees. "Best not tell Farthr you plan to spread this specific story. He'd have you roasting over the fire before morning came."

The threat gave the Kras pause, and he then nodded his little head with understanding.

The wood popped and sizzled as Seigfeld leveled his gaze over the fire, and began, "Four years ago, my sister, Anneinda, had gone missing from my home in Eris. My father called me back home to pick up her trail, claiming demons had pulled her from her covers in the night. I found tracks and followed the trail to a cavern at the edge of the Shade Fells. The cave was without light, smelled of decay, but most peculiar was the stoned walls decked with some slick lichen that burned to the touch."

"The lichen burned you?" Drada winced. She had lived her entire life in the mountains and had never found cave moss that posed a hazard to the skin.

"As surely as this fire," Seigfeld said. "I thought I had found the path to the Netherworld, and soon the chilled air billowing from the darkness only confirmed my suspicions. I tell you I had never been more afraid than I was in that terrible place."

"As is the frailty of humans," Drada huffed under her veil with surety.

Seigfeld gave his usual crooked smile and replied with a calm voice. "As is the frailty of mortals. You would have been afraid too, Drada Koehn, daughter of Vrayda."

She folded her hands to keep them from her sword. She had told herself she would not kill the man; she would keep her honor.

"By and by," Seigfeld went on, "I came upon what the Ispolini call a Witiko. Dastardly demons with a hunger for flesh, who they themselves have more bone than flesh to cover their grisly bodies. The bluish bulbs of its eyes were lit in the darkness like torchlight, its fangs were—"

"We know what a Witiko is, Seigfeld," Drada said with a click of her tongue.

Seigfeld cleared his throat. "I suspect you would."

"By the Nine Lands, I do not," Wrylyc gulped. His little hands clung to his knees to hold them steady, leaning forward with his attention fully on the human and his story. Drada held herself rigid to keep herself from shaking her head at Wrylyc. The Kras added, "I hope never to see such a beast."

Seigfeld smiled. "I would pray you never do, Kras. The beast would rip you apart, limb from torso. And, all the while, you would be alive and screaming." When Wrylyc shuddered in response, Seigfeld pressed on with his story. "I asked the Witiko about Anneinda, but the demon said nothing intelligible. The battle between us was swift. Soon, my blade found its black belly and its guts were left to stain the cave floor."

"But what of Farthr?" Wrylyc asked.

"I heard Farthr soon after killing the Witiko, fervently rustling from further down the path. He had heard the battle and sought his freedom."

"Freedom?" Drada lifted her eyebrow, beginning to understand the odd relationship between the Svet and Seigfeld.

Seigfeld dipped his head. "I found Farthr chained in a hollow in that cave, captured and meant to be eaten by the Witiko scum. He had watched handfuls of his own—and humans—slaughtered at the hands of the demons."

Drada felt her heart twist, the smoke of the fire burning her nostrils. "Your sister?"

Seigfeld turned his eyes from her. "Forever lost. Farthr agreed to help find her, unsure if he had witnessed her death among the many humans. We searched for a while, but the tunnels beneath the mountain ran long and deep in more directions than the two of us could have ever traveled in a single lifetime."

Wrylyc looked over his shoulder, scrunching his hooked nose. "I don't understand how Farthr disapproves of this story."

"He is shamed to have been captured," Drada said matter-of-factly, "and you stole from him an honorable death. He would have died with his brethren in that cave had you not come along."

"He would have been eaten alive," Seigfeld protested.

"Ah," Wrylyc grinned, "but the Svet have eaten the living, even their own battle-fallen, since their creation."

Drada recoiled, catching bile in her throat. She filled the space with words. "So, he is bound to you now because you saved him from an unsavory death?"

Seigfeld dipped his head in acknowledgement.

"Absurd," she replied. "A life of servitude is far worse than a glorified death. He should have sought more Witiko in the caves to kill."

"Oh, we killed many more in the search of my sister—"

"I hear little mourning for her in your breath," Drada challenged, folding her arms.

Seigfeld continued, "—but many paths were so thick with the demons, we were forced to retreat."

"Retreat?" Drada scoffed. "I know few who would be so eager to tell a story of defeat."

Seigfeld's gaze darkened from across the fire. "You do not know the horrors—"

"No. I do not. Because Uvil do not know fear."

The clipping of Farthr's hooves against the ground drew their attention. Towering over them, crossbow in hand, he stared at Drada with a haunting gaze, the darkness looming behind his massive breadth. His words fell on her like a curse. "You will."

Chapter III

Drada had to trust Wrylyc when he woke her to say morning had come. She had not slept well, finding herself waking regularly to keep a watchful eye on her new companions. Siegfeld and Farthr, however, had taken the chance to sleep when they could, apart from when they had taken the night watch.

For the course of the morning, mists in the Dyndaer swirled through the tall woods, speaking of impending misfortune. The three of them had little choice but to rely on Wrylyc in guiding them to Shayol Domier.

"Not that way!" Wrylyc squealed, grabbing Drada's right leg and pulling her back. "That will lead you straight into the bog. Only death that way."

Drada ogled at the moss and grime swirling inches from her feet and stretching into the darkness. The swamp held as many concentrated trees as the solid ground. "Wrylyc," Drada slurred in the thick air, pushing him away. "If this is where death resides, then here I must go. I am looking for death, remember?"

Wrylyc shook his head, "Not this death. You would sink to the depths without a chance to swallow your coin." The Kras tugged at her hand, his usual smile faded. "Come. We are almost to the ruins. Only a bit farther."

Drada studied the half-sized man, who took the hint and let go of her fingers. Spinning away, he milled onward through the vines that clouded the forest ahead. He weaved in and out of the close-knit brush like they had been carved for his passing. Seigfeld trailed immediately behind, hacking at the plants with his sword.

Drada watched the human with distrust. Seigfeld had been exceptionally quiet this morning, barely looking in her direction—at least, when he knew she was aware of him. As of now, she could not help but notice the human's blue eyes widening with awe of the Kras.

Yet he still said nothing.

Farthr sidestepped from his place in line and waylaid her. His large eyes rested on the bog that gurgled behind her. "I will follow you," the centaur said.

Drada nodded. She had come to realize last night she trusted the centaur more than the human, and had no concern having the beast guard her back. She moved onto the makeshift path behind Seigfeld.

After only a few steps, she heard a gelatinous slosh and splash from the swamp.

She spun on her heel to see a beast the size of Wrylyc abruptly draped over the Svet's back as though it meant to ride the centaur. Time stopped for a moment as the *thing* stirred awkwardly on the Farthr's posterior.

The creature's body was yellowish and molded with wide pinkish eyes. Its ears were floppy and leathery on either side of its bald head, hanging just below its cheeks. Unexpectedly, screeching and hissing, the monstrosity raised two hands full of clawed fingernails, sharper than knives, and jammed them through the hide of the Svet.

As the nails pierced into Farthr's flesh, he roared, swinging back with his crossbow and striking the beast across its gruesome face. The creature gurgled but hung on tightly in the eddying mane of the centaur's dark locks. Farthr stomped around in circles reaching for the small beast, finding no way to loosen it from his back.

"Farthr," Drada cried, unfastening her hooked blade from her belt. Moving within distance, she swung her blade, cutting open the creature's back. Blood seeped, but the blade seemed to have no effect on its grip on Farthr. She swung again to slice open its arm, and again, the monster did not loosen its grip.

Fathr suddenly lurched toward the bog.

"What is it?" she screamed.

"You mustn't go forward," Wrylyc squawked from behind Seigfeld, rocking his head back and forth to catch sight of the scene, "The myling aims to drown you in the swamp!"

Seigfeld pushed pass Drada, jerking his sovnya free. "Step aside." Using the weapon as a polearm, he stabbed the curved blade into the meaty tissue of the myling. Seigfeld groaned as he tried to pry the monster off his friend.

The myling screeched, wrestling against the strength of the human. Farthr had stopped spinning, strained by the myling's grip, its claws deep within his muscles. His hindquarters stumbled into the soggy, blackened waters of the bog. Drada knew if Farthr lost his balance they would lose him to the yellowish beast.

The Svet desperately swung at the monster, hitting it in the head. The myling rocked sideways with the impact but held firm.

In haste, Drada took the opportunity sliding across the muck to attack again. She hacked her blade through the spindly arm of the beast in a single blow, cleaving the limb just above the elbow. The myling screeched, releasing its grasp and falling to the murky flooring.

Siegfeld jerked the monster from Farthr's back with his long weapon, gripping the wooden shaft. His muscles quaked under the surprising, but evident, weight. Unable to keep the beast suspended in the air, he slammed the myling to the ground and pushed the blade the rest of the way through its molded bulk.

The myling twisted against the sovnya, blood flowing over its skin. Yellow chunks of flesh drooped from the myling's body beneath the crimson flow.

"Kill it!" Wrylyc bounced, watching the myling twitch in the muck.

Drada smashed the myling's head with her sword, ending the struggle.

"Lucky to have found company on your journey, Drada," Seigfeld frowned, jerking his weapon free from the carcass. "I suspect you would already be dead without the Kras's guidance, my blade, or Farthr's ass."

"Excuse me?" Drada's jaw fell from behind her veil. The confrontation caught her off-guard. Though she suspected the human bid to insult her for her weighted words last night. "You underestimate me."

"I think not." Seigfeld twitched his nose like he was ridding it of a foul smell. "In a single day, you have lost your war-brother, have been saved from the simargl's bite, and now, a myling's embrace. I can see why you were sent to find the name of death."

Drada tensed, her eyes locking on the blood dripping from the edge of her sword. The drops fell to the pool of blood flooding from the myling's body, mixing with the grime and mud of the forest flooring.

Seigfeld wiped his blade clean. "You appear to have an unsettled pact with death."

Farthr grated his teeth. "Leave her alone, Seigfeld. We have our duty and she has hers."

"Hold your tongue, Farthr," Seigfeld barked through thin lips. "You have been mangled, and the blame can only fall to this ungainly woman. You will not find glory dying for the cursed."

"I will live," Farthr said. The blood oozing from his punctured flesh slowed from the gaping holes.

Drada spoke over him, determined to keep her honor and not cut the human down where he stood. "I am *not* cursed."

"Bah! Yet you search for the name of death." The human clutched his sovnya and hung over Drada with a fierce gaze. "We will find out soon enough. I trust if the gloom hanging over Shayol Domier is true, we will know your nature soon enough."

"What do you mean?" Drada paused, looking at Seigfeld and then Farthr. "I thought you sought demons. What exactly do you expect to find at the ruins?"

"More than demons really. We also seek death," Farthr answered.

"Farthr," Seigfeld warned, casting a wary eye on his companion.

The Svet did not heed the warning. "Ivarr Gauthus, the master of the Crimson Sun, acts on the order of Patrician Falmagon Sej of the Kadari, and we do as we are bid." Farthr winced, his ears twitching beneath his mane. "We suspect the Old-dark is seeping into the world of the living."

Drada hooked her sword on her belt. "I don't know what the Old-dark means."

Wrylyc's hands were shaking while he offered his wisdom. "Old gods before time was recorded. The ancient gods supposedly know us better than we know ourselves and were said to be death themselves. Some stories have referred to the eight of them as the Likhyi. Their names cannot be pronounced in any modern tongue, but when translated they mirror the eight elements of this world: stone, sky, fire, sea, void, primal, profane, and sacred."

Drada's heart thudded in her chest. "Is this the name of death? The Likhyi?" The answer to her question had been sitting in the minds of her companions all this time, and yet they had said nothing.

Seigfeld snorted. "One way to find out."

Wrylyc waggled his head, and suddenly grinned. "I agree. If the two of you aren't going to kill each other, we should make haste. Shayol Domier is near."

Chapter IV

The timber gates of Shayol Domier were remnants of what they had once been, withered away between the two teetering towers of flat stones. The rotted wood had become discolored and fragmented over time with one door dislodged from the wall, overrun by the forest foliage, and the other hanging ajar. Drada squinted into the heavy vapor coiling through the dilapidated buildings and scattered trees that had grown overtime, running her fingertips along the inner arch.

The sticky mold was moist and smelled... sick.

"Be wary of anything lurking about," Farthr said, checking the bolt on his crossbow. "Far too many places to hide in a place like this."

"I will make us a torch for better light," Seigfeld said. He grabbed a thick branch and pulled flint and steel from his pocket.

Drada turned from the human, eyeing the towers on either side of the gate. One had partially caved in on itself with dark green climbers spiraling up and over the top. The walls were six times higher than Drada, and the towers taller yet. "What happened here?"

"Not far from here, twelve hundred years ago, the Ash Tree was protected by the Kadari from hordes of demonic Bukavac and an Eretik," Wrylyc said, rocking on the end of his toes. "Shayol Domier was the Kadari's main stronghold in Maharia."

"*Eretik?*" Drada echoed with wonder.

"A meddler in dark magic," Wrylyc explained. "My grandfather had said she had come back from the dead, terrorizing the living with her evil from Kalamaar to Maharia."

A wind too cold for summer brushed by them, sending a chill up Drada's spine. She shivered, holding the veil across her helm so that it would not falter.

"The battle with demons did take place here, but the rest is hogwash," Siegfeld said with a snort, seemingly unaware of the breeze. He stood upright with the fiery branch in his hand. In his free hand, he held several more sticks to transfer the light when needed. "As I said, humans had not come to Maharia when this structure was built. Maybe the Uvil or the Stuhia, but not humans. Our kind had not yet ventured as far as the Dyndaer."

"You are mistaken," Wrylyc said, pointing at a pile of collapsed stones across the courtyard. "That building once led to the Kras chambers underground where the slaves were held—where my grandfather was held. And—"

"You are not convincing anyone with your stories, Kras," Seigfeld said.

Farthr grimaced with pain. "You are too closed minded, Seigfeld. The Kras know their history better than any human."

Drada rested her hand on her sword, interjecting before Seigfeld silenced the Svet. "Where do we go to find death? The fog only swells in the darkness."

Wrylyc scrunched his nose, peering ahead where the others could scarcely see. "Why don't we go into the keep? It looks to be unbroken."

"I sense doom here that I have not felt since the Shade Fells," Farthr said. His ears twitched, squinting to look through the dusky haze covering the ruin.

Drada took the first step into the ruin, seeing the outline of the keep in the dim light. She unhooked her weapon from her belt and pulled the shield from her back. "Be ready for whatever comes." She advanced to the keep doors.

Pulling the doors open, Drada was greeted with the sound of growling and gnashing of teeth. Though, she could see little in the darkness. Seigfeld, to her right, backed away several steps, while Farthr fired a bolt into the darkness ahead of them. A screech of pain resounded and then quickened footsteps raced toward them. Farthr bellowed again and fired another bolt. A thump sounded as something connected with the ground in a heap.

"I thought you could not see in the dark," Wrylyc said.

Farthr set another bolt. "I could hear it."

"I cannot see anything," Drada said. "What did you kill?"

Seigfeld edged into the keep, holding his temporary torch with an outstretched hand. The glow glimmered over the dank earth. Sprawled out with one bolt in the side and another through the eye socket, was what appeared to be—at first glance—an oversized, hairless mutt. Grey wrinkled skin drooped from a thin body to an oversized head, where two goat-like horns cropped out from the skull.

"A Dreka," Wrylyc said. "Disgusting creatures. A single bite could take off your arm."

Drada peered at the mouth to see rows of teeth on the top and bottom gums. "Died easily enough."

"What is this?" Seigfeld asked, whipping the torch around to look at the entryway. A staircase led down with three pale brown columns on either side. At the top of the stairs sat a giant stone statue of a man with a long beard. Each fine hair was carved into the stone, but most impressive was the large hammer held in the sculpture's hand. "Dahz?"

A grin split across Wrylyc's face, and Drada heard him giggle. "Yes. The Lightbringer, who rides across the expanse in his chariot, Mioengi, holding the Hammer of Righteousness, Mulafell."

"What is a statue of the White-Clad doing here? In the Dyndaer?" Seigfeld lit another stick to give more light, throwing the first to the ground. "This is a god of men, the Protector of Men."

"My people would not have built this," Drada said.

"Like I said, Shayol Domier is a stronghold built by men." Wrylyc grinned. The Kras had difficulty keeping the look of satisfaction from his face.

Drada watched Seigfeld mull over the magnificent statue, shaking his head with confusion. "It must be true," he finally said.

Again, a cold wind chilled Drada beneath her armor. A sense of darkness pulled at her momentarily before letting go, and in moments, the feeling was only a memory. She turned to gaze at the downward staircase. "We should go down there."

"I don't know what we will find," Wrylyc said. Drada realized his face was suddenly etched with fear. Yet he took the first step near the stairs.

"Farthr," Siegfeld ordered, "stay here and keep watch for anymore Dreka." He glanced at the staircase from the corner of his eye. "You will not be able to squeeze down there anyhow."

Farthr hung his crossbow over the quiver of bolts hanging from his side. "I will make a fire. We could possibly camp for the evening."

Seigfeld frowned. "Make the fire so you may see better, but we will not stay here any longer than we must."

Drada followed Wrylyc and Seigfeld down a flight of stairs to another set of double wooden doors, heavy and well-fitted into their frame. On either side of the entrance hung faded tapestries of what appeared to be similar images of Dahz the Lightbringer.

Seigfeld pulled open the doors and thrust his burning stick into the opening. A waft of dry air, laden with the smell of death stung Drada's nostrils.

"Oh, it stinks," Wrylyc groaned, covering his hooked nose with both hands. "Something terrible."

"I don't see anything moving," Seigfeld said, taking a step opposite of the doors. The light flickered, barely illuminating the square room. The human hit his foot against the ground a few times, and concluded, "The ground is different in here." He scraped his foot across the dusty flooring. "Red rock, by the looks of it. I wonder where they found red stone in the Dyndaer."

Drada gripped her sword hesitantly, searching the room with her eyes. She could see little in the darkness.

Wrylyc said, "I see several doors."

Seigfeld pointed at the door across the room. "Follow me. We will start there."

A clang, like the sound of a blacksmith's hammer on an anvil, resounded with Seigfeld's next step, followed by a cry of pain from the human. He grabbed his leg as the small spear that cut through his thigh clinked against the wall at Drada's left.

"Don't move," the Kras cried.

Drada held her breath, watching Seigfeld—already in motion—drop the torch and fall to his knee. The moment his knee struck the ground another clang sounded, and a second spear fired into his chest.

Drada dropped her shield, snatched a hold of Seigfeld's leather tunic, and yanked him back out the doors, while Wrylyc grabbed her waist to hold her back.

"Careful," he said.

"We are under attack," she shouted. Drada rocked back as the darkness in the room above her rippled. A strange sensation Drada had never felt before trickled into her mind, like the slow drip of a rain drop from a leaf petal.

Terror.

She shook the thought away, refocusing on the unmoving shadows.

"No!" Wrylyc cried in response, hearing Farthr scuffling beyond the stairs. "We triggered a trap. Hurry. Get him up the stairs."

Chapter V

Night had come and the darkness in Shayol Domier was bottomless. The glow of the fire at the base of the statue illuminated only a hair's breadth beyond the heated embers.

Drada touched Seigfeld's forehead and recoiled her hand. His fever was blistering. The yellow seepage leaching from the wound on his leg and chest seeped more now than it had a handful of hours ago.

"He is dying," Drada said. "The poison is in his blood."

"Anneinda," he murmured, eyes closed. His voice was as faint as his breath. His body convulsed.

Drada gritted her teeth. "Humans and your use of poison…"

Farthr stood over her, crossing his arms. "A warrior of the Crimson Sun killed by a simple trap. He will find no glory in the afterlife."

"I expect not considering the feats of heroism I have heard thus far." Drada stood up, rubbing her hands together.

Farthr glowered. "He was a noble man."

"Maybe." Drada lifted her head to the Svet. "Still, I do not see any reason for us to stay here." She pointed to the dead Dreka, adding to the rotting aroma. "You found your demon, and I am not going to go beyond those doors again."

Wrylyc emerged from the stairs behind her. "I have studied the room below, and I think I discovered the source of the spears. A line, hidden beneath the dust, has been brushed on the flooring to mark the safe pathways. He stepped off the path."

Drada picked up her shield, fastening it to her back. Her eye rested on Seigfeld. "It does not matter, Wrylyc. We are not going to go into the room again. It is not worth the risk."

"The risk?" Wrylyc cocked his head. "I thought Uvil did not retreat. Are you really afraid of going in there?"

"I am not afraid." Drada snipped. "A fine line rests between courage and stupidity. You do not rush into a fire after watching another get burned."

"But you have not discovered death's name," Wrylyc argued.

"Quiet," Farthr growled. "Something comes."

The earth beneath Drada's feet quaked. Heavy stomping thudded toward the entryway of the keep. Wrylyc scooted back near Seigfeld, who exhaled to never inhale again. Farthr dropped his dark gaze to his lifeless companion before lifting them back to the wooden doors leading outside to the courtyard. The foot falls drew closer.

Suddenly, a large creature crashed into the doors, cracking them under the impact. A howling resounded, followed by several more howls, and yipping. The beast struck the doors again.

Farthr lifted his crossbow. "We might survive this, Uvil, but not without bleeding."

Drada grabbed her arm-guard once more and raised her sword at the ready. "Whatever comes, be sure its blood flows more freely than ours, Farthr. Stand with me."

The door cracked again, a panel falling away to uncover the moving shadows. The centaur released a bolt through the opening striking flesh. And another. And another.

The timber rattled as the massive, unseen beast chipped away the pieces. Wrylyc shouted. "It's a simargl. And many Dreka."

No more had the Kras identified the beasts than a Dreka leapt through a smaller opening in the door. Grey skin eclipsed the demon in the subdued light, rushing at Drada with its horned head bent with intent for ramming.

She lowered her shield and battered the demon to the side, sinking her sword into its flesh without delay. Farthr dropped a second with his bolt. A third and fourth skittered across the dirt toward Drada, gnashing the rows of sharpened teeth.

Again, Drada smacked the first with the shield, and swung her sword to hit the second. Blood sprayed. She ignored the gushing stench of death pouring out from the hideous beasts. Instead, her attention was on the simargl busting through the keep doors.

"Farthr!" she cried.

The centaur wasted no time loosening the bolt from his heavy crossbow. The bladed shaft tore through the animal's skull, felling the monster.

More bays filled the courtyard. The ground quaked once more.

Drada spun and thrusted her sword into the back of the remaining Dreka. The unearthly howl erupting from the demon's jowls caused her to fall to her knees and release her sword. She covered her ears, feeling the room spin under the echoing death bawl of the beast.

Farthr grabbed her by the shoulder, lifting her back to her feet. "Get your sword. We cannot hold this position."

"We have nowhere to flee," Drada said, shakily ripping her sword free. She breathed deep to steady herself. The image of the shadowy room below touched her mind.

"I do not," Farthr said, nodding toward the stairs, "but you can save yourself."

Drada took the centaur's meaning. "The Uvil do not retreat!"

Farthr roared with fury, firing another bolt. "Go into the underearth and find death's name, Drada, daughter of Vrayda. Bring your people glory and leave this filth for me. I will have my glory."

Wrylyc appeared between them, hastily handing Farthr Seigfeld's sovnya, and then Drada a burning torch. She took the blazing stick in her shield hand reluctantly.

"Come on," Wrylyc said. "You must stay on the painted lines or your fate will be the same as Seigfeld."

Drada pressed down the steps, disregarding the din of snarls and howls rumbling above. Waving the torchlight near her feet, she found the lines marking the path within the square room. Wrylyc practically pushed her on the first line.

"I will help Farthr distract the beasts," Wrylyc said.

Drada spun around to see the doors already closing. She grabbed at the frame while trying to balance on the safe marking on the floor. "Wrylyc, no."

Wrylyc vanished from sight. "My life has never been my own."

"You have to tell the story."

The doors creaked as the Kras continued to push. "You must tell the story now."

"You cannot die!" she screamed, her hand sliding off the grimy wood.

His final words hung in the air. "I will try not to."

The doors latched shut. Frantically, she reached for the handle, only to find none was to be found on the interior side of the door.

"Wrylyc," she cried.

Although she had expected silence, Drada was answered with a thunderous roar within the enclosed room. The ground shook. The walls tremored.

The light of her torch flickered and faded as shadow darker than pitch, blacker than the grave, spread through the room. Screams of the dead echoed in her ears. Icy claws crept up her spine and neck and cheeks. Razor teeth etched along her legs, no matter her armor or clothing. Any scream Drada may have responded with was barred in her lungs; fear froze the heart in her chest. The darkness swarmed over her like insects on decaying flesh.

She stumbled, her foot falling from the path.

A poisoned bolt tore into her leg, and then another into her side. Drada wailed, gripping the base of the projectiles lodged into her skin.

She could feel her warm blood rushing from the wounds.

The room spun. She lifted her head up hearing battle, and death, and the clang of iron on stone. And amongst the clamor whispered a voice, more ancient than any she had ever heard, speaking in a language no longer known. She strained to hear a word amongst the undertones.

She fell to her knees. Another bolt penetrated her back, tearing through her breast. The darkness was heavy as iron, weighing against her armor, her helm, even her bones. She crumbled to the floor. Physical strength left her body.

The shade enveloped her. The voice clouded her mind with a single word.

Likhyi.

Death's name had been spoken.

"So be it!" she whispered, her voice failing. With her remaining strength, Drada tore the cord from her neck. She traced the cold, smooth token between her fingers, sliding it from its binding. She would complete her quest from the other side of the veil.

Ripping off her helm, Drada shoved the quoin into her   mouth   and   gulped.

ABOUT THE AUTHORS

Joshua Robertson was born in Kingman, Kansas on May 23, 1984. A graduate of Norwich High School, Robertson attended Wichita State University where he received his master's in social work with minors in psychology and sociology. His bestselling novel, *Melkorka*, the first in The Kaelandur Series, was released in 2015. Known most for his Thrice Nine Legends Saga, Robertson enjoys an ever-expanding and extremely loyal following of readers. He counts R.A. Salvatore and J.R.R. Tolkien among his literary influences.

J.C. lives in the Midwest with his wife and two dogs and has an M.A. in English Literature. The first novel in his world, *Blood and Bile*, was released in 2017. Before completing junior high, J.C. had received his first box set of Dungeons & Dragons and devoured J.R.R. Tolkien's *The Lord of the Rings*. Since, he has been heavily influenced by a myriad of fantasy authors, such as Weis and Hickman, Robert Jordan, and Ed Greenwood.